The Time of the Clockmaker

Also by Anna Caltabiano
from Gollancz:

The Seventh Miss Hatfield

The Time of the
Clockmaker

ANNA CALTABIANO

GOLLANCZ
LONDON

Copyright © Anna Caltabiano 2015
All rights reserved

The right of Anna Caltabiano to be identified as the author of this work
has been asserted by her in accordance with the
Copyright, Designs and Patents Act 1988.

First published in Great Britain in 2015 by Gollancz
An imprint of the Orion Publishing Group
Carmelite House, 50 Victoria Embankment, London EC4Y 0DZ
An Hachette UK Company

A CIP catalogue record for this book is available
from the British Library

ISBN 978 1 4732 00043 2

1 3 5 7 9 10 8 6 4 2

Typeset by Born Group using BookCloud

Printed in Great Britain by
Clays Ltd, St Ives plc

www.annacaltabiano.com
www.orionbooks.co.uk
www.gollancz.co.uk

To all of us who are sure they were
born in the wrong time and place.

Prologue: Present Day

The normally overcrowded streets of New York were even more packed than usual that day, everyone pushing and straining for the best vantage point. I fought my way relentlessly through the crush of transfixed people wearing bright-green sweatshirts, raising their phones to take photos, while waiting on 5th Avenue for the annual parade to begin. I was searching the crowd for *her*.

One face after another passed by, and still there was no sign of *her*. It was like looking out upon a sea of interwoven greens – Kelly green, chartreuse, lime green, forest – every possible variation was present. I was wearing white, as instructed. I imagined it was to better stand out so she could spot me. It didn't help my concentration that my mission had me tied up in knots. Tension surrounded me as people pushed and shoved against one another to hold the observation points they had staked out as their own.

None of that mattered to me. I was not here for some infantile parade, annual tradition or not. This grossly overcrowded setting was merely the meeting point to which I had been directed. I had a purpose, and although this green-tinted mob was less than navigable, I pressed on. My eyes darted, scanning for that one familiar face. Babies cried, old people complained about the crush and children alternately screamed and laughed – a cacophony

1

of invasive sounds. Tuning it out completely was no easy trick, and since there was too much overlapping noise to count on sound to guide me, I was forced to trust my sense of sight above all else. So I continued searching the ocean of faces and the sea of green, but to no avail. I wanted more than anything to get out of that maddening crowd, but I knew it was not an option.

Redoubling my resolve, I pushed on. The parade's music and marching sounds were within three, perhaps four blocks from what little I could distinguish above the observers' noise. There was no sign of them yet, just the fanfare heralding their approach. The parade appeared to be mocking me, its appearance as elusive as my intended rendezvous. Why did she want us to meet here?

I bolted, trying to dodge around people, those I bumped hollering after me. I feigned ignorance or deafness and doggedly pursued my search. Something hit me in the stomach and I stopped short. Looking down, I saw the metal barrier meant to keep the crowds on the sidewalk and out of the path of the parade. There was no way around and no easy way over, so I turned and kept going. Systematically examining every form with the proper height, build and hairstyle with no luck made me feel quite discouraged, and so I paused for a moment to catch my breath and calm my nerves, but I never stopped scanning the crowd.

After taking several deep breaths, my head felt a bit clearer, so I began walking among the observers again, determined to find her before the parade was in full swing and further movement became impossible. Colliding with people who looked at me in disgust as though I didn't belong in the crowd, I could only think to myself, *If you only knew the half of what I've been through – you have no idea!*

I pressed onwards. I could see no one I recognized until I glanced to the left and suddenly there she was – the woman I'd been trying to find for so long. She was across the street from where I had been standing not five minutes before, and she was moving towards me. I began running towards her, through the jeers and shouts of folks who had been *waiting all day for a front-row position!* But she was running erratically. There was something wrong.

I waved my arms and shouted in her direction but her eyes remained fixed elsewhere, and I knew full well that no one could have heard me from where she stood, not over the roaring, swarming throng. I was relieved to see her at long last, yet now that I'd found her my apprehension heightened and I yelled louder. I began to push harder against the crowd, but it became ever more difficult to move as the parade drew closer and the mob continued to jockey for position.

I was pressed up against the metal barrier again, just as she was across the street. I smiled and started to shout her name, but the look of utter bewilderment upon her face at that moment was something I had never seen before on anyone's face. *What's the matter with her?* The thought had no sooner crossed my mind before I followed her gaze downwards and saw a red stain colouring her shirt.

I tried my best to get to her. Everyone roared as the parade came into sight and I took advantage of the distraction to clamber over the barrier and run into the street. With every step I took, I saw the red stain spread faster and faster. As I drew closer, I glimpsed a knife sticking out of her stomach and knew there was no time to save her. Everything was happening so fast, but I observed every detail in slow motion. Never taking my gaze from her as I ran, though I thought I would be sick at any moment,

I saw her eyes widen as her naturally pale complexion became almost ethereally transparent. It reminded me of how static on a television back in the days of antennas, before cable or satellite, could make ghostly images out of real figures. I extended my hands, trying to will myself to get to her in time, but I knew it was futile. Each second felt like an hour as she literally began to fade right before my eyes.

She crumpled backwards, the crowd oblivious to her as she fainted against them. I watched helplessly as she made one brief moment of eye contact with me, that puzzled look still upon her face. I wanted to scream but my voice was frozen in my throat. She managed a very brief smile, as though to let me know it was somehow going to be all right – I could almost hear her telling me that I must find a way to go on. And then she disintegrated into mere specks of dust before she hit the ground. Even now, no one around her had taken notice, all eyes still on the approaching parade. It was as if she had never existed. I knew I couldn't possibly have heard the dull clatter of the blade hitting the sidewalk, but I swear I did. It was coupled with a piercing screech, the source of which I could not identify at first, until I realized it was my own voice. I stood frozen in my tracks, terror flowing from my open mouth, horrified by what I had just seen.

'Come now, miss, it can't be that bad.' A jolly, over-weight policeman smiled as he took my arm.

Only then did I realise that I had frozen in the middle of the street.

'Yeah, it's just the high school bands leading the way, but they're trying their best to sound good, y'know?' After escorting me to what he thought was the safety of the sidewalk, he tipped his hat at me and winked before he walked off.

I stood there in stark disbelief, in the same spot where she had just dematerialized. I somehow found the presence of mind to locate the glittering knife lying near the gutter. With all eyes on the parade rather than me, I picked it up, thinking to slide it into the front pocket of my sweatshirt. Maybe it would provide some clues. I couldn't just leave it there for someone else to stumble on.

It was utterly surreal. I stood there in the mass of bodies feeling only one thing – the brutal cold of the knife in my hand, still slick with her blood.

Chapter 1

My fingers fumbled with the keys for a few seconds before I managed to unlock the door. I propped it open with my hip, clutching two large grocery bags.

'Good God,' I muttered as I struggled to get the heavy, handleless paper bags inside without dropping them.

The more eco-friendly Manhattan became, the more of a pain it was to navigate. Don't get me wrong – I thought going green was a very admirable thing, but there was such a thing as *too* green. I shuddered as I recalled the look the cashier had given me when I told him I had forgotten to bring my reusable cloth bag. He glowered down at me through his fleshy eyelids and his condescending stare immediately brought back memories of Christine – a girl I had known a long, long time ago.

As beautiful as Christine looked with those artful tendrils of her Southern-belle golden hair framing her dainty face and azure eyes, when it came to dirty looks she appeared to have mastered every variation. Last summer – or rather a little bit more than a century ago, since that was practically the same thing to me now – Christine had believed I was stealing her future husband away from her. Henley. Oh, Henley. That summer I had received far more than my fair share of her scowls. But it had been worth it.

I chuckled at the memory as I walk to the kitchen and set the bags down on the countertop. In the end, the man Christine regarded as her fiancé had married her sister. My smile dissolved into a long sigh as I remembered her sister.

If Christine was one of the most unpleasant people it had ever been my misfortune to meet, her sister, Eliza, had to be one of the best. She was unassuming and didn't have lofty expectations about life. She didn't resent her sister's prettiness. Nor was she bitter that a childhood sickness had left her blind. Eliza was content with her devout thoughts, finding God in everything and taking comfort in her belief that He had created a greater plan for all of us . . .

All of us except me, I reminded myself.

Eliza believed in heaven – a heaven that would welcome all good people, regardless of whether or not they shared her faith.

I thought back to a time long ago, a time that felt both foreign and familiar. I remembered walking into Eliza's room to see her kneeling in reverent prayer. When she finished her devotions, she told me something that had stuck in my mind ever since.

'I'll meet you in heaven someday, I know it. It doesn't matter whether you believe, you see,' she said. 'God loves you whether you believe or not.'

In that moment, hearing Eliza's reverence, I wondered whether that might be the case. Was there someone out there watching over me? Was there really a greater plan into which we all fitted? I had desperately wished for that. I wished I wouldn't always be as lonely as I felt and Eliza's words only fuelled that dream. Maybe there really was a greater plan in which I just needed to trust. Maybe there was a reason for all the strangeness in my life.

But I knew now that wasn't the case. Eliza might be in a place she called heaven, but I would not be joining her.

I slumped against the countertop, the tiles cool against my palms. Eliza didn't know everything. She had no idea that I wasn't human, that I would never die. For while Eliza had now been dead for almost a century, I was immortal.

'Miss Hatfield?' I called out in the empty kitchen. I quickly corrected myself, remembering that she would sometimes refuse to answer if I didn't call her by her first name. 'Rebecca? I'm home with the groceries.'

A silent house responded.

Realising that Miss Hatfield was out again, I put away the groceries in a leisurely fashion, all the while wondering what I would do to occupy myself till she returned. My body appeared to answer my question for me when I found myself staring at my keys on the counter again. Next to them was a simple ring set with a blue stone, flanked by two smaller diamonds.

I was surprised. Not because I had never seen the ring before – no, it was a ring I wore often, practically every day – but because I thought I had put it away. It was a gift from someone a long time ago. Someone I wanted to remember and someone who wanted to be remembered.

Shaking my head, I put it on and grabbed my keys again. I knew I needed to get out of the house. I felt as if I couldn't think clearly while inside.

Miss Hatfield's house certainly wasn't unpleasant. It looked like a normal New York brownstone on the outside. A bit run-down, perhaps, with cracks leading up the cement steps to the shabby-looking front door, but similar to all the other houses in the neighbourhood.

Maybe that was the reason I hadn't suspected anything when I first met Miss Hatfield. The house looked like an ordinary house and she appeared to be an ordinary woman.

The year was 1954 when I first met Miss Hatfield. I was eleven years old and everyone called me by a different name from the one I used now – I had once been Cynthia. Perhaps I was gullible, being so young. Perhaps Miss Hatfield had perfected her lies . . . Whatever the case, I accepted Miss Hatfield's invitation to join her for a glass of lemonade in her house. Agreeing to that changed everything.

Once she had me inside the house, Miss Hatfield adjusted a large golden clock she had hung on the wall and sneaked the last drop of an odd clear liquid into my drink. I noticed her doing these things with great curiosity – even a bit of suspicion – but, not wanting to be an ungrateful guest, I played along. Little did I know that by turning the hands of the clock, Miss Hatfield had advanced time, aging me in my mortal body, before putting a drop of water from the Fountain of Youth into my drink, thereby making me immortal.

I didn't find out what she had done until I looked into a mirror. I laughed to myself as I remembered how at first I believed that Miss Hatfield had somehow put me in another person's body. I learned later that the secrets of time travel and immortality were much more complex than something as silly as body-swapping, but in that moment I was terrified that I was no longer myself.

Bit by bit, Miss Hatfield explained to me how I could never go home again – my parents would never believe that this mature body was their daughter. Nor would I be able to stay in one time period for long, either. She told me that I was now a visitor in all time periods and no longer had a time or place in which I belonged.

When she first disclosed all this to me, I felt like my head was going to implode. I still felt like that sometimes, but I was slowly growing accustomed to it – well, as accustomed as one can get to never aging.

I opened the front door for the third time that day and was greeted by the same ruckus of the streets I had encountered that morning. Cars honked and people huddled in spring coats pushed past. There appeared to be more of them than usual. Everyone went about their lives, choosing to ignore everyone else, and they were happy.

How many couples would I see today? Thankfully Valentine's Day had come and gone, but I still spotted at least three couples on the opposite side of the street.

I looked more closely at the pair nearest to me: a tall man in a grey coat with a blonde-haired woman on his arm, throwing her head back as she laughed at something the man must have said. They were walking away from me. Arm in arm. Hands entwined. Steps in sync.

I shook myself out of it and started down the street. I noticed that sections of the street were being closed and lined with metal bleachers. The St Patrick's Day Parade was tomorrow – of course! That also accounted for the extra people who had appeared to descend upon the city out of nowhere.

I let myself blend into the crowd as Miss Hatfield had taught me. *Act as they do. Walk as they do. Feel as they do, and you become them*. I didn't pause. It was just like being in a play. I was merely acting different parts, but somehow that made me feel less alone. For once it was as if I knew what was expected of me, and what I had to do. The half hour walk was a familiar one, and the cold spring air made me walk all the faster. I passed St. Paul's Cathedral at a brisk pace, dodging around the tourists.

The concrete gave way to what looked like a small park in the city. Surrounded by trees, you wouldn't know it was the New York City Marble Cemetery until you entered it. There was only one path through, as if whoever built it didn't want people lingering and loitering, but I would have known my way without it.

I didn't even have to count the rows of headstones to know where to turn. I hadn't memorized it. It was instinctive.

At last, finding the large marble gravestone, now slightly worn away by the passing years, I let myself fall to my knees. My head hung low. I was unable to bring my hands up to cradle it; they felt like weights at my sides.

I knew the words on the tombstone by heart: *Henley A. Beauford. Innovative Businessman & Loving Husband.*

My fingers found the ring I wore on my left hand and fiddled with it, turning it quickly three revolutions.

It felt as if it hadn't been that long ago. A few months, perhaps? But in regular, mortal time almost a century had passed since I first met Henley.

I let my fingers come up to trace his name. I thought I knew everything there was to know about this man when I fell in love with him, but I still found there were trivial things I knew nothing about. Like his middle name. What did the 'A' stand for? I hadn't thought to ask him.

I turned to the tombstone beside his. *Eliza P. Beauford. Loving Wife & Daughter.* I smiled because Eliza would have known those things about her husband. She would have taken good care of him, too.

If there was a heaven, I wondered if they were both watching. Did they forgive me for keeping so much from them? Did Henley forgive me for everything I put him through?

I turned away from the graves and glanced around. I wasn't sure what I was looking for. All I saw were trees around me, and all I heard was the wind. I stood up on shaky

11

legs and walked a few steps to a nearby bench. I couldn't see the cars and buildings of the city, and I was at peace.

There, on that simple wooden bench, it could have been any time period. I half-expected Henley to saunter over in his usual way with that gleam in his eye I had grown to adore. I closed my eyes and brought his image to mind. He would bring a hand from his pocket to brush a strand of dark hair from his eyes. His touch was always so gentle. He would sit mere inches away from me, almost but not quite touching. And he would look at me the way he always did, those clear eyes of his seeing directly into me.

I wondered what I would say if he were here. *Sorry, I forgot to mention that I was immortal. By the way, since I found out that Miss Hatfield is your mother, you're actually half-immortal, too . . . Not that it matters, since you're dead.*

I sighed and opened my eyes. I reached into the pocket of my jacket to pull out a slip of charred paper. I always carried it with me, and taking it out just to hold it had become a habit. I already knew the words on the piece of paper: *To my darling Charles. With all the love in the world, Ruth.* It was a note from Henley's mother, Miss Hatfield, to his adoptive father, Mr Beauford. I was careful as I unfolded it, given that it was now a hundred years old.

I remembered how my hands shook upon first seeing the photograph the piece of paper contained. There, in a lavish dress with her beautifully curled hair piled on top of her head, was Miss Hatfield. There was no mistaking her, yet every time I saw that photo, I couldn't help but draw a sharp breath.

It did make sense to me now, how Miss Hatfield had encouraged me to pose as Mr Beauford's niece, and didn't mind too much my staying with the Beauford family far longer than expected. I recalled her asking about Mr

Beauford's son, just once. It all made sense, yet I couldn't muster the courage to bring it up with Miss Hatfield.

I knew my reticence was silly since I had already uncovered what I thought was most of it. And I had a right to know, because it did concern me . . . But for some reason it felt horribly wrong to ask, as if I would be trespassing somewhere I didn't belong.

I had almost resolved to ask her, but later, when we had more time. Miss Hatfield always appeared to be rushing out of the house, sometimes even disappearing for a couple days.

I heard a sudden noise nearby, like the crunch of leaves underfoot, and my head snapped up as I slipped the piece of paper back into my pocket. The noise alone wouldn't normally have startled me, but it did sound very close by. I looked around, but all I saw was an alarmed bluebird hopping out onto the path in front of me. I guessed I was just being more paranoid than usual.

'I knew I'd find you here.'

Hearing the familiar voice, I turned my head in the opposite direction from the bird. Miss Hatfield was walking towards me between two rows of graves. It didn't faze her that she was in a cemetery, or that she was walking above the bodies of people who had probably been alive when she was living in her original time period.

'It's useless to dwell in the past,' she said. She didn't even have to glance at the graves nearby to know that I was at the Beauford family plot. 'We're not like them. You know that.'

And I suppose I did. I knew what she was saying was true. I even left Henley, telling him that I didn't love him, just so he might forget me and live a normal life. I loved him enough to want that for him.

I glanced at Miss Hatfield and wondered how much she knew. She knew that Mr Beauford had adopted her son, and she had briefly seen me with a young man, but I didn't think she had connected the two. But then again, Miss Hatfield was full of half-truths and mysteries.

'Rebecca?' She looked at me.

'Yes, Miss Hatfield?' I said.

'Yes, *Rebecca*,' she corrected.

She always made a point of wanting me to use her first name, yet I couldn't help but call her 'Miss Hatfield' in my mind. When I became immortal, I left the identity of Cynthia behind and became Rebecca Hatfield – the same as all the other immortals before me. We took on a single identity that existed in any time.

'Let's go home.' Her eyes darted about. 'I don't feel safe. I never feel safe in any time.' She whispered so low that I had to crane my neck to make out her words. She was normally suspicious, but lately she had become even more so than I was used to. 'Come along home, Rebecca,' she said. 'We should dress for the gym. And remember to avert your eyes. People easily remember the faces of those with whom they make eye contact.'

I mumbled assent, but Miss Hatfield was already too far ahead to hear.

I watched her as she made her way back through the rows of graves. She who could not die walked so casually among the dead. It was perverse and unnatural. Not at all the way things were meant to be.

Born in the 1940s, I was supposed to be in my seventies. I looked down at my hands, almost hoping to find a wrinkle, but I found none. Smooth. Young. For ever. Everyone else would age while I remained unchanged.

Chapter 2

'Have you been going to the gym as I requested?' Miss Hatfield asked me that afternoon.

Miss Hatfield's normal walking pace was almost a jog for me and I struggled to keep up with her enough to hear the ends of her sentences.

I was about to admit that I hadn't been going as much as she wanted, but Miss Hatfield answered for me. 'Of course not. I'm glad I'm taking you with me now. I bought the gym membership for a reason, you know.'

I did know the reason, but it wasn't to work out. It was to be *seen* working out. Miss Hatfield believed that being recluses would make us more noticeable. Although it sounded contradictory, it made sense in its own way. We had to do all the things ordinary people did: go to the gym, make small talk with the receptionist, be polite enough to look normal – so normal that a regular person would simply forget us. The goal was never to befriend anyone. Appearances were what mattered to Miss Hatfield. Truth was always secondary.

'The woman at the front desk has been asking after my sister lately,' she said. 'I told her you had a dermatologist appointment on Wednesday morning. A skin rash. Nothing serious. Just a minor thing from when we were upstate this past Saturday.'

'What were we doing? Hiking?'

'Of course not. It's March and much too cold for that. We stayed at the Mohonk Mountain House on Saturday. It's a spa resort.'

A spa resort. That was the last thing I could imagine Miss Hatfield doing. But then again, she would do anything and everything to try to look normal.

'Got that?'

I jogged up to her as she waited for the light to change on East 64th Street. 'Dermatologist on Wednesday morning. Skin rash. Resort on Saturday. Just us?'

'Just us. What type of skin condition did you have?'

I tried to think fast. 'Poison ivy?'

'At the resort? Don't be silly. And that can take about two weeks to clear up completely. It was an allergy we didn't know you had to shellfish that you had at the restaurant,' she said, then took off walking at her fast pace again.

She bounded up the stairs and through the frosted glass doors of the gym, her ponytail swinging. It would never have crossed my mind that she didn't belong in New York at this time. I followed her through the glass doors.

'I see you two ladies are already dressed and ready to work out. Are you here for the class?' The woman at the front desk looked slightly more orange than when I last saw her a couple of weeks before.

'I'm afraid not,' Miss Hatfield said. 'We're just here to use the ellipticals and maybe an erg. Some sisterly bonding time.' She smiled at me, and it scared me how genuine Miss Hatfield sounded. 'By the way, I love your tan,' she said, turning back to the woman at the desk.

The woman sneezed.

'Bless you.'

16

'Excuse me. But, yeah, thanks. They had a sale on airbrush tans at the salon across the street.'

'We'll definitely have to check that out,' Miss Hatfield said.

'You should. They work magic there!' The woman smoothed her hair back. 'How was the resort, by the way? The Mohonk Mountain House, you said?'

'Oh, it was fun,' I said. 'Well, except for the nasty rash I came back with.'

'Your sister told me about that. What caused it in the end?'

I shrugged. 'The dermatologist said it was probably some sort of reaction to the shellfish I had at the restaurant.'

'We didn't even know she was allergic to anything,' Miss Hatfield chimed in.

'What a shame . . . Anyways, enjoy working up a sweat today, ladies.' The woman pulled a tissue from behind the desk and blew her nose.

'Oh, we will,' Miss Hatfield called over her shoulder.

Once we were out of earshot, I said, 'We're not actually going to the salon, are we?' I had to ask.

'God, no. Of course not. She looks like a tangerine.' Miss Hatfield grabbed some hand sanitizer from an automatic dispenser.

I didn't understand. As immortals I thought we couldn't get sick. 'Better to be safe than sorry?' I asked.

'Don't be absurd,' Miss Hatfield said, climbing onto the elliptical next to me. 'Immortals don't get sick or catch diseases.'

'That's what I thought . . . But the hand sanitizer?'

'No chance of dying of disease or old age, but as usual we have to *look* normal,' she hissed. 'The people in this time are germ-obsessed. We need to follow suit. And remember, you can still die from physical harm, so I

17

wouldn't recommend dropping one of those heavy weights on yourself.'

'Yes, ma'am,' I muttered under my breath.

'Now, no more talk of this in public.'

I set up my elliptical and started moving in silence. I wondered how long it would take me to start lying to people so seamlessly. If it wasn't so alarming, I would have been quite impressed by Miss Hatfield's skill. I guess she had centuries of experience. Maybe I would get that way once I had centuries of experience, too.

Miss Hatfield interrupted my thoughts. 'If you're going to look dazed, at least look sweaty and dazed as if you've actually done something.'

I almost laughed. That was such a typically Miss Hatfield thing to say.

'Sometimes I don't understand you,' she said. 'Your strange little smiles . . . It's like you're seeing another world behind those eyes.' She sighed.

I was glad I was as much of an enigma to her as she was to me.

'I chose you specifically to give you this gift of a whole other life because I saw something in you that reminded me of myself when I was turned.'

I was surprised that Miss Hatfield was bringing this up right after she had asked me to drop the subject.

'And do you regret that now?'

'No . . . If anything, I see even more of myself in you now.'

'I'm not sure I'd call every aspect of immortality a gift,' I said.

'Keep your voice down.'

I looked around at the people running and pedalling furiously around us. There weren't that many of them and most were out of earshot. The closer ones had earbuds in, probably with the volume cranked up.

18

I thought Miss Hatfield would ask me what I meant, but she already knew. 'There are drawbacks, yes. Things you have to sacrifice. But I've given you another life. A chance to be happy. You weren't happy at all in your old life.' Miss Hatfield looked straight ahead as she maintained a constant tempo.

She was right that I hadn't been happy in my previous life as Cynthia in the 1950s. But back then I still had family. Parents. Friends. I had a life.

Now . . . I wasn't sure what to call my existence. This sneaking from time to time, as if we were fugitives slipping from hiding place to hiding place.

'I don't know if I can call this a life,' I said.

'Be grateful.' She didn't even glance at me when she said it.

Miss Hatfield waved to her left and I turned to see an athletic woman patting down her afro.

'That's the woman who's going to teach our Pilates class next Friday.'

I shook my head. Miss Hatfield was too much.

That evening, we had supper in front of the television. Miss Hatfield was the one to suggest it, and that was unusual in itself.

Miss Hatfield always preferred Google News and Twitter to television because she said they were a quicker, more efficient means of staying current with events and brushing up before going out each day. Television, on the other hand, she regarded as a useless thing we had to pretend to watch to keep up with the latest reality TV shows.

So imagine my surprise when she brought our Chinese takeout to the couch in front of the dusty television.

'Um . . . What do you want to watch?' I asked. I figured it would be easier to have her choose a channel rather than me picking a show and being chastised for my poor taste and opinion.

'I don't know. Just pick something,' she said.

Miss Hatfield never *didn't know*, much less admit to it. Was this a test of some sort? I wouldn't put it past her.

I flipped through the channels before settling on a sitcom. The show revolved around a family – a patriarch with his new younger wife, his two grown kids and their families. I hadn't seen it before and couldn't recollect reading anything about it online. I didn't even know what it was called since I had tuned in partway through. My eyes flickered over to Miss Hatfield to see what she thought of the show I had picked. She looked engrossed already, trying to figure out the family dynamics while biting into a pot-sticker.

'Do you think those two are related?' she asked, pointing to two of the kids.

'I don't know. It's hard to tell.'

I grabbed a carton of fried rice and sank into the couch.

This episode appeared to be mainly about two gay parents worrying over their newly adopted baby's behavioural development. Most of the comedy was derived from the parents panicking over things the baby either did or didn't do, like talk or walk.

Miss Hatfield shook her head. 'I don't understand why they can't be content with their baby's abilities. She's healthy. They should be thankful that's the case and that there isn't anything more seriously wrong with her.'

'Perhaps they're worried that the baby not talking might indicate a greater problem . . . like a disease or something,' I offered.

'Still, it seems foolish.'

'They're just worried for their child,' I said.

'I know, and that's why they're foolish – they're investing all this time and energy in something so trivial.'

'But it's their *child*.' I was struck by the fact that she saw the baby's health as trivial.

But all she said was, 'There's more to worry about in life.'

I paused, then said: 'I should think that as a parent, you'd worry about your own child, and that would be a primary part of your life.'

'Even if one worries, there's only so much one can do.'

I supposed I should have expected this kind of cynicism from Miss Hatfield. Technically, only a couple of months had passed since I rejoined Miss Hatfield after leaving 1904, but it felt like an eternity with her, and perhaps I ought to have anticipated this response. After all, she did essentially give up her child . . . But I couldn't blame her for that. She knew she was immortal, and I guessed she didn't want her child to have to deal with that growing up. At least, that's what I would have thought in that situation.

'You have to take care of yourself first. Even if that means seeing to your own needs before those of family,' Miss Hatfield said. 'Those who think otherwise are either weak or deluded. Maybe both.'

I put down the carton of food I was holding. 'What if you take care of yourself by supporting the people you love?' I pointed at the screen. 'I mean, they all look so happy to just be around each other. Even when they're worried beyond belief, they seem satisfied just being with family. Maybe that's how they take care of each other – and themselves.'

Miss Hatfield shook her head slowly, but this time she was looking at me instead of the television screen. 'You're still young. Your views will change as more time passes.'

I was doubtful but remained silent.

She turned back to the TV show.

I wished I had picked another programme. Not because Miss Hatfield had her own opinions – I was used to that by now – but because hearing Miss Hatfield's disregard for family made me hurt more than I had in a long time, since first leaving the people I loved. I didn't want to become *that*. Watching the family bicker and laugh together forced what I was missing back into my thoughts. Sure, it was apparent on the street, with families walking their dogs together and couples sitting on the benches hand in hand, but here, actually sitting down to watch a family interact, I had nothing to distract myself with. I couldn't change the channel or leave the room; I didn't want Miss Hatfield to know that this was affecting me. It was in plain sight and I had to watch.

We watched a couple episodes of the show and at some point all the characters drove each other crazy. The kids argued, the siblings argued, the parents argued . . . But in the end, none of it mattered because they always made up. They had this bond with each other that nothing could break. And as long as they had this bond, they always had family to return to. I was envious of that.

Miss Hatfield stood up, straightening her shirt. 'Have a glass of milk. I could heat it up for you. It'll make you sleep better.'

'Sure.' I knew this was as tender as Miss Hatfield could be. I couldn't live on this affection alone, but I knew I had to. This was all I was going to get.

Chapter 3

I opened my eyes but couldn't see a thing. All around me were light and colour, shapeless and inchoate. I blinked, trying to refocus. When I rubbed my eyes, I felt wetness on my cheeks. Perhaps I had cried in my sleep again.

Looking up, I could see the thin outline of the curtains covering the window above my bed. As I blinked away my tears, the picture became clearer and I soon saw the individual rays of light coming through my curtains and scattering upon the opposite wall. I sat up, pushing the covers off my legs abruptly. I almost knocked over the small jewellery box I kept at my bedside as I walked heavy-lidded into the bathroom.

I turned the shower on and just stood there for a moment, listening to the water pelt against the glass. If I couldn't be in the one place and time I wanted to be, at least I could enjoy a hot modern shower. I slid into the shower carefully, the warm spray against my skin so relaxing that it almost made me forget all my problems. But all too soon I knew I had to get out and reluctantly turned off the water.

As the steam in the bathroom dissipated, so did the makeshift fantasy I had created for myself in which I was normal. I wasn't normal and that was a fact I couldn't run away from . . . no matter how hard I tried.

I rubbed my face with the bath towel. If only I could scrub everything away and start over. I dropped the towel and moved to the sink to peer into the tiny mirror. Standing as close as I was, my face filled the entire frame and I didn't quite recognize myself. My breath fogged up the mirror and my fingers drew lines on it as I dragged them over its surface. They traced down the cold glass to the mirror's ledge, where they froze.

My fingers pushed up against something familiar. I knew what it was immediately. I knew the shape and feel of it better than I knew any other thing. But I couldn't believe it was here and had to look down to be certain.

My eyes confirmed what my fingers had felt. It was my ring – the one with the blue stone flanked by two small diamonds set into the centre of a silver band. But I could've sworn I put it away last night . . . In fact, I was certain I had placed it in my jewellery box for safe keeping.

Wrapping myself in a towel, I ran over to the bedside table and opened my jewellery box. Everything appeared to be the way I had left it and nothing else was missing.

I returned to the bathroom sink and examined the ring. It looked the same as it always did, just seemed to have been taken out of my jewellery box and moved.

I frowned but put the ring on anyway. I knew I should tell Miss Hatfield about the strange occurrence . . . but then she'd ask me where exactly I had gotten the ring..

When she had first seen me wear the ring, she had assumed that I had bought it for myself. She had told me that I shouldn't buy small objects such as jewellery that a regular person wouldn't notice because it was a waste of money; a small object wouldn't help me fit into this time period.

I had let her scold me. I couldn't tell her that Henley had given it to me. She would be so upset that I had become attached to someone, let alone fallen in love with him. And the fact that Henley was her son . . . Well, it *really* wouldn't go over well.

Moving over to my closet, I pulled out the first shirt and pair of jeans I could find. I was starting to put them on when I heard my phone buzzing on top of my dresser. Miss Hatfield had insisted that we have cell phones in this time to further blend in. 'It's the twenty-first-century mode of communication,' she said. 'Everyone has one on their person at all times, so we must, too.'

I picked up my phone expecting it to be Miss Hatfield. I frowned when I saw I had received a text message from a blocked number.

11:00am
St Patrick's Cathedral. South-west corner.
Wear all white.
Be prompt.

I wondered if Miss Hatfield had borrowed someone's phone or blocked her own number somehow. Knowing she worried about privacy, that didn't surprise me in the slightest, and no one else had this number.

Tossing aside the shirt and jeans I had just pulled out, I searched for a white top and white trousers and hurriedly put them on. I had overslept and taken my time in the shower. It was past 10:30 and I had to get to the cathedral.

Wondering what Miss Hatfield could possibly want with me dressed head to toe in white, I rushed over to the bathroom sink to stick a toothbrush into my mouth and try to make myself appear somewhat put together before meeting her. She always hated me looking anything less than respectable, but I guess that was the nineteenth century in her.

As I was flitting from one side of the room to the other desperately trying to get ready, I happened to glance out

25

of the sliver of window not covered by curtains. Green. Confused, I pushed the curtains aside. There was no such thing as that much green in Manhattan.

The sidewalk in front of the brownstone was awash with a sea of people all dressed in green – green clothes, green hats, green face paint. Everyone was heading to the St Patrick's Day Parade.

I realized how out of place I'd look among them, but then I got it. That was exactly what Miss Hatfield wanted. She wanted to be able to spot me easily. I found it a bit strange, since I would have thought that making me noticeable was the last thing she'd want . . . but then again, Miss Hatfield was always mysterious and often did things I considered unexpected.

I made sure to stick my phone in my pocket in case she contacted me again. I spent a few minutes searching for my keys but, realising that I must have left them in the kitchen the day before, I made to leave my room. A ping from my computer stopped me.

Sitting down in front of my laptop, I saw that I had new email. I clicked to pull it up. My body went cold.

I love you, and always shall.

I swallowed, unable to do much more. I tore my eyes away from the words just long enough to find out who the email was from. It was from me.

Dazed, I looked again, but I wasn't imagining things.

To: Rebecca Hatfield
From: Rebecca Hatfield

I quickly checked my sent mail and found the exact same email there, too. According to my computer, I had sent myself the email. But I knew I hadn't. And I knew where I had heard those very words before.

I shut my laptop and abruptly stood up, knocking over the chair in my haste. What if Miss Hatfield had sent the email? What if she already knew everything that had occurred between Henley and me?

I glanced at my phone to check the time. I had twenty minutes left and St Patrick's Cathedral wasn't *that* far. I had to find out who it was from.

Taking a deep breath, I opened my laptop again. I found the email and clicked reply.

Who are you?

I pressed 'send' before I could change my mind.

Almost immediately, I heard a ping and felt my breath catch. I opened the new email.

Who are you?

The words I had typed just moments ago stared back at me. It was silly of me to think – to wish – for something that could never happen.

I exhaled a breath I had forgotten I was holding and was about to close my laptop again when I saw that a blank new email was open. Thinking I must have just clicked 'compose' without meaning to, I almost shut the window, but then I felt something odd.

It was as if the keys beneath my fingers were moving . . . but my fingers weren't pressing down on them. They appeared to be moving on their own. I looked closer at the keys and saw that they were indeed moving. Shocked and horrified, I snatched my hands away from them. But they kept moving.

Wide-eyed, I glanced up at the screen.

I think you know exactly who I am.

I had barely finished reading when I felt something on my hand move. Startled, I looked down to see the ring on my finger turn. One full revolution.

My mouth dried up. I glanced over my shoulder. Nothing. I knew I was acting silly but I so desperately wanted it to

27

be true – and no other explanation made sense. At first, I couldn't bring myself to say his name. Finally it came out, small and wavering.

'Henley?'

I didn't know what was more surprising – the fact that I wholeheartedly expected an answer, or the fact that I actually received one.

I must say I was hoping for a more pleased reaction. I really did miss you, Rebecca – or should I say dear cousin?

I heard a chuckle – Henley's chuckle – as distinctly as if he were speaking right into my ear. I spun around, expecting to see him standing there with his hat and gloves in hand as he always had. But he wasn't there.

Henley wasn't standing next to me. He wasn't in the room.

As if sensing my confusion, Henley spoke to me again, this time in a gentler but more serious tone. *I know*, was all he said.

I wondered what exactly it was that he knew. That I was more confused than I had ever been? That Henley was here . . . but at the same time, not here?

I wanted to say all that. I wanted an answer. But all that came out of my mouth was one word.

'Henley.'

Rebecca. There was a pause during which all I could hear was my own breathing. *You have no idea how much I've longed to hear you say my name again.*

'You're . . . you're not here.' I felt stupid saying it, but I couldn't get past that fact. 'I can't see you.'

I know you can't. And if I could fix that, I would. I guess you could say that I don't have a body.

'You don't have a body.' I felt a dull ache in my brain as I scrambled to try to understand what he was saying.

28

I'm here, Henley said. *Well, at least I* think *I am . . . Wherever 'here' is.*

'What can you see?'

A silence followed that lasted so long I grew worried I might have lost him.

I can see everything. Henley's voice tickled in my ear and I could've sworn I felt his breath against my face.

'What do you mean? Do you see this room?'

I see exactly where you're standing. The room. Everything. I see it in this time. In past times. In future times. And it's not just this room or this house I see. I can see Central Park, San Francisco, Paris . . . Anywhere, really.

I staggered a few steps back.

Maybe you should sit down, Henley was quick to say. Just as he spoke, I saw the chair in front of me turn and move towards me. He made it sound as if his sudden return were nothing, but my mind was buzzing.

I always imagined how you'd react, but you're pale as a ghost.

'A ghost,' I repeated. 'You're a ghost.'

I suppose you could say that, Henley replied. *I guess anything that's alive without a body must be a ghost.*

'And you didn't bother to tell me all this time that you were still—' I was about to say 'alive', but that wasn't the right word. 'Still out there?'

I tried, Henley said. *Of course I did. But I didn't even know where – or what – I was, at first. I even tried contacting you in 1904 in the séance parlour because I thought you would be there.*

I shook my head, trying to make sense of his words. 1904? The séance parlour?

I remembered that occasion well. We had visited Miss Dorothy Jones's Séance Parlour to take Henley's mind off his ailing father. Séances were a popular entertainment back then. Henley was there – physically there – and Willie, a childhood friend of Henley's. The three of us sat in a dark room with a woman who was supposed to be some sort of psychic medium. It was all for fun. Willie joked with Henley the entire time.

And when the medium's sister started convulsing, we all thought it was an act.

'Is there a spirit here among us?' I remember Miss Jones asking.

'Yes.'

'Do you want to introduce yourself to us?'

It was so quiet I could hear everyone's breath, including my own.

Then came the words that jolted us all: 'I am Henley. Henley Beauford.'

Rebecca, you're pale.

'What did you expect?' I tried to steady my breath. 'You... It was you talking in the séance, wasn't it? I mean, *really* you.'

Yes, he said. *I tried to contact you through the medium or her sister, but it felt as if I was being sucked into . . . no, falling into her sister's body. I was terrified. I had no idea what I was doing. And I certainly didn't find out what I could do until much later.*

'I can't imagine how that would feel.'

It felt as if I was in a coma-like state. I could hear the world around me. I could see everything happening too. But I couldn't participate in it.

'How did this happen to you?' It came out all hushed like a whisper.

The last thing I remember . . .

Henley was silent for so long that I had to prompt him. 'What is the last thing you remember?'

30

Well, I remember dying.

I must have looked alarmed, for Henley quickly said, *No, nothing bad. I just recall retiring for the night. It hurt to bend down with my stiff back – that's what age does to you – but I straightened my slippers before climbing into bed.*

'And then?'

And then I fell asleep. But it was like a sleep within a sleep – I closed my eyes and slipped into a dream, and then I fell into something beyond my dreams.

It was strange hearing what dying was like. 'Just like that?'

Just like that. At least that was my experience . . . And then I woke up and found myself as I am now. Conscious. Thinking. But not quite alive . . . or dead, for that matter.

'How does it work?'

Henley understood what I was asking. *I can't easily focus on one small thing, but for some reason, I'm beginning to be able to focus on you. It's like a bird's-eye view of the world in every time that has passed, and every time that will come.*

'Like seeing the future,' I said. 'What can you see in my future?'

It doesn't . . . work . . . the same with people like you.

'Then you know about me?'

Yes. When I look into the past and the future, you're not there. I see every person in every moment they ever lived, but there's only a thin outline of you in the time you're currently visiting.

'What do you know about yourself?' I was hesitant to ask because I wasn't sure whether he knew that Miss Hatfield, an immortal, was his mother.

As if guessing my worries, Henley simply said, *I know about my mother.*

'So you know that Miss Hatfield – Ruth – was immortal when she gave birth to you?'

31

And that I'm half-immortal because of it? Yes. I suspect that might have something to do with my current circumstances.

I wondered what else I should ask. I had often imagined this moment and how it would be – what I would say if I could talk to him just one more time. In my dreams, we talked for hours and I told him everything. But now that it was actually happening, I found I couldn't remember a thing I wanted to tell him.

'Do you forgive me?' I asked after a while. 'For leaving, I mean.'

I thought I heard him draw a breath.

I do, he said. *But I wish you had told me you're immortal.*

I nodded, unable to speak.

I had to find out second hand why you left. Henley laughed, and I knew he was trying to lighten the mood. *Luckily, being in all times and places at once, it was easy to overhear you talking to Miss H – my mother.*

Henley's voice was strained and I knew that if I could see his face, his brows would be furrowed. His voice sounded like the Henley I remembered. I knew he had grown old and eventually died, but without his physical body, he sounded as young as he was when we first met.

What are you thinking? Henley asked.

'Oh, nothing. Nothing at all.'

My phone beeped, giving me a jolt. Wondering if it was another text from Miss Hatfield, I glanced at the screen. No, it was just the phone service provider with the monthly bill.

I looked at the time. 11:02 AM.

I had forgotten I was supposed to meet Miss Hatfield. She would be furious if I didn't show up.

As if on cue, I heard Henley's voice in my ear.

Somewhere you need to be?

32

'Yes,' I blurted. Hearing his voice still startled me. 'I'm late to meet Miss Hatfield!' I said, grabbing my keys.

I guess I'll be there, too. His voice took a dark turn. *I don't really have a choice.*

I thought about Henley always being there – wherever 'there' was. He would always be watching; he would always be listening. I wouldn't have to lose him ever again. I shook my head, trying to clear my mind, as I raced out of the house. I had to get to the cathedral on time.

I was overwhelmed as soon as I stepped through the front door. A throng of people swept me up and carried me with them. Everyone except me was wearing green. Taking a deep breath, I began to push my way forward, fighting to go where I wanted. I knew I didn't have much time left.

I wanted to call out to Henley to see if he could help, but calling out would only attract attention and I wasn't sure whether others would hear his disembodied response. I looked up to see if I could catch a glimpse of a street sign, but with the crowds of people swirling around me, I couldn't see a thing.

I tapped a man in front of me, who was wearing a large leprechaun hat, to get his attention. I saw him flinch from my touch, but he still looked over his shoulder to see who had poked him.

'Excuse me,' I said. 'Do you know what street this is?'

'Fifth Avenue,' he said, and turned back to his friend.

I impatiently tapped him on the shoulder again. 'I know that – what's the cross street coming up?'

The man gave me a deadpan look, but still peered ahead to check. 'Forty-Eighth Street.'

I muttered a thank you, but I was pretty sure he didn't want to hear it.

The cathedral was only a couple of blocks away, but even so, I tried to move through the crowd as quickly as I could. After a few minutes of pushing and shoving, I looked up to try to check the street sign, but instead my head fell back as my eyes took in St Patrick's Cathedral and followed the spire up and up.

'South-west corner,' I mumbled to myself, bringing my attention back to my surroundings as I dodged through the crush.

The meeting place was right across the street, so I began looking for Miss Hatfield. I scanned the crowds for a slim woman, not overly tall or curvy – physically she was utterly forgettable. But Miss Hatfield always wore her hair up and, try as she might, she never succeeded in making it look like anything other than a Gibson Girl hairstyle of the early 1900s. That, combined with the stiff, precise way she walked, made her look different from the other women of this time.

The sound of church bells interrupted my thoughts. A stillness spread through the crowd as everyone tipped their heads back to gaze at the cathedral before them. For a moment, everyone was silent, listening to the bells mark the hour. The bells clanged together, a sharpness in their sound. When the bells fell silent, everyone turned towards me – or rather towards 44th Street, where the parade began.

The sound began slowly – an echoing reverberation began in everyone's throats, which turned into cheers and soon became a roar.

I wanted to block it all out. To concentrate. I narrowed my eyes and continued to search in earnest. My eyes stopped at person after person. All wearing shades of green. Plastic necklaces. Hats. Striped trousers. But I didn't see her.

34

I looked behind me at the chilly wall I was now pushed up against. Banana Republic, it proclaimed. In front of me, a mass of people filled the sidewalk. Some poured towards the coming parade. Others surged forward in hopes of finding a better view. I knew Miss Hatfield had to be across the street somewhere.

A stocky woman pushed past me, hitting multiple people at once with her green bags. I pressed my back against the wall to let her through.

'Henley,' I whispered. 'Can you see her?'

There were so many people crammed on the sidewalk that no one took any notice of a young woman talking to herself in front of a Banana Republic. Better yet, no one noticed a bodiless voice responding.

I can't see your kind well, remember? An outline isn't much to go by, he said, knowing immediately who I was asking about.

I thrust myself forward into the horde of people and began clawing my way past strangers. The more people bumped into me, the more I bumped back. *She has to be here somewhere.*

The dank smell of sweat and oily face paint made me want to cough. I felt a young girl's hot cheek against my shoulder and another man's sticky back press against my side. My white clothes were already stained with splotches of the green paint smeared on everyone's bodies. But still I shoved myself towards the looming cathedral ahead. As I forced my way closer, it appeared to grow bigger before my eyes. I trained my attention on it, trying to keep myself from drowning in the crowd.

A shooting pain drew my attention down. I realized that I was finally at the front of the crowd and my stomach had hit one of the metal barricades the police had set up in order to keep people out of the street. The roar of the throng was so loud now that I hadn't even heard the *clank* as my body hit the metal. I knew the parade must be getting closer.

I scanned the sidewalk across from me and saw a flicker of a pale face moving erratically through the green. That had to be Miss Hatfield. There was no question about it. But the relief I felt turned cold – I knew immediately that something was wrong. There wasn't anything normal about Miss Hatfield's motion. Her movements looked . . . broken.

She was running. But she wasn't running towards something or someone. She was running *away* from something.

I yelled but my voice was lost in the crowd. As the parade drew nearer, the people around me grew louder. Not knowing what else to do, I frantically waved my arms, hoping that it might get her attention.

It worked. I saw her head snap towards me and her eyes appeared to focus on my face. Then she glanced back again, behind her. But I had already seen the expression on her face.

Miss Hatfield pushed her way towards me, her gaze locked with mine. Our eyes remained focused on each other until she was directly across the street from me. In that one second, all that separated us were two flimsy metal barriers and an empty street.

As the cheering grew louder, I stood still and watched her.

Miss Hatfield took one final glance behind her before locking eyes with mine again. I smiled and started to call her name, but a look of confusion on her face stopped me. As she looked down, my gaze followed. We both saw the red stain colouring her shirt.

I felt cold metal scraping my leg as I clambered over the barrier in front of me. I tried my best to run to her, watching the red spread faster and faster. No one else appeared to notice Miss Hatfield, their attention on the approaching parade. My eyes were drawn to a knife sticking out of her stomach and I thought I would be sick at any moment.

I saw Miss Hatfield's face drain of all colour, her expression one of utter bewilderment. I watched her fall into the throng. Her eyes flickered back to me and her lips twitched into a faint smile one last time before she disintegrated into mere specks of dust.

She was consumed by the crowd before she even hit the ground. No one around her had noticed a thing, all eyes on the approaching parade.

I wanted to scream but had no breath left within me. The crowd roared all around, and though it was impossible, I thought I heard the dull clatter of the blade hitting the sidewalk.

A policeman took my arm. He was smiling, saying something, but all I heard was a noise like an endless buzz as he guided me towards the place on the sidewalk where she had just been standing.

I stood there for a long time afterwards. The people around me watched the parade, but I was blind to that. My eyes wouldn't leave the spot where Miss Hatfield had so recently stood.

I somehow found the presence of mind to bend down and take the glittering knife lying on the sidewalk near the gutter.

I turned it over in my hands, the sheen of blood making my hands shake uncontrollably.

I knew what had happened, but I couldn't understand how.

Chapter 4

You have to go.

I heard that familiar voice, but right at that moment I couldn't pull it into focus. I heard the words but couldn't place their meanings, much less respond to them.

Rebecca. Do you hear me?

I wanted to shush the voice and wave it away.

Rebecca. It's not safe here.

But it was so insistent.

Rebecca! Are you listening?

'Shh . . .' was all I could manage.

Listen to me. It's not safe here.

I felt something in my mind click and I almost heard the *snap* as everything fell back into place.

'Henley?'

Rebecca. I know you're in shock, but you can't stay here.

I heard his words but their meanings were delayed.

I don't know exactly what happened, but you have to get out of here.

Out was all I heard and I agreed. I had to get out.

My limbs felt wooden. For a moment they wouldn't respond, but then all of a sudden they were moving and propelling me in the general direction of home. Miss Hatfield's home.

The streets were still littered with people, although the worst of the crowds had dissipated once the parade

38

passed by. It was easier to move and I found myself running home.

I scrunched up my face. My mind was numb. I couldn't bear to think, for fear I would relive what had just happened. It was as if my brain had shut down and my body was simply going through the motions.

Rebecca, Henley called again. *I know it's hard, but I need you to concentrate. Focus on getting home.*

Home. I nodded when I saw the familiar door I had watched Miss Hatfield open hundreds of times. I half-expected her to open it again, but instead I dug through my pockets for my keys. As I lifted them up to the door, a clanging sound drew my eyes to them.

The keys were striking each other. Clanging. Over and over like the bells of the cathedral. I couldn't make them stop. My hands were trembling uncontrollably.

I felt a strange pulling sensation on the other end of my keys and saw them grow steady. I knew Henley was helping me and briefly shut my eyes, happy for him to take over. At last, we managed to push the key into the lock and open the door.

I sighed with some kind of relief, returning to the familiar safety of the house. I succeeded in locking the door behind me, but when I turned back, everything was different from what I remembered.

The normally slightly cluttered parlour was in complete disarray. Photos from the walls were strewn on the floor, their frames splintered. A vase which usually graced the corner of the room was also shattered on the floor. The pea-green couch Miss Hatfield appeared fond of was tipped over, its cushions scattered and among the wreckage.

'I . . . is there anyone here?' I breathed.

Is anyone still here? was probably closer to what I meant, but Henley understood.

No, was all he said.

I gingerly stepped through the mess and soon saw that all the rooms were in a similar state of disarray. I did not need to be concerned about breaking anything since everything was already shattered and torn. I didn't even worry about hurting myself; I already knew I was numb. Not knowing what else to do, I automatically went to the place where I felt safest – my room. Of course it was trashed the same as every other room, but it was the only place I could think of going.

My jewellery box was crushed under my bedside table, which in turn was lying unnaturally on its side. The sheets had been stripped off the bed and the mattress was half on the floor. The contents of my closet were strewn about like dirty autumn leaves.

I found one clear corner of the room to sit in. One quiet patch in the midst of havoc and confusion. I drew my knees up to my chin, trying to make myself small enough to be insignificant. I wanted to mould myself into the walls, hoping that somehow I'd get lost in the tumult.

I . . . I don't know why I didn't see this coming. I could almost hear Henley pacing in front of me. *I should have seen the person who did this. The person who killed Miss H –* my mother.

I couldn't understand it, either. If anyone might understand, it would be Miss Hatfield . . . But she was gone now.

I remembered one of the earliest serious conversations I ever had with her, when she listed all the ways the women who shared our name had died. The first Miss Hatfield drowned herself. The second burned to death in a fire aboard a ship heading to Wales. The third was executed during the Salem Witch Trials. The fourth died in an asylum, probably due to a 'treatment' gone awry, after telling her fiancé what she had become. The fifth

Miss Hatfield killed herself with a cake knife in front of the sixth – *my* Miss Hatfield.

'Don't you think it strange,' she said, 'that each Miss Hatfield dies soon after she finds the next one? Is it really a coincidence, or is it time trying to protect its secrets? Is it destiny?'

In my naivety I asked, 'You don't mean that you'll leave me?'

'Not willingly, but I can't control destiny.' I remembered her gaze was downcast, and for a moment she refused to look me in the eye. Then, suddenly, her head snapped up. 'I'll do whatever I can to prepare you for what's ahead.'

Curled up in that corner of my room, I desperately hoped she had done enough to prepare me.

'Oh, God.'

At first I didn't realize the voice was mine. The words just slipped out and I couldn't stop them. Once uttered, the words hung there in the still air.

'Oh, God. Oh, God.'

For the first time since witnessing her death, I felt tears in the back of my throat. In the panic and the rush, I had forgotten to cry.

But I knew instinctively that now was not the time. I sat up straighter, imagining that Miss Hatfield could see me, and addressed Henley.

'You see everything, right? Everyone in every place in every time, except me and your mother,' I said.

I do.

'This . . . person came into the house.' I attempted to lay out the facts. 'I suppose that's not hard to do. Break into the house, I mean.'

Henley didn't respond.

'Anyone could do it. And this intruder was obviously looking for something.'

41

That would explain the dishevelment.

'He didn't bother covering his tracks, that's for sure.'

What could this person want?

'I didn't take a close look, but nothing appears to be missing.' I had registered that the clock was still on the kitchen wall, and my fingers moved of their own volition to the ring on my finger. 'Nothing important, anyway.'

This isn't a petty burglary, though. Are you certain that nothing of value was taken?

I thought through the things Miss Hatfield and I kept in the house. 'There really isn't much of value here,' I said. 'But you're right – the fact that nothing's missing suggests this isn't a regular break-in.'

It still doesn't make sense.

I wanted to ask when things ever made sense but refrained, knowing it wouldn't help at all.

I would've seen him. I would've seen the break-in – if something was going on here, I would've seen it.

There was silence again and I hugged my knees closer.

'Because you can see everyone in all times,' I reiterated.

Yes . . . Well, except for you. I only see you in the one time you're in.

I let out a breath. 'And Miss Hatfield.'

And Miss Hatfield, Henley confirmed.

I swallowed. 'Then he – or she – has to be like us.'

The room was quiet for such a drawn-out period of time that I almost thought Henley had abandoned me.

What do you mean? he said after a while.

'They have to be immortal,' I said.

Henley paused again. *That doesn't make sense.*

'That's the *only* explanation that makes sense.' I stood up, hearing shards of glass snap under my sneakers. 'If this person was mortal, you'd have seen them breaking into the house. Even if you'd been distracted by something else, in some part of time there would be a person breaking into the house and you would be able to see it even now.' I began to pace around my room, not caring if I stepped on anything. 'Watch the house. What do you see?'

It looks fine. And then it's destroyed.

'Just like that?'

Just like that.

'If you can see everyone clearly except immortals, the fact that you're unable to see whoever did this can only mean that they were immortal. The intruder probably fled to a different time immediately afterwards.'

That does make sense . . . and I couldn't see Miss Hatfield being stabbed, so it's likely that the intruder was the one who murdered her.

I froze at the word. Murderer. That was exactly what he was.

'An immortal murdered Miss Hatfield.'

I felt a heaviness in the pocket of my sweatshirt and reached in to feel cool metal. I drew the knife out. I had forgotten I'd brought it with me. I had no idea what to do with it, but it just hadn't felt right to leave it there. I gripped the knife, wishing that Miss Hatfield was magically not dead and that she would return at any moment to scold me for my posture. She was gone when I needed her help most of all.

I put the knife down on an empty patch of the floor. I couldn't stand holding it any longer. I didn't want anything to do with it. All I wanted was something to take me out of this nothingness that shrouded me.

Rebecca. Henley called me out of my thoughts. *If this person is in fact an immortal, you're not safe. They're going to be looking for you.*

43

Chapter 5

Do you have everything you need? Henley sounded even more agitated than I was.

I threw my phone into a navy duffel bag I had found in the closet near the foot of the stairs. I wondered if it belonged to Miss Hatfield, or perhaps one of the others who had come before her. But there was no sense in wondering, since I would never find out.

I ran into the kitchen to fetch the most important object in the house. My fingers cradled the golden edges of the clock as I lifted it gently from its wall mount. I remembered Miss Hatfield explaining its incredible capabilities to me, her fingers lingering on the clock's face just as mine now did. I touched the clock in the same way all six Miss Hatfields before me had and countless after me will touch it.

Rebecca.

Henley's insistent tone brought me back to the present and I returned to my bedroom to place the clock into the bag. My eyes were drawn to a skirt I had thrown onto the foot of my bed that morning which had started inching towards the duffel bag. Once there, it wrapped itself around the clock.

'Good thinking, Henley,' I said. Breaking the clock would be utterly disastrous.

The clock was my only means of travelling from one time to another, but more importantly, it was a way for me to stay sane. I didn't have my own time and therefore was only a visitor in any time period. The longer I stayed in one particular time period, the more uneasy I began to feel. It was like a growing knot in my stomach that progressed from mild discomfort to incessant restlessness, and finally to insanity. I physically couldn't remain in one time for too long; that was the reason I had been forced to leave Henley.

Shaking my head, I began to turn to my closet to pack some clothes, but Henley stopped me.

We have very little time. Rebecca, I don't think you understand exactly how much danger you're in.

He was right. I didn't understand. But neither did he. I knew I should be worried, but oddly he appeared to be more concerned than me. It was almost as if I couldn't be bothered with it.

You've got to go now.

I tucked the duffel bag under my arm and walked briskly out through the front door. I didn't want to run because I knew that would call attention to me. I smiled grimly, thinking how like Miss Hatfield I sounded.

I raised my arm to hail a taxi. Luckily, there were always taxis in the neighbourhood going to and from the more busy business districts, and I caught one without having to wait too long.

'Where to, miss?'

'JFK, please.'

The driver glanced into his rear-view mirror and eyed my small duffel bag. I definitely saw him frown.

'Only that tiny luggage?'

'Yes,' I said, and left it at that.

I spent the rest of the journey to the airport sitting in silence. I was glad the taxi driver didn't try to make conversation. I needed time to myself. I desperately needed to think.

I brought to mind once more everything I knew about the immortals and the business of time travel. All the evidence suggested that the intruder was an immortal – in which case, like me, he could posses the ability to travel in time. Consequently, travelling to a different time would make no difference to my safety – he would still be able to find me.

I paused my whirling thoughts and glanced at the driver, but he had turned the radio up in response to my silence. If he only knew the kind of trouble I was in . . .

The car jerked to a halt and I pitched forward.

'Here you go.' The driver turned and waited for me to open my purse.

I had just enough to pay in cash after I fished for a few extra dimes that were living in the very bottom of my trouser pocket.

He thanked me, then eyed my light-looking duffel bag again with a frown as I opened the door. 'Have a safe flight.'

Side-stepping a crowd to avoid being trampled, I made my way towards the ticket counter.

'Next in line, please.'

I glanced around to make sure it was me, but Henley must have interpreted that as hesitation as I felt something push me forward.

Catching myself on my stumbling feet, I hissed, 'Stop it, Henley!'

Gathering what little remained of my dignity, I looked down at the smiling face of an older woman behind the counter and smiled back. Her foundation creased further into the lines around her mouth. I hoped she hadn't heard me admonishing Henley.

'Where are we off to, sweetie?'

Even standing on the platform behind the counter, the woman was a few inches shorter than me. Faint lines traced her features and her cheeks sagged a bit, giving her face a pleasant roundness. I realized the woman was probably in her mid-sixties to early seventies – the same age I was . . . or technically *would be*, were my years not fixed in time.

'Sweetie?' The woman's smile faltered, but it was nothing like the frown the taxi driver gave me.

I realised she had asked me a question. 'Pardon?'

'Where are you flying to today?'

'Oh . . .' I looked around and tried not to panic. I should have thought of this before I left the house, or even in the cab.

I scanned the other side of the counter, passing over an unopened box of blue pens and a work timetable with lunchtime highlighted in pink before my eyes stopped on a stack of travel brochures. *¡Bienvenido a España!* the one on top proudly proclaimed. *Visit Madrid! You'll love it here!* I wondered if it was a sign.

'Yes . . . uh . . . I'd like to buy a ticket for Madrid, please.'

'Oh, how nice.' The warm smile was back as she started typing. 'We can fly you to Heathrow and you can connect there to Madrid. By the way, the weather's gorgeous in Spain this time of year – it's not too hot or wet yet . . . Let's see.' The click of her typing stopped and she sighed. 'Oh, sweetie, I'm afraid all the flights to Heathrow today are full. You see, they only leave at 8 a.m. in the morning and the rest of the flights are 3 p.m. and later. I'm s— Oh, maybe . . . Yes, I think there's a few seats on this one. It'll be arriving late, though, about 1 a.m. You'll have to catch a flight to Madrid the following morning. The Heathrow flight was supposed to be leaving this morning at 8:36. It was delayed five hours due to maintenance and a few passengers transferred off it.'

'That's fine,' I said quickly. I would have said okay to just about anything then.

'Very well. I'll get this set up for you.' The sound of her typing resumed. 'Would you like to book your return flight as well?'

'No thank you,' I said. I contemplated whether there was ever going to be a return.

Since I would be arriving at one in the morning, I figured I could book into some nearby airport hotel. I would worry about that when I got there.

Digging into my purse again, I pulled out the credit card Miss Hatfield had provided for emergencies only. If this wasn't an emergency, I had no clue what would be. It was a mystery to me how Miss Hatfield had obtained a credit card, but it was no surprise that she managed to do it. I also dug out the battered passport Miss Hatfield had given me. One of the first things Miss Hatfield had done in this time period was apply for a passport. According to her, there was no such think as too much 'just in case' preparation. She worked for weeks straight to forge baptismal certificates and hospital birth certificates. I saw letters from the DMV to obtain drivers' licenses. The deaths of young women in New York were circled in the obituaries for a time – I had guessed that was connected to how Miss Hatfield had obtained a social security number. Although she wasn't particularly handy with a computer, she'd had centuries to become proficient at forging and obtaining official documents and 'borrowing' the social security numbers of already deceased people. I just held my breath and hoped her work was good enough.

The woman at the counter was quick to swipe my card and soon enough the freshly printed boarding pass was in my hands.

'Have a wonderful time in Spain, sweetie,' the woman said. 'Next in line!'

The security line was a nightmare. A baby screwed up its face and unleashed a yowl from hell. A platinum-blonde woman took five minutes to simply remove her strappy sandals. But thankfully my turn eventually came. I placed my bag on the conveyor belt. Barefoot like everyone else, I walked into the tube-like machine like the people in front of me had. I was told to put my hands up while a sliding bar scanned me from left to right, after which a uniformed woman took a glance at my boarding pass and waved me along.

'Whose bag is this?'

I turned to see a uniformed man holding my duffle bag up.

I must have looked guilty or nervous, or maybe even both, because the man looked my way and motioned me over.

'Miss, I'm going to search the bag.'

I mutely nodded. No one else's bag was being searched.

'Where are you off to, miss?' The man unzipped my bag and started rifling through the clothes I had packed.

'Um.' I looked down at my boarding pass. 'Gate thirty-eight.'

He laughed. Glad something I said was amusing.

'No, I meant where are you off to on this trip.'

My face heated up. 'London first. Then connecting to Madrid.'

'Business or pleasure?' he asked.

'Mostly pleasure.'

The man partially pulled out the golden clock from between layers of clothing in my bag. 'Beautiful clock.'

'Thanks,' I said.

'You know, my aunt collects antiques. This must be worth a fortune in the condition it's in.'

'Well, now you know why I didn't want to check my luggage.' I tried to smile at him.

'Of course,' he said. 'But might I suggest different packaging next time. Like bubble wrap?'

He zipped my bag up without putting everything back the way it was, and handed me my bag. 'Have a nice day.'

I shuffled over to a bench to reorganize. I checked the clock before bundling it up in my shirts again. I made sure I still had my phone and put it in one of the side pockets.

Then came the long trek to the boarding gate.

Good God, JFK is huge.

'You're telling me.'

I had never been in an airport before – the need hadn't arisen either before or since I'd become immortal – but navigating it was a breeze as long as I remembered to pay attention to all the signs. After all, I'd seen the shtick movie characters did before reuniting with their loved ones.

'Gate thirty-eight. Flight to London, Heathrow,' I read.

It was close to boarding time and the area around the gate was packed with families trying to console crying babies and young couples who couldn't keep their hands off each other. Unable to find a single empty seat near the gate, I remembered seeing charging stations with seats at other gates and decided to top up my phone before boarding. I glanced around and spied one at a nearby gate. Two of its seats were already taken, but there was an empty third. I was only a few steps away when a man swooped in without looking and took the seat.

50

'Dammit.'

The man looked up at me with wide green eyes. 'I'm sorry,' he said. 'I took your seat, didn't I?'

I muttered something unintelligible and was turning away when he stood up.

'Here – why don't you take the seat?' He moved his things aside. 'I don't really need to sit to charge my phone anyway.'

I was about to refuse, as I would have done on any other day. But this wasn't any other day and the weight of everything that had happened pressed down on me. In that moment, all I wanted to do was take a seat, and so I did.

'Thanks,' I said, finally setting my duffel bag down between my feet.

'No probs. You're the one who looks like you need it.'

I wondered if I really did look that tired. I hadn't seen myself in a mirror since leaving the house.

'Say . . . I was about to get a Starbucks. You in?' A strand of the man's curly dirty-blonde hair came loose from his quiff. 'You clearly need some caffeine in you, and as much as I'd like to take credit for treating a beautiful woman, I actually have a gift card I need to use.'

'Thanks, but I'm fine.'

'No, seriously – I got like five Starbucks gift cards for my birthday. It's as if my friends think that coffee is the only thing I live on. I even have one of those treat receipt coupons that might get me a free drink.' He grinned and his green eyes flashed, reminding me of Henley. 'So what do you drink?'

He was so much like Henley in some ways, but the complete opposite in others. He was kind, and to a complete stranger no less. His eyes crinkled at the corners

51

when he talked, just like Henley's. But his laugh was entirely different.

'I'd like a strawberries and crème frappuccino, please.'

He laughed. 'That's hardly coffee.' Nevertheless, he headed off to buy me one.

A coupon? Free coffee? The men in this time seem very frugal.

I couldn't help but feel a little self-conscious for the man, but I just smiled.

I opened my duffel bag to retrieve my phone and its charger. My phone was sitting neatly in one of the side pockets, but I couldn't find the charger. I came to the conclusion that I must have left it behind in my hurry to get out of the house.

I sighed and glanced at the two businessmen seated around the charger with me. Neither of them had the same phone. I checked the phone Starbucks-boy had carelessly left behind, connected and charging but, unlike mine, it was a BlackBerry.

I thought about asking around as there had to be some people using the same phone as me, and who therefore probably had compatible chargers on them, but decided against it. Asking to borrow a stranger's charger would draw attention to me . . . and for what? It wasn't as though I had anyone to call – the only contact on my phone was Miss Hatfield.

I zipped my duffel bag again and looked towards the Starbucks near the gate. Starbucks-boy had his back to me as he waited for the drinks, but I recognized him by his flannel plaid shirt and grey skinny jeans. He stood with his arms draped on the counter, relaxed. There was something so easy and uncomplicated about him. I wanted to be like him.

52

Soon he came back carrying two drinks.

'I hope you like whipped cream,' he said, holding mine out towards me.

I smiled in response, looking briefly at the name on my cup.

'Yeah, my name's Samuel, by the way. Sam to most people.'

'Well, thank you, Sam.'

I reached for my duffel bag to pull out my wallet, but he stopped me.

'Gift card, remember?'

'Are you sure?' I asked, though I knew I didn't have enough cash to pay him back after the expensive taxi fare.

'I'm definitely sure.'

I took a sip of my frappuccino and drew out the silence.

'So where are you heading?' He looked up at the sign above the gate number. 'London?'

I shook my head. 'I'm connecting to Madrid.'

'That sounds like fun. What are you up to there?'

I wondered what I would do once I arrived. It would be a good idea to lie low and remain inconspicuous for a bit, at least. Maybe I could also learn more about Juan Ponce de León, the man who discovered the Fountain of Youth and who was part of my legacy now . . . After all, Spain was his home country. Maybe it was some sort of fate that led me to glimpse that particular brochure at the ticket counter?

'Sightseeing . . . you know, the usual things,' I said. 'How about you? Are you going to London?'

'Sadly, no.' He pointed to the gate across from the one we were at. 'Paris.'

'Sightseeing?' I guessed.

'Nah – I wish.' He ran his fingers through his quiff and

quickly brushed it forward again. 'I signed up for a course there. I'm studying photography at Tische and thought I deserved a creative break. I mean—'

'Attention, ladies and gentlemen. This is Flight DAL4371 from JFK to London, Heathrow. We are now inviting Economy Class passengers to begin boarding at this time. Please have your boarding pass and identification ready. Thank you.'

'That's me,' I said quickly. I grabbed my duffel bag and began to turn.

'Could I get your number?'

I sped up, pretending I hadn't heard him.

Chapter 6

Everyone was quiet, listening to the plane's engines scream in their ears as it descended.

My palms were sweaty as I tried not to think about this hunk of flying metal crashing to the ground. I knew I had to start thinking about finding a place to stay the night. I was so wound up from the day's events and flying that I had sat rigid the entire flight. All I wanted to do now was lie down.

There was a loud whining noise as the plane seemed to decelerate. I looked around at the other passengers to see if this was normal. Everyone continued reading their books and talking. I heard the thud as the plane's wheels hit the Tarmac, followed by an uneventful few minutes as passengers shifted in their sheets wanting to deplane.

'Please make sure you have all your carry-on items with you as you exit the plane.' A flight attendant with too much red lipstick ushered us out. 'Thank you for choosing to fly with us. We hope you enjoyed your flight.'

I got off the plane on unsteady feet, not used to being on solid ground that wasn't travelling at some 550 miles per hour. People pushed past me, eager to retrieve their suitcases from baggage claim and get out of the airport. Some were home; others were visitors here, just like me.

The air in England smelled different even inside the terminal. Gone was the odour of baked, pockmarked concrete, and I thought I could almost detect notes of Miss Hatfield's perfume – something from older days brought into the rapid-moving present.

I passed Immigration and Customs without much of a delay. The people behind the desks looked tired and barely looked up at me.

I headed for a uniform-clad man seated at another desk.

'Do you need some help, ma'am?' he asked.

I wondered if I looked as lost as I felt.

'I have a connecting flight in the morning, and I'm afraid I need a place to stay the night,' I said.

'As your flight was delayed, we can give you a voucher to stay at a nearby hotel, if you'd like. There's a free shuttle bus.'

A bed. Finally. With all the excitement of the day and the uncomfortable flight, that was exactly what I needed to forget the fatigue bearing down on my shoulders.

'That would be wonderful.' Something in his expression told me that my smile looked strained.

I spent the entire ride to the hotel staring out of the window, trying to catch my first glimpse of England. It was black outside and the road melted into the sky. Every so often, we would pass a streetlight. They were so bright, like giant spotlights dotting the road, but all they lit up was the road ahead and the occasional building. I was so tired that I could only clearly see my pale face staring back at me. Nothing struck me as different from New York; it was the same darkness, and the uneasiness had followed me here, too.

The hotel was also in Heathrow, and soon enough I was dealing with a sour-looking teenage boy at check-in.

'How many nights?' His mouth appeared to be fixed in a permanent pucker even when he talked.

'Just one – I have a connecting flight in the morning. They gave me this voucher because my flight was delayed.'

'Room 125.' He handed me a flimsy plastic key-card.

'Thanks.'

As I suspected, Room 125 was on the first floor. With its yellow wallpaper, single window and art-free walls, it wasn't much to look at, but I supposed I should have expected that from a last-minute hotel room near the airport that took airline vouchers.

'Well, I guess this is it.' I tossed my bag onto the bed.

You'll be safe here for the time being.

I held my head in my hands. I couldn't begin to describe how *good* it felt to hear his voice.

What are you thinking?

'About you.' I was telling the truth. 'I missed you.'

What, during those seven or so hours you were on the plane?

'You know I don't mean just that.'

There was a pause. *I know.*

'So much has happened so quickly. And just when I had gotten you back, too. I'm still trying to wrap my head around everything else.'

The murder, you mean?

It still felt strange to use that word. 'Yeah . . . but also you being here.'

I can understand that.

'Why did it take you so long?' It was a question I had been considering since this new Henley had first spoken to me. 'I thought you were gone for good.'

When I died . . . I didn't know where I was. I thought I had reached some kind of afterlife, but it wasn't exactly what I thought heaven would be.

'What was it like?'

Like watching a multitude of scenes projected onto millions of tiny picture frames.

'Like a control panel with lots of television screens?'

Henley laughed. *I guess you could say that. I've had to learn a lot about technology during the last hundred years.*

I ignored that. I didn't know whether Henley was trying to change the subject or just try to get me to smile, but either way, this was serious. I tried to figure out how to phrase my next question. 'And . . . where are you now?'

In a dark room watching all this play out.

I was surprised by how quick and definite his answer sounded.

I don't have a concept of how long it took me, but I started to learn to focus myself into one time and one scene. With everything going on at once, it's all colour and noise, but if I focus I can make some sense of it.

'Like you're doing now?'

It took practice to get to this point. It took practice to find you.

'What do you mean?'

He chuckled. *Miss Rebecca, you're a hard one to find and you don't even know it.* Henley paused. *It's like watching what you would call a video. Two people are having a conversation, but where one of them should be standing is just blank space. It's as if someone cut you out of the scene, leaving a Rebecca-shaped hole. I can hear you, and I can see your outline if I concentrate, but otherwise it's as if you're not present in any time.*

I guessed we were almost even, save for the fact that I couldn't see Henley at all.

It took me a while to learn how to reach out to you.

'By typing on my computer?'

Not just that.

'Like when you moved the ring you gave me into the kitchen and the bathroom?'

I learned many things, including that I shouldn't talk when people are around because they can hear me when I focus my voice in one place. Henley laughed darkly. *I scared many a person that way. Who knew ghost tales could be made true?*

I had been wondering if it was just me who could hear him.

Then I started trying to touch things, to move them. It was difficult at first to manipulate objects without falling through them . . . It still is.

I knew things were hard for Henley, but he had to understand things were challenging for me, too.

I could hear footsteps through the ceiling from the floor above and the sounds of doors opening and closing in rhythm with the whirring of planes flying overhead. I stood up to inspect the walls to give myself some time to think. They were a peculiar yellow; I couldn't tell if they had always been that way, or if the sickly colour was the result of age and sun. No matter. I was only here a night, and since it was already dark out, I figured I would get some sleep. It wasn't that late by New York time, but I was exhausted by the day's events. Add the fact that I had been too nervous to sleep on the flight since it was my first time on a plane and I was utterly worn out. I didn't want to stay awake thinking any more.

I shut the curtains, then unzipped my bag to check that the clock was still intact after being jostled on our journey. Although it had been tossed around a bit, surprisingly neither the glass nor the metal case had a single scratch. I set the clock on the left-hand bedside table. The dim lights of the room reflected against its golden rim, and that sight was comforting to me. It was one small thing that hadn't changed, even after Miss Hatfield had died.

Thinking about the past?

Henley's voice startled me.

'Yeah,' I breathed. 'There's a lot to come to terms with.'

I walked over to the room's single window and opened the curtains just long enough to close the window. The window was big and I was surprised to find it didn't have a lock. Realizing I had nothing to change into, I turned off the light and slipped between the covers clothed.

Despite how tired I thought I was, sleep didn't come easily. The yellow of the room was replaced with darkest black, but I still saw shadows behind my eyelids. When the shadows morphed into crazed patterns, a fevered dream began. It didn't make sense. There was no story or plot. Just images. Faces. Miss Hatfield's blanched skin. The hotel clerk's scrunched-up mouth. Henley's furrowed brow.

I wasn't aware of tossing in my sleep, but when I woke, the sheets were twisted and my clothes were plastered against my sweaty body. Cool air touched my face and I felt the perspiration gathered on my upper lip. Suddenly chilled, I looked towards the source of the breeze. Through the slightly parted curtains, I saw that the window was open.

Frowning, I got up to shut it again. There was a satisfying click, but I recalled hearing that same sound when I closed it before . . .

Just as I was getting back into bed, I heard a noise. That is, I *thought* I heard a noise. I froze, but hearing nothing else in the dark save for the drunken shouts of a man making his way up from the hotel bar, I lay down again. It was probably just my paranoia mixed up with how tired

I was. A lot had happened in only a couple of days and I needed time to digest it all.

There was a crash and I shot up in bed. My fist clutched at the sheets as I tried to get away from whatever was in the room with me. I groped around for the light but I couldn't remember which wall the main switch was on. With the curtains shut and the lights out, all I could tell was that the sound appeared to be coming from somewhere on my left.

Rebecca, get away from the bed!

I followed Henley's direction, but instead of moving away from the intruder, I blindly launched my body towards the left side of the room and the source of the noise. The clock was somewhere on the bedside table, and it was the only thing that mattered now. Scrabbling in the darkness, I felt the solid wood of the table and the cold metal of the clock.

I also felt a stranger's hard body reaching over me.

I could hear the voices of other hotel guests in the corridor outside, all too preoccupied and loud to guess or probably even hear what was happening in a room a few doors down from their own.

I tried to hit him. There was nothing skilful about it – I just lashed out and struck him wherever I could. But he was strong and shoved me towards the wall.

I heard the sound of breaking glass before I felt the sharp pain on my forearm and realised the glass face of the clock must have broken. Something wet and sticky began to drip down my arm, but I didn't have time to think about that as I mindlessly groped around in the dark for the clock.

Another stab of pain as the intruder stepped on my hand. I cried out, and as he stumbled, unbalanced, I was able to push him over.

I think he fell, but I was too disorientated to be sure. More crashes followed, and Henley might have been yelling. Still no one came to find out if anything was amiss. I wondered if they thought it was the drunken man I had heard earlier yelling and knocking things over in his room.

All of a sudden, the floor felt harder and colder than it had been a few moments ago. I picked myself up, intending to run after the intruder, but I had no idea where he was. I heard a thud on the far side of the room and figured that was the intruder jumping out through the window. He had escaped.

I groped my way across the room to shove the curtains aside but concluded they must have been torn down in the scuffle. Outside was as dark as the room. Darker than I remembered; I couldn't see any airport lights or street-lamps. I tried to find the light switch again, but was so turned around I had no idea where it was.

Not thinking straight, crawling on my hands and knees, I searched the floor for the clock. The carpet felt rougher than before, but I assumed that was because my hands were now cut and bruised. I ransacked every corner of the room but still couldn't find the clock. It was lost.

For the first time since Miss Hatfield turned into dust before me, I heard my heart. It was deafening and my head thrummed with its beats. I just wished it would stop.

Without the clock, I was stuck. I wouldn't turn into dust. No, my fate would be much worse than that. I would slowly watch myself go insane, all the while knowing it was happening but powerless to do anything about it.

I shivered from the suddenly piercing cold. I wanted to call out. To call for Miss Hatfield or Henley. But my voice was trapped inside my throat and all I could do was gasp.

Everything was so dark, I couldn't tell whether my eyes were open or closed.

Rebecca?

I wanted to respond, but my throat felt tight.

Rebecca? He seemed to be getting further away.

I wanted to call out for Henley not to leave me. He couldn't leave me. What would I do without him?

It was so dark that I began to see colours – or rather, flashes of light. Were they real? Were the colours behind my eyelids? Henley seemed to have stopped calling.

Chapter 7

It was the sound that woke me – or rather the *lack* of sound. The whine and thrum of planes were distinctly absent, as was the sharp ringing of telephone calls and people's loud conversations barely muffled through the wall. No sound. No motion. All was still and flat.

When I stretched out my legs, pain shot through me. I'd woken crumpled on the ground in a foetal position, but my cheek wasn't pressed up against the hotel room's discoloured carpet. Instead, I felt a cool dirt floor against my skin.

My eyelids felt like lead and forcing them open proved as difficult as sitting up without screaming. Looking down at my body, my nakedness made me gasp. My clothes were nowhere in sight. Even the small action of moving my neck made me want to double over in agony. Then I noticed my surroundings and stiffened.

The yellow wallpaper was missing. In its place were rough wood walls that sloped towards each other in a perpetual balancing act under an almost pyramidal thatched roof. The structure's floor was bare dirt. Sunlight coming in through the open window revealed an uneven bed of straw occupying the far corner of the room and a small chest in another. The clock was nowhere to be seen.

Ignoring my body's protests, I stood up and stumbled towards the wooden chest. It was simple in design, latched but not locked, and I flicked it open easily. I rifled through layers of linen inside it, only realising they were clothing after I found a woman's shift and a man's white shirt.

My blood ran cold in my veins as I realized what was going on: in the struggle with the intruder, one of us must have hit the clock and accidentally turned its hands, causing me to travel in time. That was why the hotel room had felt so different after the scuffle. I cursed myself for not having realized earlier. It also explained why I was naked – my jeans and T-shirt wouldn't have survived the trip. I was in a different time and my modern clothing hadn't been made yet.

My next thought was for Henley – had he come with me? And when was this, anyway?

'Henley?' I tried. 'Henley?'

Are you all right?

His voice was loaded with concern. I remembered he could only see an outline of me and therefore didn't know if I was hurt.

'Yes, I'm fine.' I stretched and cringed.

I think you have a different definition of 'fine' from mine.

Though Henley couldn't see me per se, that didn't mean he wasn't paying close attention to the outline of my body and its movements. But the bright side of his not being able to actually *see* me was that he couldn't see that I was naked, either.

Throwing on the shift, I quickly rummaged through the rest of the clothes. I wanted to collect what I thought I would need and leave wherever this was before anyone found me, but I was also looking for clues as to where – or rather *when* – I was.

65

I added a petticoat to the shift, followed by a reddish-brown gown that laced up in the front. There were other clothes I didn't know how to wear, but I figured this simple ensemble would be fine for my purposes . . . whatever they might turn out to be.

I found a pair of leather shoes and hurriedly put them on. They were half a size too small, but they would do.

'Thankfully the clock has to be somewhere . . .'

I was talking mostly to myself, but Henley replied. *Does it always come with you?*

It was easy to forget that even Henley didn't know all the details of time travel that I had learned through Miss Hatfield.

'That's just how it works. The clock always comes with me to the time which I'm visiting.'

It goes where you go?

'It's more that the clock's just so old that going back and forth in time doesn't change it. It's always been the same . . . It wouldn't just disappear, so the intruder must have taken it with him.' I ran my fingers through my hair. 'Can't you just . . . see?'

You mean look for a small clock in all of space and time?

It did sound absurd when he put it that way. 'Is that a no?'

Rebecca. Imagine looking into a doll's house for a miniature clock. Now multiply that doll's house by a few billion to account for all the houses and all the clocks that have ever existed or will exist in time. Now can you see how absurd and impossible your request is?

'But you found me.'

And it took a while. And a gap in time is slightly – only slightly – easier to find than this needle in a haystack. Besides, that was you. You have this . . . draw. It's hard to explain.

It's like I can focus on you a little better than the rest of the world.

I was glad Henley had found his way back to me, but it was impossible not to wish he could be a little more helpful. It looked like it was going to be up to me to find the clock.

I tried to put the contents of the chest back the way I had found them, but knew the owner would probably realize a few pieces were missing. I had no grand plan, but it was obvious I needed to leave before the house's inhabitants returned. I opened the door and a gust of cold wind flew into my face. It cut right through the coarse, homespun dress and I hesitated in the doorway.

'Look, I have to get it back.'

For once, Henley didn't say I was being hasty or foolish. He didn't say anything.

Gone were the planes screaming through the sky, the asphalt, the smell of wet concrete. In their place was a startling green that made the wide sky appear brighter. Seeing no obvious alternatives, I began walking.

Heathrow really was a heath in whatever time this was. Everything in the landscape was rough, from the coarse grass to the wiry purple and yellow flowers dotting the scenery. Leaves and stems scratched at my ankles and snapped where I walked. The too-small shoes I was wearing pinched at the toes. The footprints I left behind me in the damp ground trailed back to the little house, which was now almost a speck on the hillside.

Ahead I could see a tree by the bank of a narrow river, its top and branches flattened as if the sky weighed heavily on it. Having nowhere else to go, I began to walk towards it. All too soon I was standing on the riverbank, still without a plan.

What are you going to do now?

I bit my lip and concentrated on Henley's words. I couldn't begin to tell him how nice it was to hear a familiar voice.

'I . . . I don't know.'

Don't cry.

I didn't realize I was tearing up until he said that. He had probably heard it in my voice, and now hot tears were sliding from the corners of my eyes. I gasped for breath, but my lungs wouldn't expand.

I felt gentle hands around my shoulders and my body sank into pure warmth.

'Don't cry.'

It was an unfamiliar voice and unfamiliar frame I sank into, but it felt safe, for some reason. It was a fatherly gesture, something I couldn't remember receiving for a very long time.

I gulped in air, and as it rushed into my lungs, I realized he smelled like a father too – like *my* father . . . or rather Cynthia's father. The stranger smelled like the husky smoke of a pipe, and I could vaguely remember a time when my own hair smelled lightly of that smoke. It was always after my father hugged me as he came home from work.

'Please don't cry.'

The stranger held me close for quite a while. Only when he released me did I get my first look at him. He was old. His beard wasn't greying – it was completely white. His wispy hair matched his fragile frame and his skin hung limply over his bones. I was surprised that such a feeble-looking man had been holding me up without apparent effort just a moment before.

'No need to be frightened,' he said, watching me glance him over. 'Just tell us where you're off to and we'll see you get there.'

'Are we taking in strays again?' The new voice sounded younger and harsher than the old man's.

Over at the river bank, a younger, dark-haired man was tying up a rowing boat.

'This girl's obviously lost,' the older man said. 'It's our duty to take her home.'

'Lost?' The younger man jumped from the boat and began to walk towards us. 'Are you sure about that? Perhaps she's just run away from home? I mean, look at the way she's dressed!'

This made the older man avert his gaze, but I could see his brows were furrowed.

'Father, have you even thought to ask the girl yourself? Surely she can talk.' By now the younger man was standing next to me, and although he addressed his father, he was looking at me.

The older man finally turned back. 'My dear girl, are you lost or running?'

I opened my mouth to answer, but then paused. Was I lost or was I running? Both, I supposed, but I could never explain that.

'Lost.'

The old man nodded, satisfied with my answer.

The young man scowled. 'Even so,' he continued, as if I wasn't there, 'it's not our job to take her home. We have other things to do. Other things that actually pay.'

The old man did not appear to hear him. 'What's your name, girl?'

'Rebecca,' I said. 'Rebecca Hatfield.'

'And how did you get here, Mistress Hatfield?' The young man squinted at me.

369,000 pounds of flying metal called an airplane, I wanted to answer. *And, oh yeah, time-travel*, but all that came out was, 'I was travelling.'

'Travelling?' The young man threw his arms up. 'Through here? Why? There's nothing here! Where on earth were you going?'

'I–I . . .' I could tell he didn't believe me and I panicked.

'Oh, do be gentle with the girl,' the older man said. 'It's obvious she's been through a lot. She must have stepped out of a carriage to stretch her legs and accidentally been left behind.'

'*Accidentally* left behind? And a carriage? Across this heath?'

'What other explanation is there? I know she's not dressed like much, but I think she's one of those *important* people. Why else would she sound the way she does? Why don't we bring the girl along?' The old man said. 'We can accompany her into town and enquire after passing carriages.'

'She isn't ours to worry about,' the younger man hissed.

'She is now.'

'I never asked you where your home is,' the old man said.

It was the first time in hours that any of us had broken the silence.

'Far from here,' I said. I hoped he wouldn't continue questioning me, but of course he did.

'I supposed so,' he said. 'Your accent . . . It's certainly not from these parts.'

I'd assumed it would only be a matter of time before they picked up on the way I talked. I realized I had an American accent in a time where there probably were no Americans yet.

I glanced at the young man sitting behind me. He hadn't spoken since we got into the boat and made no effort to join the conversation now, but I knew he was listening to our exchange.

'Are you from the north?'

'No,' I responded. 'From the west.'

'Ah, near Liverpool?'

'A bit farther west.' He didn't need to know exactly how far west I'd come from.

'And what's it like there? Where you come from?'

The first thought that popped up was the St Patrick's Day Parade in New York. Not really knowing how to respond, I said the first thing that came to mind. 'Very green.'

'And what's your home like?'

'It's a . . . brown stone building whose steps I trip down every morning.'

'Steps?'

I wasn't sure if I'd said something wrong. 'Yes . . . steps.'

'And what about windows?'

'Oh, we have windows.'

'Many of them?'

I thought back to Miss Hatfield's brownstone. 'I suppose you could say that.'

'There you go!' He suddenly turned to the young man. 'Told you she was mighty important. I had a hunch.' Then the old man nodded thoughtfully and surprised me by not questioning me further.

The next time he spoke was when the boat stopped at a moderately large village.

'Give me your hand, Mistress Hatfield,' the old man said, 'and just hop across. Don't fall in the Thames.'

I looked down at the wide gap between the boat and solid land. All I could see was dark water. 'Just hop across,' I echoed. Easier said than done.

'Oh, come here.' The words were barely out of the young man's mouth when I felt strong hands lift me up and over the gap.

71

Upon collecting myself, I muttered a quick thank you.

The young man shrugged. 'We'd have been waiting all day for you,' was his response.

The old man led me by the hand through crowds in what looked like a marketplace of sorts, dotted with small lean-tos. I saw an entire wagon filled with meat and another just with turnips. The people between looked over their shoulders at me and whispered among themselves as they watched me being led by the old man. I knew I must have looked a sight as I walked through the streets in a dress I might not even be wearing correctly.

I don't like him.

'Keep your voice down,' I hissed.

I didn't want anyone to hear Henley, especially the old man or his companion. I had no idea what they would do if they witnessed me talking to a disembodied voice. Leave me here? Burn me at the stake for being a witch?

I don't like the old man or his lackey. I mean, what do they want with you?

'Probably nothing,' I whispered under my breath. 'Plus they're the only shot I have to get somewhere.'

You don't even know where they're taking you.

'I don't really have a choice, do I? Anywhere is better than being left here . . . Now hush!'

We stopped when the younger man found a particular lean-to and went inside alone. So preoccupied was I with everyone staring that I hadn't noticed he'd been looking for something. The young man emerged from the lean-to a few minutes later accompanied by a rough-looking woman. They both glanced at me, but neither moved to speak to me.

The woman was heavyset and seemed to make the ground shake as she circled me. Over and over she pulled at her tightly curled hair so it straightened and sprang back into place, making me more nervous each time. Though at first glance she looked like a hefty housewife, there was something unquestionably predatory about her, and I felt myself shrinking in response.

She turned briefly to mutter something to the young man, before squinting at me.

'Speak,' she demanded in a gravelly voice that matched her appearance.

'I'm sorry?' I didn't know what she wanted.

'Oh, she's definitely not from around here. A foreigner. You're right about that. There *was* a report of a flipped carriage early this morning . . . Though where she got those rags, I don't know.'

'My garments and trunks were stolen.' I figured it was worth a shot.

'Including the clothes off your very back?' Her arched eyebrow made her face look all the more intimidating, and it took everything I had to maintain eye contact with her.

'They were bandits. They made me change out of my fine clothes and into these.'

'An unusual twist in the story,' the woman said. 'If anything, it proves how foreign you are to these lands. That and the dreadful accent . . .'

There was a pause and I held my breath. Did she buy it?

'You. Follow me.' The arched brow was lowered. Without waiting for a response, she turned on her heel and headed off towards the far side of the marketplace.

Not knowing what else I could do, I followed her.

The old man did the same, saying, 'She's definitely someone important. Someone higher up. Listen to the way she speaks. Maybe some far-off duke's daughter. Better yet, a foreign Bohemian princess—'

After not more than a few steps, the woman stopped abruptly in front of me. She turned and looked down her nose at the old man.

'I want the girl *alone*,' she clarified in her grating voice.

I took the old man's hand in mine. I noticed for the first time just how cold it was and how it shook ever so slightly.

'Thank you,' I whispered to him. 'Thank you so much.'

I kissed him on the cheek and even the young man gave me a last taciturn nod. I attempted to smile, then I followed the woman.

I was uncertain of everything – where I was, the exact period I was in, who I was with – but I knew I had to do something. Given the way people were dressed, I had to be in some far-off century – before even Miss Hatfield was born in the 1800s. I had to find the clock. I had to at least try.

Chapter 8

'Hurry up now.' I suspected that the woman I was following was as tightly wound as her coiled hair. She tutted at me without even turning back when I lagged as little as two steps behind. She walked quickly, I chased her, and the late afternoon sun trailed us both.

'Come on.'

I trained my eyes on the back of her head and willed myself to keep up with her. Though her legs looked stubby, they appeared to move twice as fast as mine.

Henley had fallen silent in her presence. With just the woman and myself present, his voice would have easily been heard.

When she stopped to open a wooden door in the side of a large building, I almost ran into her.

Though the woman hadn't looked at me for a while, she did so now. 'We don't have time for clumsy.'

I didn't know why she was being so short with me. I figured she was just that sort of woman as I hadn't done anything to offend her, so far as I could tell. I held my tongue and followed her through the door.

I was immediately startled by how warm it was inside. One wall was dominated by a large fireplace in which three people could have crouched. A large pot hung over the fire, but even that looked tiny in comparison to the

75

flames that looked set to consume it entirely.

Though the fire was the main source of light in the room, I also noticed small rectangles of light at the top of all four walls, two on each wall. They were the only windows, and they couldn't have been more than a foot across. People were scampering around with armfuls of vegetables and heavy pots. I was surprised I didn't feel claustrophobic. I watched a woman take two live chickens from a cage and tuck them under her arms. They were still squawking as she made her way past me.

'You.'

Recognising the gruff voice of the woman I was supposed to be following, I quickly returned my attention to her.

'Less daydreaming. More walking.'

I quickened my steps to show her I was at least trying to keep up, but she only muttered something under her breath.

Exiting the kitchen, we entered a narrow hall with a few doors on each side. They were all made of the same dark wood and loomed over me.

'Wait here.' She disappeared through one of the doors before I could answer.

Though the doors looked sturdy, I could hear voices behind the one she had just closed in my face. The woman's thick, abrupt voice was joined by a second, definitely female. Not as throaty, but still firm. I couldn't make out a word they were saying, but I knew they had to be discussing me.

Minutes dragged by as I stared at the door. It was simply a door, with no intricate carvings to distract me. But as I squinted at it, I began to see patterns and designs in the grain of the wood. I sighed, feeling the long hours since I had last slept – properly or otherwise.

The door swung open at last and the burly looking woman stepped out, followed by the other woman. The second woman was wrapped in an austere dress – it was a dark-grey colour and was cut unflatteringly, making her look rather square. Her hair was plastered back against her scalp into a tight bun, and she pursed her lips as she looked me over from head to toe.

'I see,' she said. After pausing for a moment, as if contemplating her next words, she added, 'Follow me.'

I couldn't help but feel glad when we left the other woman behind.

Assuming this woman wouldn't want to wait for me any more than the previous one had, I did my best to never be more than a step behind her. She led me down numerous corridors filled with oil paintings, still lives and portraits of people looking stiff and posed. Leaving the corridors, we passed through a number of interconnected rooms. Not having time to examine them closely, they all looked the same to me – square rooms with sparse decorations and furniture covered with white sheets. Judging by the number of people who worked in the kitchen, it seemed as though there were lots of people working at the house, but it also seemed as if no one actually lived there.

Finally, the woman stopped in a room where the furniture wasn't covered by white cloths. A breeze from somewhere ruffled a few papers on a table.

The woman moved to a door on the far side of the room. 'Who should I tell Lord Empson is calling?'

'Excuse me?'

'Your name, my lady.' The woman looked annoyed, as if already regretting her decision to allow me into the house.

'Oh!'

My eyes darted around the room wildly. I didn't know exactly what I was looking for, but I needed a clue. Something. And quickly.

Eleanor Shelton.

'Pardon?'

He had said it softly, but she heard.

I smiled, grateful that Henley had stepped in.

'Eleanor Shelton.'

The woman nodded and disappeared through the door. I was alone with Henley at last.

'Thanks,' I whispered, taking care not to speak too loudly. If I had learned one thing in 1904, in Henley's time, it was that the walls always have ears. You could never be too careful. 'But who's Eleanor Shelton?'

Someone you'll need to know a lot about quite soon.

Henley's familiar chuckle echoed through the room. It sounded as if he was standing right next to me and across the room all at once.

I turned to survey my new surroundings. There were two small cream-colored couches, one of which I decided to sit on to avoid looking restless. Glancing around, I saw a small fireplace, complete with golden poker, and a wall of books. I was close enough to the bookshelves to see that most of the titles on the spines were in foreign languages – Greek and Latin, probably. I laughed quietly, wondering if this Lord Empson actually read these books, or if they were just for appearances.

There you are, chuckling to yourself while I'm hard at work making sure you have a cover story.

My head snapped around at the rustle of papers.

'Henley! You scared me! What if someone comes in?'

That's what happens when you leave me to do all the work.

Henley was shuffling through a pile of papers on the desk at the far end of the room. A book from the shelf behind me flew past my head onto the desk, where its pages started flipping without any help from a human hand. It looked like there was a ghost in the room.

I shook my head. I wondered if I would ever get used to this.

Here we go.

'Did you find something?'

A whole lot of something, Henley said. *I gave you the name Eleanor Shelton earlier because I noticed some papers – letters mostly – in which she was mentioned.*

'So you were riffling through papers while the woman was still in the room?' I thought back to the breeze ruffling the loose pages on the table.

Apparently she lives rather far away, Henley said, not answering my question. *So I figured that maybe this Lord Empson's never met her before. It's an enormous assumption, I know, but it's all I had to go on.*

'So she's a real person and not a fictional character.'

Precisely. I figured it would make him want to see you a bit sooner.

'And I'm guessing Lord Empson is the owner of the house?'

Master of the house, Henley corrected me. *Yes, and Eleanor Shelton is the daughter of his business associate.*

More papers and books flapped around my head. They travelled at such speeds that I was amazed they didn't make any sound when they landed on the table.

'What kind of business?' I figured I should know my dear Papa's line of work.

Fur trade. From Russia through Lithuania.

'Lithuania?'

The Grand Duchy of Lithuania.

'The Grand what?'

79

The Grand Duchy, Henley said. *It doesn't lose the 'Grand Duchy' part of its title till 1795.*

'Well what year is it now?'

Only 1527.

'1527? It's 1527 right now?' I heard my voice start to rise. 'Only 1527? What do you mean, *only* 1527? And how do you know that?'

I'm knee-deep through his expense records and personal letters, so I'm pretty sure it's currently 1527 where you are.

I felt dizzy. I was thankful I'd had the foresight to sit down.

It could have been worse, Henley said.

'How? This is the furthest the clock turns. I don't see how it can get any worse.'

You could have been dropped off in a war zone or something.

'Is that supposed to make me feel better?' I hissed. 'I don't know anything about Lithuania – twentieth-century Lithuania or the Grand Duchy of Lithuania. It sounds like a made-up fairy-tale kingdom!'

Relax. And try to get as much of this information into your head as possible: you're Eleanor Shelton, the daughter of Nicholas Reginald Shelton. Your father is in a partnership with Lord Empson and trades in fur. The fur comes into the Grand Duchy of Lithuania from Russia, then is sent by Baltic trade to England, where it's worn by terribly fancy women.

I wanted to tease Henley for the mini history lesson he was giving me, but I was too preoccupied with trying to remember everything.

'What kind of furs?'

The standard: mink, sables . . . you know.

That was precisely it – I didn't know.

As your father's only daughter, it's safe to say you're an heiress, but as a woman in this time, it's unclear how much

– if any – of that money you'll actually inherit. You've never met Lord Empson before. I don't think.

'You got all of that from just a few papers?'

A few papers and some educated guesses.

I knew that if I could see Henley now, he would be wearing one of his smug looks.

Before I could say another word, the loose papers and ledgers on the desk began to fly about the room. Books slipped into gaps left on the shelves and papers dived into stacks quicker than they had first leaped out of them. I heard the doorknob turning as the last book slipped back into its place next to a dusty Latin tome.

A slender man with a large silver chain around his neck strolled through the door. With each step he took towards me, the chain chimed.

'My dear Eleanor.' He approached me with his arms outstretched.

'My Lord Empson.' I bobbed down in the best curtsy I could muster.

'No need for formalities.' Lord Empson took my hand as I stood. 'I feel as though I already know you.'

I felt my eyebrows rise in relief. As Henley hoped, he'd never met Eleanor Shelton. If he had, my deception would have been over before it truly began.

'How are you transitioning to England? If I had known you were coming, I would have sent people to meet you at the port. It's just like your father to plan this at the last moment – as you know, he's always like that.'

'The weather's quite different from what I'm used to, but it's growing on me.'

Lord Empson rewarded me with a smile through his thick, greying beard. 'Certainly warmer here, especially in this season. My dear, you know your father always wanted to show you England, ever since you were born. It's his true home and country.'

He walked over to his desk and I decided to sit back down on the couch.

'This isn't your first time in England, is it?'

I hesitated. 'No, it's not.'

'Good. Good. At least Niki hasn't deprived you of that. I always told him that living in the East was a good idea to keep a closer eye on our business, but it's still no place to raise a child – a daughter, no less. I told Niki he should keep you here so at least you wouldn't develop an accent from the East. But you know your father – he does what he wants.'

I watched Lord Empson pick up a sheet of paper lying on his desk. He frowned at it and glanced at me before replacing it in one of the stacks. I hoped Henley had managed to put everything else back where it belonged.

'Have you just arrived? I was hunting this morning – I hope you haven't been waiting long.'

'Yes I have . . . just arrived, I mean.' My face grew warm when I realized what I had said. 'You haven't been keeping me waiting at all,' I said quickly.

The corners of Lord Empson's eyes crinkled as he tried not to laugh. 'If your father had given me a bit more notice, I could have secured a place for you at court and made proper arrangements. You see, we're quite in the middle of things, I'm afraid. But do write to your father to let him know you've arrived safely.'

I didn't know what to say so just nodded mutely, hoping it would come off as looking thoughtful.

'The court's moving to the Palace of Placentia in Greenwich. Almost everyone is already there, including my wife. Since it's only about two hours from here, I thought I'd check up on the house and sort out some affairs before rejoining her. And I'm quite glad I did – look who I found!' He gestured to me to come closer and I took a few steps forward. 'I promised Niki that I would secure a place for you in court should you ever visit. It's my fault, really, for not believing he would spring this on me at the last minute, as he does everything else.'

Lord Empson paced the floor in front of his desk. 'You must be introduced properly, of course.' He paused, spinning on his heel towards me. 'I believe I can place you with my aunt, the Countess Grenville. That would befit your station till something else can be arranged . . . And for tonight, we must ready a room for you – Helen!'

No more than a couple minutes passed before there was a knock at the door. A young servant girl came in and immediately curtseyed.

'See to it that you and the others prepare a room for Lady Shelton tonight. And quickly,' Lord Empson said. 'Have the cook prepare something for her.' He looked at me apologetically. 'I'm afraid I just had supper moments before you arrived.' His eyes seemed to take in my full form once more, and he eyed me from head to toe, before turning to Helen again. 'Also pull out one of Lady Empson's dresses for Lady Shelton to wear tomorrow.'

'My dresses—' I began.

'Were stolen along with the rest of your things,' Lord Empson said. 'I know. I've been told. Such ruffians.'

Helen was still standing with her head bowed, until Lord Empson dismissed her.

'That will be all.'

Lord Empson resumed his pacing in front of me.

'We must place you in front of the right people at court . . .'

83

From where I sat in the middle of the room, I could see Lord Empson's mind working while he paced, churning as he talked half to himself.

Lord Empson suddenly drew close to me. 'The Lithuanian court still remains very faithful to the Pope, does it not?'

'Um . . . yes?'

'I thought so. You must be careful with your faith here. There are rumours about court that the king intends to break with His Holiness.'

I made my eyes big, hoping I looked appropriately shocked. I knew his words were scandalous but couldn't begin to guess what the situation entailed for me.

'Yes, well, still rumours. They could be all talk.' He sounded as if he was trying to convince himself. 'Just be careful.'

I promised him I would and he looked reassured.

Just then, a timid knock sounded.

'Yes?' Lord Empson called.

Helen scuttled in. 'A room has been readied, my lord.' Her eyes didn't leave the floor.

'Well, do escort Lady Shelton to her room then.' Lord Empson turned to me. 'I do hope it is to your liking. I'm afraid it probably won't be much since we had to make do without prior notice. But please use Helen as you see fit.'

His wording of *using* another person struck me off guard. 'Y-yes, certainly,' I croaked out.

'I will see you in the morning, my dear.'

I managed a curtsey and followed Helen out.

The room Helen led me into had a four-poster bed and a chair and table set by a lone window on the far side of the room. That was it. The lack of furniture made the room seem empty.

Helen stood there as if expecting me to say something.

'This all looks very nice.' I tried.

Helen smiled, but didn't move from her position by the door.

There was silence as I perched on the edge of the bed. I wondered if she would get the hint and leave.

Finally, after a few minutes had passed and Helen didn't seem to get the hint, I asked, 'Could I have a moment alone?'

'Certainly, Lady Shelton. Shall I bring up supper when it is ready?'

'Yes, yes.'

I heard the door shut behind me.

Remember, you need to actually dismiss your servants.

I flopped onto my back on the bed. Pain I hadn't even noticed soared up from my feet. I had blisters upon blisters from my too-small shoes. '*I* don't have any servants. Helen belongs to Lord Empson.' I bit my lip. I hated the way that came out.

You're blending very well into this time period, aren't you?

I ignored his jab. 'This whole time period's a mess. *I'm* a mess.'

Well, what can you do about it? Henley said. *Not much. Just learn and adjust. That's all you can ever do.*

Before I could answer, there was a knock at the door.

'Come in,' I called.

It was Helen, carrying a tray of food. I sat up as Helen carefully walked over to the table and set the tray down. I followed her over to the table. It looked to be a stew of some kind and I felt my stomach growl in appreciation. I couldn't remember the last time I ate.

Helen took a step back and motioned toward the chair.

I sat down. I glanced up at her, but Helen just watched me. I suppose she was going to stand there and watch me as I ate. Picking up the spoon, I started my food.

The stew had some sort of meat in it and it was delicious. I was so hungry and eager to eat that I burned my mouth – it was still so good. With each spoonful, I forgot that Helen was there. I couldn't afford to be self-conscious; I was too hungry for that.

When my spoon scraped the bottom of the bowl, I almost wanted to ask Helen if she could get me some more of the strew, but I knew Miss Hatfield would classify that as 'unseemly behaviour' and 'definitely not befitting a woman of my class'. Instead, I sat back and looked to Helen for a cue as to what to do next.

'My lady, would you like me to help you get ready for bed?' she prompted.

'That would be a fine idea,' I said. 'What with all the travelling today.'

Helen helped me take off my dress, leaving me in the white slip that I wore underneath, and even combed out my hair. If she thought of my dress as peculiar, she didn't betray anything. Maybe the woman who had gone to fetch Lord Empson had filled her in on my story?

I thanked and dismissed Helen when she was done.

As the door closed once more, I crept into bed.

Henley knew I was exhausted. It must have been written across my face.

Goodnight, Rebecca.

Once again I found myself in a time period that was not my own, pretending to be someone I wasn't, and once again Henley was helping me in my deception. I was grateful that Lord Empson appeared to be practically falling over himself to find a place for me and get me settled, but my priority was the clock. I needed it to return home – wherever home was now, but that was a problem for another day. Luckily, my mission and Lord Empson's travels looked likely to coincide. I knew the clock wouldn't be lying around in any old village marketplace. The person who attacked me wasn't the sort to hide away in the sticks, I was sure. My best bet was court, and Lord Empson was going to take me there. All this needed to happen but, for now, it was bed.

Chapter 9

The next morning, I was awakened and quickly dressed by Helen. I was still so tired, I barely noticed what she had dressed me in – something blue-ish and heavy, with lots of layers – I wondered if I had gotten any sleep at all last night. The embroidery scratched my skin as Helen pulled part of it over me.

Breakfast appeared in my room as I struggled to pry my eyes open. It consisted of a loaf of white bread, salted beef, and what smelled like beer.

As with dinner, Helen stood by as I tried to eat quickly.

'His lordship has asked me to tell your ladyship that the carriage is ready and awaiting you.'

I nodded, mouth full. I probably looked like a barbarian to Helen, but I was just so hungry from last night.

When I was finished, Helen led me to the study I was in yesterday. Lord Empson stood as I came in.

'My dear Lady Shelton,' he greeted me. 'I hope you slept well.'

I remembered to give him a quick curtsey before answering that I had slept well.

'And I trust you had some breakfast?'

'Yes, I did. It was delicious.' I omitted the fact that I didn't touch the beer.

'Anything for Niki's daughter.' Lord Empson patted my

88

hand. 'Now then, we have the carriage readied out front. I despise rushing you out like this, but I'm hoping you can get to court in time for the opening feast today.' He took my arm and led me out the door of the study.

We walked thorough narrow corridors, panelled entirely of the same dark wood of the study, and past an area that looked like a parlour or a sitting room. A servant was ready at the door to open it for us, and through the door, I could see a black carriage with two horses.

'Here you are, my dear Eleanor,' Lord Empson said as he gave me a hand into the carriage. He passed me a folded piece of parchment paper with a large wax seal on it. 'And a letter of introduction to the countess, of course.' As I took the letter from his hand, he paused before adding, 'I will join you shortly. In the meantime, do look after Aunt Marian.'

I thanked him and promised him I would.

Helen climbed in and took the seat across from me in the carriage.

Lord Empson turned toward her. 'Remember to tend to all of Lady Eleanor's needs – every last one of them. She should be your priority. Goodness knows, Niki always insists on the very best for his daughter.'

'Yes, my lord.'

Lord Empson gave me one final nod before signalling the carriage driver.

Soon enough, the steady jostle of the horse's movements evened out and Lord Empson was but a speck in the landscape.

'Would you like me to draw the curtains, my lady?' Helen asked, watching my gaze drift to the window.

'No, thank you, Helen. I enjoy looking out at the countryside.'

I had decided that all carriage rides were the same. No matter what time period it was, they were always uncomfortable. Sixteenth-century carriages were actually quite similar to those from the early twentieth century. In terms of horse-drawn travel, not much had changed – or rather *would* change. Once you accepted that discomfort was inevitable, the ride was always easier.

Lord Empson had said that the journey would take about two hours. Since Helen didn't look comfortable making conversation with me, I spent the majority of it looking out of the window. Though all carriages were the same, carriage rides were made different by the scenes passed and left behind. Instead of the ice cream parlours and hat shops I'd seen on rides with Henley, now there was nothing to observe but tree after tree.

'My lady?'

My eyes opened at the unfamiliar voice. I sighed. It was only Helen. I realized I must have dozed off, leaning my head against the side of the carriage.

'My lady?' she said again.

'Yes, Helen?'

'We're here, my lady – welcome to the Palace of Placentia.'

When I looked out of the carriage window, a gasp left me.

So this was it, the current home of the court and hope-fully *my* home for a while. This was the Palace of Placentia.

The palace lived up to its billing. In all its grandeur, it truly was a palace. Stone walls rose as high as I could see, and as soon as we were through the gates we were surrounded by dozens of people – ladies walking in pairs catching up with the latest gossip, page boys running errands, and important-looking men strolling leisurely.

'My lady,' a footman said as he took my hand and helped me out of the carriage.

I wasn't yet accustomed to being around people dressed in sixteenth-century garb. To see it on so many people made me feel as if I was at a costume party or Renaissance fair.

A small smile threatened to break out onto my lips at the thought of this all being somehow an elaborate ruse . . . I wished it were true. Everyone would take off their costumes and I would be back in Manhattan with Miss Hatfield.

'This way, my lady,' Helen said.

I was reminded by her obvious familiarity with the place that Helen probably spent a good portion of every year at court and therefore must know a lot about it. I followed her up a short flight of stone steps and then through several rooms. I knew we hadn't arrived at the front entrance, but the hallways were nonetheless lavishly decorated. Tapestries and paintings dotted the walls. Wood carvings spanned the ceilings and flowed onto the backs of doors.

'The Lady Eleanor Shelton is here to see the Countess Grenville, by request of Lord Empson,' Helen whispered to a young man who seemed to have materialised out of nowhere.

I handed him the letter I had been holding the entire trip. 'From his lordship.'

The young man bowed and slipped into the next room. Shortly after, the door opened for us.

'Lady Eleanor Shelton,' he said, announcing me, though the countess already knew who I was, of course.

I looked back to see where Helen was, but she had moved to a spot next to the door. I walked in alone.

The room was small and very simple – dark wood being the primary colour and material that stood out to me. There were a few chests on one side of the room, but a vanity was the main furniture in the room. The countess was seated at the vanity at the far end of the room with her back towards me, but her cool blue eyes held my gaze via her reflection in the mirror in front of her. She was holding the letter from Lord Empson, its elaborate seal already broken.

'Lady Eleanor Shelton,' she pronounced, eyeing me through the mirror.

The countess looked as if she had been a beauty in her youth. She wasn't old yet, by any means, but her flaxen hair shimmered with more strands of silver than blonde and the corners of her lips were swallowed up by the fine lines that had begun to span her face. What made her look even older was the stiff, black dress she wore. There was a bit of black embroidery along her sleeves, but compared to everyone else I had seen so far, hers was the most spartan costume.

'Yes, my lady.' I wasn't sure what to do, so I bobbed down in a quick curtsy.

'You're the daughter of his lordship's business partner?' The countess turned to look at me.

I supposed she meant Lord Empson, so I nodded.

'Are you mute, girl? There's always something wrong with the pretty ones.'

'No,' I said.

'No, what?'

'Um . . . No, my lady.'

'Very good, though that "um" was unnecessary. Never start a sentence with "um". It doesn't do anyone any good.' She gestured to the letter now lying on the vanity. 'It says here that you were brought up in the Grand Duchy of Lithuania. That explains that terrible accent, but I would still expect manners from you. Your parents are English, are they not?'

'Yes, my lady.' I really hoped that she – or anyone else at court, for that matter – wouldn't expect me to start speaking Lithuanian.

'And you had an English tutor? Or maybe a governess?'

'Yes, my lady.'

'Well, they did a dreadful job.'

The countess stood and began to walk towards me. I stumbled a few steps back.

'I suppose his lordship expects me to take you under my wing. Guide you. Counsel you. Teach you some manners.' She stopped a few inches away from me and lifted my chin with the tips of her fingers. 'I was once a pretty little thing like you. But do you know what happened?'

I couldn't trust my voice. I wanted to shake my head, but I was trapped by the countess holding my face up to hers.

'Do you know what happened?' she repeated. 'I was used. By the likes of Lord Empson and others like him. They're all the same. I was used, and when I was no longer needed, I was discarded like a child's plaything.'

Both her harsh words and her firm fingers beneath my chin made me uncomfortable. Finally, she released me.

The countess glared at a young servant girl in the corner of the room. She was standing so still that I hadn't noticed her before.

'You. Out.'

The girl quickly curtsied and scampered from the room.

With no one else present, the countess turned her full attention back to me. 'I'll help you,' she said. 'I'll do *exactly* as his Lordship wants and take you under my wing as my personal gentlewoman.'

'Thank you so much.'

'Joan,' the countess called.

The young maid who had been kicked out of the room only a few seconds ago came rushing back in. I wondered if she was used to doing this sort of thing. Maybe she was the countess's right-hand woman, doing all her menial tasks for her.

'Joan, show Lady Eleanor to a room and make sure Lord Empson's girl –' I realized she meant Helen '– keeps it to Lady Eleanor's liking.'

I guessed I was to be just another one of the tasks on Joan's list now.

The countess turned to me. 'There will be a feast tonight. You'll be introduced to many important people so wear your best dress.'

'Um, I don't have any.'

'Any what?'

'Any dresses.' I bit my lip.

'None at all? Well, that certainly is a problem.' The countess made a show of letting out an exasperated sigh.

'My trunk . . . got lost at the port.'

'Lost? At the port? And now you're without a stitch of clothing? Well, this might be a blessing in disguise. I imagine things are done differently in Lithuania – it's practically the middle of nowhere, after all. Joan, send for the dressmaker as well.' The countess waved us out. 'The feast will be at four.'

'Four? Isn't that a bit early?'

'Of course not. This is court. Things are done differently here.'

I curtsied out of the room, murmuring another thank-you.

'Don't thank me,' the countess called after me. 'If I were a better person, I wouldn't help you.' She laughed then, which only unsettled me further.

*

94

'Here you are, my lady.' Joan rubbed her nose with the back of her hand, making it red. 'If there's nothing else you require right now, I'll be off to find the dressmaker.' Helen lingered behind her.

'Very well,' I said, beginning to look about the room. On our way here, we had passed a couple other rooms, and I realized this all was part of the countess's small wing of the palace. Each room had a door or two that led into the next almost like nesting dolls.

When I didn't hear the door close behind me, I turned to find the mousy-haired girl still standing there with Helen by her side, looking at me. I realized she was waiting to be dismissed formally.

'You may go now.'

Joan curtsied and left.

'You too, Helen.'

Helen curtsied and followed Joan out the door.

'What a strange woman!' I said as I collapsed onto the four-poster bed in the middle of the room. The bed was a bit short for me and my feet dangled off the end.

The countess, you mean?

'Yes, the countess. I wouldn't be surprised if she tried to kill me in my sleep!'

Oh, Rebecca, she wasn't that bad.

'Not that bad? You only say that because you weren't the one talking to her directly.'

I rolled over and sat up on the side of the bed with the bedside table. A pitcher of water and a basin had been placed on the table, and I decided to freshen up before I had to meet more people. The only furniture in the room other than the bed and table was a vanity much like the one the countess had been sitting at and a few wooden chests placed by the wall next to it.

'What do you suggest I do now?' I asked Henley, changing the subject.

Play along until you can find the clock. Do you have any other choice?

I knew he was right.

'Where might the clock be?' I wondered aloud. 'It was made in 1527 – this year we're in – so it would probably look brand new. It's more likely to be at court – no regular commoner would be able to afford such an elaborate object. Plus it would stick out like a sore thumb in a villager's home.'

Not to mention there aren't too many clocks in this time period, not even at court. They're expensive – even more so for a gold one like that.

'Can we narrow down who at court could own such a thing?'

Certainly none of the servants.

'That goes without saying. Who among the gentry?'

It could be anyone.

I was afraid he would say that.

We don't know enough about any of them yet to work that out.

'It's not as if I can go from person to person saying, "Hello. Nice to meet you, your lordship. Do you happen to own a golden clock about this big? If so, would you kindly hand it over, please?"' All I could do was guess, and it turned out that Henley was in the same boat. Although he could see all time periods unfolding simultaneously, it was very difficult for him to make sense of what he was seeing. He'd described it being like watching millions of tiny ants at once and trying to home in on a single ant. Consequently it was all guesswork for him, too.

I think you should check the countess's bedroom and sitting room when she's out – maybe even all of the countess's chambers

– since they're right there two doors down. The person who attacked you and took the clock is either keeping it with him, or he's hidden it among someone else's possessions – with or without their knowledge.

I didn't like the idea that the countess might be in league with Miss Hatfield's killer. And unpleasant as she was, I couldn't even imagine her *being* the killer.

I can keep an eye out while you search the countess's rooms. At least then you'll eliminate one person. And we have to start somewhere.

Henley was right. Though I hadn't paid much attention, the room in which I had met the countess was lavishly decorated. It wouldn't be out of character for her to keep a large golden clock in one of her other chambers. Her bedroom, perhaps?

In the meantime, you just need to continue putting on an act, Henley said. *People will treat you according to how they think you should be treated. If you show them that you're a force to be reckoned with, they'll respect you.* Henley laughed. *Besides, from what I remember, you're quite the actress.*

I was going to reply with a smart riposte when I heard a timid knock at the door.

Put on an act, Henley whispered in my ear. I shivered, though his breath was warm against my neck. He would always have that effect on me.

'Come in. Do come in.' I tried to imagine what the countess might say.

'I'm sorry to bother you, my lady, but I have Mistress Cobham here to see you.'

'Thank you, Joan.' I turned to the rosy-cheeked woman Joan had brought. 'Mistress Cobham, I'm afraid I have quite the task for you today.'

97

'Whatever you would like, your ladyship.' She patted some loose wisps of grey hair back into her coif.

'I'd like an entire wardrobe.'

Mistress Cobham's hand froze. 'An entire wardrobe?'

'Yes. An entirely new wardrobe.'

Mistress Cobham appeared to recover from her shock quite quickly . . . or at least regain the ability to hide it. 'Of course, my lady. Her ladyship did mention that . . . Though I didn't think she was serious.'

I barely managed to conceal my surprise. I'd been under the impression that the countess had delegated the task to Joan. 'She did?'

'Yes, my lady. She requested five linen smocks with thread-work, of course, scarlet petticoats, two kirtles. And gowns. Lots of gowns. All to be paid for by Lord Empson.' Her curious eyes bored into me, obviously wondering what kind of connection I, a foreigner, could have with Lord Empson.

'The Countess of Grenville is *always* serious,' I said in what I hoped was a haughty enough voice.

'I'm terribly sorry, my lady, but I only brought a small selection of fabric for the gowns.'

'Well, let's see them. There's no use having you come in on another day with the rest of the fabric. We can make do with what you have.'

Mistress Cobham excused herself with a deep curtsy and left the room momentarily. She returned with a trail of young men shouldering yards and yards of fabric. They slipped through the door one by one, following her like ducklings. There were seven of them in total.

'Here we have the silks and satins. I brought the colours currently in fashion, my lady. I also have gorgeous linens and velvets directly from Paris. I've heard that all the ladies of the French court are wearing them this season.'

I nodded, suddenly overwhelmed. There were now eight people in the small room in addition to myself and Joan, and I found myself backed up against the bed.

'Green,' I blurted out.

'Green?' Mistress Cobham's entire face flushed as she began looking erratically around. 'My lady, with green currently being out of favour, I'm afraid I didn't think to bring—'

One of the men stepped forward from a corner with a bundle of green fabric.

'Yes!' Mistress Cobham said. 'The green silk. It isn't as popular this season, I'm afraid, but—'

'I'd like to have a gown made in that.' I remembered Henley saying that he liked me in green.

'Are—'

'Mistress Cobham.' I made my tone as stern as I could.

She closed her mouth.

'And I would like one made of the blue velvet and one with the black satin.' I pointed to two of the men. 'Everything else I'll permit you to choose for me. My only request is that I need them all as soon as possible.'

Mistress Cobham opened her mouth to protest, but I took her hands in mine before she could say a word.

'Truly, Mistress Cobham, I trust your judgment in this – you know what everyone's wearing.' I smiled. 'Now I must leave you. I promised her ladyship that I would attend her at this hour.'

It was a lie, but I had to get them out.

The men gathered up the bolts of fabric and filed out of the room, following Mistress Cobham as before.

You never were a girl for shopping. I never understood that about you.

I had no idea how he did it, but Henley always managed to make me smile.

99

'Can you see if the countess is in her quarters?'

She's not there at the moment. She's at chapel with Joan. You'll have exactly seven minutes until they come.

'Perfect.'

I slipped out of my room, careful not to make a sound so I didn't attract the attention of Joan or any other servants the countess might employ. I closed the door behind me to make it look as if I were still in my room.

At the first door I could find, I made sure the coast was clear just in case, then opened it and crept inside. Judging from a table with a chess set and another with a deck of cards, I guessed this was a room the countess used to entertain guests. All the other rooms of hers must be adjoining.

There was no dust on the mantel – Joan had made sure of that – but nor were there any knick-knacks lying around, the things made a room feel well used. One glance around the walls and I was certain the clock was not here.

In the next room, I was immediately struck by how warm it felt. It wasn't the actual temperature of the room that hit me, but rather that the whole room emanated a sense of comfort that the countess's other rooms lacked. The sun-bleached red curtains were weighted down with huge tassels and the chairs around the fireplace were upholstered with a similar orangey-red hue. It was as if all that was lively and energetic about the countess had been poured into this room and sealed within.

I knew I had to continue looking for the clock before Joan or anyone else found me snooping about. Henley had told me I had exactly seven minutes until the countess and Joan would come in . . . How many minutes ago had he said that?

Reluctantly tearing myself away from the cosy room, I decided to try the door on the other side of the corridor.

Peeking in, I saw that I had found the countess's bedroom. It was laid out in a similar way to mine: a four-poster bed sat prominently in the centre between two neatly kept bedside tables. Unlike my room, a wooden wardrobe stood against the one wall and a few wooden chests were scattered about. There was a single chair by the fireplace but no vanity, since that was in the room where I was first introduced to the countess. Everything was simply made. Nothing was too elaborate.

Rebecca. It was a warning from Henley.

I noticed two silver frames on one of the bedside tables – I could spare a quick look before I had to go. They stood out as the only items in the room not made out of wood.

Rebecca!

A miniature painting of a handsome man filled one, while the other held a blond little boy.

'Are you finding everything to your liking?'

Startled, I spun around and almost toppled over when I came face to face with the countess.

'I see grace is not something taught in the Grand Duchy of Lithuania,' she said. 'But no matter. You'll be here long enough to pick *that* up, as well as a few other things. Maybe even a suitor or two. That's always the case with young girls sent to court.'

'I'm sorry, your ladyship,' I said.

'For what?'

For snooping, I wanted to say. But I had a feeling she knew that already and just wanted to hear me say it, so I held my tongue.

The countess smiled at my silence. 'My husband would have liked your stubbornness. He would have said that you have spirit . . .' She trailed off as her gaze drifted to the portraits on her bedside table.

101

'Is that him?'

'Yes. The Earl of Grenville,' she said. 'Or rather, the late Earl of Grenville. And the boy who would have grown up to be the next earl.' She picked up the boy's portrait. 'George was the only one who made it past his first few months, but even he couldn't withstand the plague.'

'I– I'm so sorry.'

'I'm not the only mother to have lost her children.' The countess shook her head. 'Lord Grenville took it far worse than I did.'

'And . . . his lordship? How did he pass?'

The countess swallowed audibly.

'I'm sorry. I'm intruding—'

'Nonsense,' the countess said. 'It's been five years already. Seven since George's death.' She cleared her throat. 'My husband . . . He died of the sweating sickness.'

'I'm so sorry,' I said again.

Instinctively, I took her hands in mine. I felt her stiffen and thought I had overstepped my bounds, but she did not withdraw. The countess's slender hands felt small in mine, small and cold. I gave them a squeeze, since it was all I could do to try and comfort her.

'Now, now,' she said, attempting to smile again. 'I'm sure you don't want to hear about death from an old thing like me.'

I laughed. The countess talked as if she was in her nineties when she couldn't have been much beyond her early forties. Of course, that was probably considered a ripe old age in this period. And when you added time travel to the mix, and the fact that I was technically not supposed to be born yet, she appeared far older to me than she could possibly imagine.

But she couldn't comprehend how little age now meant to me. If only she knew how much death I had already seen.

102

'I came to find you to give you something to wear to the feast,' the countess continued. 'Mistress Cobham has been to see you, correct?'

'Yes, she has.'

'And you ordered enough dresses from her?'

'Plenty,' I said.

'Good. Good. It's the least his lordship can do to pay for them.' She sighed and I could tell she was thinking about something else. 'But since those dresses won't be ready for tonight, I thought we could have you wear one of mine.'

The countess crossed the room to the wardrobe and opened it. It was filled with black dresses. She frowned and closed it, then opened a chest by the foot of the wardrobe.

'Here it is,' she said as she draped a shimmering white dress onto the bed. 'I hope this will do.'

Speechless, it was all I could do to nod.

'I'm quite fed up with your nodding,' the countess said, even though I really didn't think I had nodded all that much. 'I hope England can knock this Lithuanian custom of nodding out of you.'

'It's beautiful, my lady,' I said.

'I am glad you like it. It suited me well when I was younger. I'm sure it will look becoming with your youthful countenance.' She made to turn away from me, but stopped. 'Lady Eleanor, would you accompany me to chapel tomorrow?'

'I would love to.' I wasn't sure that was true, but it was the least I could do now I had seen this other side to her.

'Good, good.' She clapped her hands together. 'Joan!'

Joan appeared. I wondered how thin the walls must be for Joan to be able to hear the countess calling at any moment.

103

'Yes, my lady,' she said with a curtsy.

'See to it that Helen dresses Lady Eleanor in time for the feast.'

'Yes, my lady.'

'I hope you won't be late.' And with that, the countess whisked out of the room.

Chapter 10

Are you ready to do this?

I had come to notice that Henley tended to whisper into my ear only if I was all by myself or in the middle of a loud crowd. They were situations on opposite ends of the spectrum, but they were both times when no one was paying attention to me.

'I don't think it really matters if I'm ready or not,' I whispered under my breath.

True. I could hear Henley's smile in his voice, but I wished I could have seen it. *You look beautiful in that dress.*

'You can't even see me or the dress properly. How do you know what I look like?'

You always look beautiful. Besides, I can see a little glimmer of colour. White becomes you.

Henley was always one for flattery. I didn't know if this was the way with all the men brought up in his time, or if it was just him.

Henley continued, *You know I always dreamed I would see you in a white dress one day . . . though maybe not like this, going to someone else's party.*

I rolled my eyes at Henley's flirting and his attempt to put me at ease. Nevertheless, his endeavour was welcome. I watched yet another couple enter arm in arm through the large double doors in front of me. Did I ever do things *when I was ready?* I took a deep breath and walked towards the doors. As I neared, the men on either side opened them dramatically to let me through.

When my eyes adjusted to the dimly lit room beyond, I was amazed that so many people could fit in one – albeit crowded – space.

The entire room was haloed in the light of candles. They were everywhere. They shone from tall candelabras standing at attention on either side of the room, and from sparse metal chandeliers that swung gently above the throng, leaning in as if to listen to the conversations below. Long wooden tables had been set up in two rows with enough room between them for dancing.

Further still into the room was a large chair, where a handsome man perched on the edge of the seat. He was engaged in conversation with a woman to his left, but his eyes periodically drifted to survey the room. Sure, he wasn't as fat as I remembered from his portraits and his striking looks in the flesh were something entirely new to me, but I knew his face.

A memory surfaced from so long ago that it almost felt as though it had happened to someone else in another life. Well, in a way, it sort of had. I wasn't Lady Eleanor Shelton then. I wasn't even the seventh Rebecca Hatfield. I was eleven-year-old Cynthia. It was 1954, the year I never got to finish living. I was in the school yard during recess with a textbook I had borrowed from an older girl who said I could look at the pretty pictures if I wanted to. I remembered flipping through it until I came to a full-page photo of a painting. The painting only had one figure in it – a man. He stood with his hands on his hips, and even in black and white he looked so powerful, so sure of everything, that in that instant I wanted to be him. I remembered his face. Henry VIII.

'I see you've made it to the banquet room without getting too lost.' The countess breezed up to me. She was wearing a black dress as usual, but had changed into a grander one with a fuller skirt and silver embroidery. 'I don't think I would have found you in this mess if you hadn't been wearing that dress. Lord Dormer was positively beside himself, asking everyone the identity of the ravishing young woman in pure white.'

I quickly glanced around to see that although there were many other women in the room, some twirling their skirts on the dance floor and some already seated, they were all wearing richly coloured gowns. I was the only one wearing white.

'It appears you've already bewitched your first victim,' the countess said.

I looked around for a man who could be Lord Dormer, but instead my eyes were drawn again to the man on the throne at the far side of the room.

'I see you've also found the king.'

I blushed, but I couldn't tear my eyes off him and how he moved. He leaned down towards the young woman to better hear something she said.

'All the ladies do it.'

'Do what?' I found myself asking.

'Stare.' The countess laughed. 'Don't be ashamed. The king's brother, as oldest and first in line, was born to rule. As for the king – well, you can see what he was born to do. His brother's death merely forced him to do it more regally.'

'Countess Grenville, might I interrupt?' A slightly balding, pear-shaped man walked up to us.

'Certainly, Sir Gordon,' she said. 'Might I introduce the Lady Eleanor Shelton, daughter of Nicholas Reginald Shelton. This is Sir Anthony Gordon.'

107

I curtsied as he bowed.

'I've heard quite a lot about you,' he said.

My eyebrows went up. 'You have? Hopefully good things.'

Sir Gordon let out a rumbling laugh. I couldn't help but watch as his belly jiggled.

'Most certainly good things,' he said. 'From the countess as well as Lord Dormer.'

'Lord Dormer?' This time it was the countess's turn to laugh. 'How like him to praise people he hasn't met.'

'Well, that should be amended, don't you think?'

The countess and I both turned to see a tall man impeccably dressed in red velvet and adorned in gold. His red beard was tinted here and there with grey.

'My Countess?' he added, bowing to kiss her hand.

I could have sworn I saw the countess blush as she made the introductions.

Lord Dormer flamboyantly kissed my hand, causing many people nearby to turn and watch. I knew they were already trying to figure out who I was.

'My Lord Dormer,' Sir Gordon began, 'we're quite thrilled to have you back from the French court, but if you're going to show us up with your French manners, we might have to ship you back.'

Lord Dormer's beard twitched with a smile. 'I'm afraid the French won't take me back after witnessing my terribly English manners. Besides, then I'll miss having the pleasure of dancing with English girls.'

The countess frowned. 'Didn't I tell you that Lady Eleanor is from the Grand Duchy of Lithuania?'

'Yes, yes. You've been sure to mention that more than a few times. I was talking of a different English lady.' Lord Dormer held out his hand to the countess. 'It would be dreadful manners to turn such a kind gentleman down.'

I tried to stifle my giggles as I waved the countess off.

'Are you sure you won't need me?' she asked.

'A few dances won't hurt.'

'A few? Whoever said I would give him a few? One will be enough . . . maybe two.'

The countess's dark skirts whirled around her ankles as Lord Dormer spun her away.

'Phillip's quite the charmer, isn't he?'

I had forgotten that Sir Gordon was still standing beside me.

'Lord Dormer? Yes, I suppose he is.'

'You should have seen him when he was younger,' he said. 'There wasn't a girl who wouldn't fall for those fluttering eyelashes.' He patted his belly. 'Then, of course, there were people like me on the sidelines.' Sir Gordon roared with laughter. 'But Phillip always helped me out with the girls. He's a wily charmer, but he's loyal.'

Sir Gordon grabbed two goblets filled to the brim with wine and shoved one in my direction. I stepped to the side just as red wine sloshed over the edge of the glass. Given the pure white of my dress, that had been a close call, but Sir Gordon seemed not to notice.

'Thank you,' I said, taking the cup.

'While they're both having fun toying with each other, permit me to introduce you to some people. Court is a ruthless place and the only way to survive is by cultivating friends in all the key places.' He took my arm. 'Of course, having Lord Empson as an ally is a definite advantage.'

'I suppose we all need people we can trust,' I said, thinking of Miss Hatfield. I didn't know why she came to mind all of a sudden. Now that she was gone, Henley was the only confidant I had. I couldn't lose him, too.

'Precisely so,' Sir Gordon said. He squeezed my arm. 'Here comes Lady Simnel. Her husband was a friend of Prince Arthur's and she's one of the queen's ladies, so she's quite important.'

I followed his gaze to a short woman decked head to toe in gold.

'Lady Simnel!' Sir Gordon called out. 'I didn't see you there. I must be going blind to have missed such beauty!'

I was amazed by how easily Sir Gordon switched on his enthusiasm. It was as if he came alive all of a sudden. There was no transition, and it looked effortless.

'Might I introduce Lady Eleanor Shelton? She's the Countess of Grenville's lady, freshly arrived at court. Perfect timing, too, don't you think? A breath of fresh air is always welcome!'

I smiled and curtsied as Sir Gordon went on as if he had known me for ever, and Lady Simnel and a few other women examined me with their flitting, bird-like eyes.

Sir Gordon led me on his arm from person to person like a new prize. All his introductions went the same – he showed me off, I remained silent and everyone else scrutinised me.

'Ah, there you are.' Eventually the countess rescued me.

'Tired of dancing already?' Sir Gordon actually looked disappointed.

'They're about to start the feast and we thought we should be seated early,' she said, then excused both herself and me.

'Sir Gordon didn't talk your ear off, did he?' she asked when we were out of earshot.

'More introductions than talking to me directly.'

For once, the countess looked sympathetic. 'We're to be seated there.' She pointed to the middle section of one of the tables on her left. 'I believe you're on my right.' The countess began skirting dancers as she walked towards our seats. 'Look at all those young pairs still dancing. They'll dance till the last possible minute!'

I wanted to ask what was wrong with that, but the way the countess sniffed as she passed the couples told me it was something she disdained, so I kept quiet.

'Here we are.'

Two young men dressed in green and white livery pulled out chairs for us. I recognized the Tudor rose stitched onto their tabards.

'Oof.' The chair looked far softer than it was and I slammed down into my seat.

'A lady does *not* make animalistic sounds at the table.'

I couldn't help but grin at how automatic the countess's reply had sounded. Maybe she was getting used to having me around . . .

'My dear lords and ladies, please take your seats.' The king was standing at his place at the far side of the room and began a speech welcoming his court to the Palace of Placentia. 'I hope you find the palace as bountiful in sensory pleasures and as abundant in simple joys as I have in years past . . .'

'I don't suppose I've seen you here before,' a voice whispered, surprisingly close to my ear.

'I don't suppose you have,' I said.

'So you are new at court, then?'

My eyes darted up at the man now sitting next to me. His mop of curly brown hair matched his day-old stubble, and he reminded me of Sam, the Starbucks-boy I had met in the airport. But somehow, I didn't think this man owned any flannel shirts or had skinny jeans in his closet.

111

'Is that a smile I see on the young woman's face? What a mystery.'

He sounded so much like Henley that I unconsciously rolled my eyes at him and turned back to watch the king.

'Oh,' he whispered. 'Fire, as well.'

I stayed silent, trying to listen to the king's speech but unable to focus on it.

'I had better be careful,' the man continued. 'Beauty *and* fire – I might find myself quickly ensnared.'

I turned towards him again, but finding myself mere inches away from his intense gaze, I promptly forgot what I was about to say.

'Cat caught your tongue?' He smirked.

I stuck my tongue out at him. 'No, it's obviously still here.'

I knew I was supposed to try to fit in and this certainly wasn't appropriate court behaviour the countess would approve of, but something about the man made me do it. I held my breath, wondering if he would be offended.

He laughed. 'Witty, too? Very dangerous.'

I let out my breath and tried to ignore him, turning again to hear the rest of the king's speech, but he was done and sitting back down. I made sure to clap along with everyone else.

'You don't fool me,' the man next to me said in a voice low enough that I was the only one to hear it. 'You're not like everyone else. You're strange. Wonderfully strange and different.'

'A toast to the king!' someone was yelling.

'Hear, hear!'

The room dissolved in a clattering of goblets and raised voices.

Chapter 11

'You had quite the night, from what I saw.' The countess was sitting alone in the first pew before the altar. 'You had such a busy evening that I thought I had better tell Joan to let you sleep.'

I walked down the aisle towards her. My shoes tapped against the tiled floor but she didn't raise her head.

Last night had been magical for me. It was my first glimpse of court behind the strict rules and conventions the countess insisted upon. While she sat and chatted politely with her neighbours, I gaped openly at the myriad flamboyant dresses, each more extravagant than the last. After the meal, Sir Gordon and a few of the other men to whom he and the countess had introduced me asked me to dance, but the countess declined on my behalf and shooed them away before I could respond.

'We can't have you embarrassing us – and yourself – with your lack of dance knowledge. I'm sure the customs and popular dance steps are quite different from Lithuania.' And the countess was right. There was no way I would be able to keep up with the complex dances they were doing. Each song had so many specific intricate steps to go along with it, I wondered how anyone remembered them all.

It was a glimmering world in front of me. Miss Hatfield would have loved the dancing.

113

My second sudden memory of Miss Hatfield during the feast caught me off guard. It hurt to breathe for a moment, but I pushed it away.

I focused on the mosaic of colours in front of me on the dance floor. I was a part of this world now. It could only be described as magic.

When I returned to my room, I didn't know if it was late at night or early in the morning. Helen appeared in my room to help me get ready for bed, but I dismissed her after she unfastened my gown, so I could talk to Henley.

That guy was such a . . . a . . . I don't even know what he is. I just don't like him. He shouldn't have acted that way with you. I don't like any of them.

'You make it sound as if they were doing something horrible. All they did was ask me to dance.'

And I didn't like that, either.

I almost laughed. 'Jealous much?'

Do I have a reason to be?

I didn't like Henley in this mood. He became so unreasonable.

I just shook my head and ignored him, getting ready for bed.

I was so tired, I barely remembered getting in bed. Before my eyes flickered shut, I remembered thinking about the stranger I had sat next to at the feast. I never did learn his name. I thought he would ask me to dance and then introduce himself, but oddly I hadn't seen him again that evening. I admit the disappointment I felt took me by surprise.

The next morning, having overslept, I ran into the chapel.

'I hope I haven't kept you waiting too long,' I said as I took a seat by the countess.

'I've been here a few hours. But no, not waiting. Never waiting.' She lifted her head but still did not turn towards me. 'Prayer does so much for the soul, does it not?'

'I wouldn't know.'

The countess turned to me now and studied my face. I had no idea what she would find there.

'I appreciate your candour with me,' she whispered, 'but do be careful with your words around others. This isn't like your home in Lithuania. You may have a sympathizer in me, but not everyone will feel that way. One must do the things one must to survive – including putting on acts.' The countess tipped her head to the side. 'Now tell me, Lithuania is still very much Catholic and loyal to His Holiness, is it not?'

'Yes.' I remembered that this was one of the first things Lord Empson had asked me.

There was a pause, and then she asked, 'What *do* you know of prayer?'

The directness of her question caught me off guard, especially after saying I knew nothing about prayer. 'Prayer? Well, I think religion—'

'No, not religion,' she said. 'Prayer.'

'I do pray,' I began. 'I pray in the only way I know how.'

'And how is that?'

'I talk and hope that someone, somewhere, is listening.'

'And is He listening?'

'I . . . I don't know.' I felt embarrassed as my voice broke.

For a while, neither of us said anything. I was worried that I had offended the countess and felt she was unsure how to respond to my lack of faith.

'I know.' The countess's voice was soft. 'Even though I still consider myself a Catholic, at times I think He has abandoned me. Left me to nothingness. That maybe a

115

life is just a life, nothing more. And then I feel empty. For what is a life without meaning, and what is meaning without Him?'

I watched her glare at the altar. Perhaps she thought that if she stared hard enough, it would speak to her.

'But I simply cannot believe that there is nothing after all of this.'

'All this?'

'Life,' she said. 'It can't just start and end without any reason. Yet we're all thrown into life and snatched out of it. I know such thoughts are un-Christian, and that the Bible tells us there is more, but sometimes the thought still rises. I pray to keep it down. Piety is virtuous, and I admire those who have it.'

'Sometimes I'm afraid that no one's watching over me,' I found myself saying. Though my voice was small, it still managed to echo in the chapel.

'There has to be someone . . . something there. We have to believe in that.' The countess's knuckles were white as she gripped the ledge of the pew. 'There has to be – I shouldn't be saying this. We shouldn't be having this conversation.'

I knew that need. It was a need to believe in something greater than yourself. A need to know that your life wasn't insignificant. That although at times it felt random and meaningless, you were living according to some bigger plan. That someone was watching over you. And when it all ended, that something else would begin.

I knew that need because I had it, once. I used to believe there was someone on the other side of my prayers, listening to my pleas and hearing my hopes and wishes as I whispered them on my knees before I went to bed. I still had that need, but I knew no one was listening for me any more.

116

When Miss Hatfield died, she disappeared into dust. And to the world, it was as if she had never lived, for I had taken her place. When I became an immortal, I turned to dust in God's eyes. Without death, the promise of heaven and hell became meaningless. There was only an endless existence on Earth for me until I turned to dust and someone else took over as Miss Hatfield. No one was watching over me. Life had no meaning for me.

'Eleanor,' the countess said.

I was taken aback by the countess addressing me without any title. It wasn't like her, but then again, I was beginning to learn that the countess was full of surprises and contradictions. I wasn't sure if she was opening up to me because I was a foreigner, apparently a Catholic, or if she simply needed someone to confide in.

'Yesterday, when we talked – I couldn't help but feel that you've lost someone, too,' she said.

I thought about Miss Hatfield and what she would have said if she'd had the chance to meet the countess.

'You're young,' the countess continued, 'but you've suffered great loss. I recognize that in you because I have those shadows in myself . . . He meant a great deal to you, didn't he?'

I was surprised that the countess had picked up on my loss of Henley instead of Miss Hatfield. I had lost Henley once when I was forced to leave him in his time, but he had found his way back to me. He was here again, and that was much more than the countess could say of her husband.

'Let the Church be your sanctuary, as I have tried to make it mine,' the countess said. 'Do not let the seeds of doubt be sown in your mind the way they have in mine. Though we may pluck the weeds with all our might,

117

their roots remain an everlasting labyrinth just below the surface.'

It was far too late for that, but I pretended to absorb her advice.

'In an ever-changing world, faith is all we really have. So cling to it.' The countess stood. 'Remember, you're always welcome to seek refuge here.' She looked to the confessional, sitting empty and ajar. 'You never know, someone just might be listening.'

The countess made her way back up the aisle, leaving me in the pew. She threw open the doors and the blinding light from outside engulfed her. All of a sudden, I was alone.

A draught blew the length of the room and I shivered. The chapel felt colder than any other building or room I had come across in this time. Light tinted by stained-glass windows played on the altar, casting jewelled hues on the golden decor, but that light was harsh and cold.

I stood to leave the chapel but stopped in my tracks. Although I knew this wasn't a place for me – of all places, this was where I least belonged – for some reason I was drawn to the confessional.

There were so many things I could never dare tell another person. They would think I was insane, or worse, they would be repelled and think me a monstrosity – something that was never meant to be. There were things I couldn't even tell Henley, like how scared I was – for our relationship, our future together . . . Did we even have a future together with him in his current state? Of all people, I couldn't bear to isolate him so I chose not to bring it up instead. Being half-immortal, Henley saw everything in all times, but he couldn't see my thoughts. He didn't know exactly how frightened I was.

I opened the intricate wooden door to the confessional and stepped into the cramped space. I just wanted to feel as though someone might be listening. Maybe what I needed was to voice all of my fears aloud.

I knelt down on the built-in wooden bench. It had a thin cushion, but it wasn't very comfortable. Then again, I supposed kneelers weren't meant to be comfortable.

I took a deep breath. How did this work? Did I just begin talking? What did they always say in the movies at the beginning of a confession?

'Forgive me, Father, for I have sinned. This is my first confession since . . .' I paused. 'Well, for a long time.'

'What would you like to confess, my child?'

I froze. I hadn't expected a priest to be listening. I wondered if I should continue, or whether I should step out.

I steadied myself on the kneeler. It was too late to step out.

'My child?'

'I . . . I feel as if God has turned away from me,' I began. 'That He's not up there watching over me any more.'

'And why not?' the priest asked. 'Our Lord loves everyone.'

'Because I've done something . . . and it's changed me.'

'Changed you how, my child?'

'It's made me unlovable.'

My words hung in the stale air of the confessional. Finally, the priest spoke again.

'How have you changed yourself?'

'I . . . It wasn't me who did it,' I said, thinking about the day Miss Hatfield mixed a drop of water from the Fountain of Youth into my lemonade, for ever changing me by making me immortal. I had never wanted it.

'What did you do to change yourself?' The priest's voice was more insistent now, and there was something else in his tone. Something I didn't recognize, and it scared me. 'What did you do?'

'I can't say.'

There was another pause, and when the priest spoke again, he appeared to have composed himself.

'My child, to be forgiven, you must confess your sins.'

I knew what he said made sense, but this was something I couldn't tell anyone. God knew. He saw enough to turn His back.

'I'm sorry. I can't say.'

I heard a sharp intake of breath near my ear.

'Man must not try to imitate the divine, for life cannot mimic God without ending in failure.' The priest's voice started to rise and shake. 'This is not natural! *You* are not natural, and God does not keep the unnatural. Heretics may burn in hell, but you will fall further.'

I turned my head to peer through the intricate dividing screen but couldn't see a thing. I heard the click of a latch as the door on the priest's side opened and closed. I opened my door and stepped out, but it was too late. He was gone.

Chapter 12

The balls of my feet thudded against the stone steps. I grew dizzy as they spiralled up and up, but I didn't want to pause to catch my breath or look back. I had no desire to know what I would find behind me.

My encounter with the priest had terrified me.

Calm down, Henley kept saying. *You're acting unreasonably. That was a comment anyone could have made.*

But I ignored him. It was easy for him to say that I was 'acting unreasonably' when he wasn't the one who had been confronted with the priest's accusing voice. Henley was there, but he wasn't *really* there – there in flesh and body. He hadn't *really* felt what I had in the confessional.

I felt my body pitch forwards as the stairs ended. I threw my arms out to steady myself, but it was too late and I hit the stone floor with a thud. It felt as though all the bones in my body crushed together and I let out a groan through gritted teeth.

'My lord,' a voice said above me. 'What an entrance!'

A strong arm picked me up, but I snatched my hand away as soon as I saw who it belonged to. It was the man from the banquet.

'I was about to ask if you were all right, but I see you are sufficiently recovered to show your fire again.' When he threw his head back to laugh, a lock of his hair fell into his eyes and I fought a strong urge to brush it away.

'Thank you for your assistance, but I had best be on my way now.'

'Always so serious,' the man said. 'But what's the rush?'

'The Countess Grenville wishes to see me.' I made to curtsy and leave but his hand gripped my wrist.

'We both know that's a lie.'

I froze. His grip on me was tighter than before.

'You don't have to tell me everything, but never feel that you have to lie to me.' His voice was fierce at first but grew softer as he spoke, and his hard amber eyes melted into the honey colour I remembered so well from the banquet.

I tugged my wrist away. 'I need to go now.'

The man released me and his laid-back drawl of a smile appeared again. 'Where's that fiery pride of yours? Did you lose it when you fell?'

I gave him a cold look, but he appeared not to notice.

'What's your name, dear lady?'

'Didn't you just say that I don't have to tell you everything?'

The man let out a long sigh and comically pouted. 'Have it your way,' he said. 'But in the meantime, your dashing white knight – who just rescued you – is named Richard Holdings.' He bowed.

'My dashing white knight?' I laughed. 'I thought knights were supposed to save damsels in distress, not distress them further.'

'I try my best, but I'm somewhat new to the whole trying-to-catch-maidens-falling-out-of-thin-air concept,' Richard said. 'Now, what is this pretty damsel's name?'

'No,' I said.

122

'No? What do you mean 'no'?'

'Nice try, but no.'

'My lady!' Helen appeared as if out of nowhere, but I suppose there were only two real exits from the chapel. I had never felt so grateful for her presence. 'My lady, the countess asked me to call for you. She told me you were at the chapel. She wishes to see you straight away.'

I glanced at Richard and we both fell into a fit of giggles.

'So now she really is calling,' he said.

'Yes, and I had best respond.'

'Till we meet again.' Richard swept into a mock bow and I laughed at how cheesy he sounded. 'And don't think we won't meet again. I have ways of making fate work in my favour.' He winked and I could feel Helen turning red on my behalf next to me.

'Don't be too certain of that,' I called over my shoulder as I followed Helen back to the countess's quarters.

I don't like that man, I heard Henley mutter in my ear.

'He's harmless,' I said aloud.

'You say that now, my lady,' Helen replied. Remembering herself, she quickly looked down. 'Oh, but what do I know?'

'There you are.' The countess stood up from her place near the fire. 'Taking ones own time seems to be a very Lithuanian custom.'

'I was enjoying the gardens,' I muttered.

The countess waved my words away. 'I sent for you as I thought you'd like to see who finally made it to court.'

As if on cue, the door behind me opened and Lord Empson walked through with his arms outstretched.

'Lady Eleanor!' he exclaimed.

In spite of his welcoming arms, I thought the countess would probably deem it inappropriate for me to hug him

123

so I curtsied instead, which appeared to please both of them.

'How are you enjoying court?'

I opened my mouth to respond, but before I could get a single word in, Lord Empson continued.

'I trust Countess Grenville has seen to it that you are well taken care of and are meeting the right people.'

Lord Empson walked over to the countess as if he had only just noticed her. He took her hand and kissed it.

'My dear Aunt Marian, I trust you are in good health?'

I'd almost forgotten that the countess was also his aunt.

'Joan and I are keeping well.' The countess withdrew her hand. 'Though we would be keeping better if you would increase my allowance. Even after letting the other girl go, the money is still stretched thin.'

Lord Empson's smile looked forced now. 'Maybe it wouldn't be so thin if you scaled down your dress budget.'

'My dress budget? I haven't bought a single—'

'We will discuss this later.'

Lord Empson's voice turned icy, shutting down the conversation, and the countess didn't dare say another word. This was a side of Lord Empson I had not seen before and it scared me. But as quickly as his temper appeared, it was gone.

'Lady Eleanor, I hope you'll do me the honour of dining with me tonight. My wife was telling me how much she is looking forward to meeting you. I'm afraid she's feeling slightly under the weather so we will be eating in our rooms, but I still hope you'll join us.'

I glanced towards the countess.

Seeing the direction of my gaze, he added, 'Of course, Aunt Marian, you're welcome to join us, too,' Lord Empson said smoothly.

The countess dipped her head in a slight nod.

'I'd love to, my lord,' I said.

'Very well. Eight o'clock, then? My wife *will* be pleased.'

Lord Empson bowed out of the room, leaving me alone with the countess.

'I'm convinced his wife is a saint,' I heard her say as she turned away from me. 'I've already instructed Joan to ready a gown for you for supper. I'm afraid it won't be much, but it'll be the best we can do.'

I thanked her, telling her that it would surely be more than enough.

'Lord Empson also brought a few samplers so you can practise your sewing. I had Joan put those in your room as well.'

'Samplers?'

'Yes, samplers. You can go and work on them now before supper.' Seeing my alarmed face, she paused. 'Or you can walk the gardens.'

'I think I might take a walk,' I said quickly. I wondered if my distaste for sitting around in my room was that apparent.

'Take Lord Empson's girl with you – Helen, was it?'

I excused myself and crept back out to the main corridor. I had no intention of taking anyone with me, but the countess mustn't find out. Seeing that no one was around, I saw a chance to talk to Henley.

'Now that we know the countess doesn't have the clock, what do we do next?' I hoped Henley would have a simple answer.

We obviously have to continue searching for it.

'Of course, but how do you suppose we do that?' I was impatient to get on with it, but I knew that inappropriate behaviour would lead to questions about my identity and background. I couldn't afford that kind of scrutiny. 'We need a way to get into more rooms.'

Perhaps you could gain entrance by befriending the servants. They're always about.

'That would look suspicious. As Lady Eleanor Shelton, I'm not expected to *notice* the help, much less befriend them,' I said. 'But you're on to something. I can't risk stealing into most of these rooms. I need to be invited, and to do that I must befriend more of the important people.'

At least then your chatting and loitering about would have a purpose.

I was going to give a smart retort, but I decided it wasn't worth it. Instead I turned a corner into a crowded corridor, and that silenced him.

I passed dozens of people, all walking with their heads down. They all looked busy, as if they were late to meet with someone or other. The ladies occasionally lifted their heads to glance at me. Some gave me shy smiles, but most of them stared, obviously noting me as a newcomer.

I thought about asking them where the main gardens were, but didn't want to draw more attention to myself than I already had. Thankfully, before long the corridor I was in brought me to some doors that opened out into the gardens. They were comprised of only two colours: green and white. Rows and rows of white rose-like flowers grew near my feet. Neatly trimmed grass lined the gravel pathway and short trees with fragrant white flowers dotted the scene.

'You, there. Girl!'

I turned, not because I thought the speaker was calling for me, but because I was curious to see who was shouting. Across the path was a rotund woman dressed in a shade of green that almost blended into the gardens.

'You, girl!' she called again.

I looked over my shoulder to be sure no one else was nearby. 'Me?'

She cackled. 'Of *course*, you! Who else would I be calling to?' There was no mistaking it, in truth – she was looking straight at me.

'I'm sorry—'

'Come closer, my dear. I can't quite hear you! These old ears aren't what they used to be.' She trilled so loudly that I was sure people in their rooms inside the palace could hear her. I warily made my way towards her, not knowing what she could possibly want.

'Now, who might you be?' the woman asked. She looked me up and down. 'I make a point of knowing all the ladies' maids at court and I don't believe I've seen you before. Of course, I was unable to attend the king's opening feast last night due to an upset stomach. I'm sure my absence was noted, as I was told my company was missed.'

The woman's voice had an uneven pitch and her words rang uncomfortably in my ears as she carefully pronounced her vowels. Her dress was a brighter green than I first thought. Instead of a serene shade it was almost electric, but the green of the gardens had softened its appearance. I also noticed her sleeves were trimmed with bright pink to match her hot-pink slippers.

'I'm Lady Eleanor Shelton, my lady,' I said, giving her a quick curtsy. 'I've just arrived and I'm serving the Countess Grenville.'

'Countess Grenville?' I saw the woman's eyebrows shoot up. 'The girl from the Grand Duchy of Lithuania, of course. My . . . You must have some interesting connections to warrant that.'

'Connections?'

127

'Are you related to her in some way? Maybe by marriage?' she pestered on.

'Oh, no. Nothing of the sort. My father does business with Lord Empson.'

'Lord Empson. Of course. But business? Oh my . . . You don't mean *actual* business, do you? Trade and that sort of thing?'

'Well, exactly that, as it happens. He and my father are in the fur—'

'Fur! So it is actual business! To think Lord Empson's mixed up in *business*. The Countess Grenville must be so disappointed. They must really need the money. It probably means they're not getting enough from their lands. Do you know if they've sold any of their holdings?'

I had quickly come to realize that this woman only stopped talking to ask questions.

'I don't know,' I said. And truly, I didn't, but even had I known, I probably wouldn't have told her.

'Oh, my dear child. To be swept up with all that *business* – how horrible for them!' The woman folded me into her arms and I felt instantly muffled by her heavy green sleeves. I flinched at the suffocating smell of her perfume and wondered if she felt that. If she had, she made no remark.

'You know, I don't think I introduced myself properly.' The woman finally released me, if only to get a better look at my face. 'I suppose you've heard of me from the Countess Grenville?'

'Perhaps . . .' I began. Seeing her upset expression, I realised that wasn't what I was supposed to say. 'I'm sure she mentioned you, but I think it must have slipped my mind.'

'Oh, yes. I imagine so. It must be so overwhelming to come to court after your . . . *primitive* childhood.'

128

I narrowed my eyes, trying to judge if she meant to offend me. The woman's face remained creaseless and I concluded that she had no idea how her words sounded to others.

'I am Lady Anne Sutton.'

She stood there, obviously waiting for some kind of response, so I awkwardly curtsied again.

'You mustn't tell anyone that we didn't have someone introduce us. Imagine the talk that would result!'

I doubted anyone would care, but I nodded anyway. Though I had only just met her, I already knew Lady Sutton well enough to decide that it would be far easier simply to agree with her on almost everything.

'Well, then, now that we've had our introductions, come and eat with me tonight.'

'I beg your pardon?' My face must have betrayed my surprise.

'Supper, my dear. Have supper with me. We must fill each other in on all the going-on of court, of course.'

'Of course . . .' I muttered.

'Very well. Supper tonight at seven-thirty. I'll have a maid—'

'Why, my lady, fancy running into you here.'

I recognized the accompanying chuckle and turned to face Richard Holdings yet again.

'Following me?' I murmured. I probably didn't even need to lower my voice on account of how hard of hearing Lady Sutton appeared to be.

'Oh! Lord Holdings!' Lady Sutton appeared to be talking even louder than before, and I wondered if that was so she could hear herself speak. Or maybe it was to attract the attention of anyone who might be passing so they'd see who she was talking to?

With his tousled brown hair that curled at its ends, the young man before me didn't look like a 'Lord Holdings' to me.

'My lady.' His eyes lingered on me before he took a curt bow.

'Lord Holdings, are you acquainted with Lady Eleanor Shelton?'

'I do believe I am.' His eyes held mine a second longer than necessary. 'Lady Eleanor Shelton.'

'What was that?' Lady Sutton stepped even closer.

'We have been introduced,' he said.

'How marvellous! I was just telling Lady Eleanor that she absolutely *must* have supper with me this evening. Will you join us?'

'I'm afraid I'll have to decline tonight. Christopher—'

I saw my opening. 'Lady Sutton, regrettably I won't be able to attend, either – I've already promised to dine with Lord Empson and his wife.'

'What a shame . . . What a pity! We must simply move it, then. Supper is just not the same when eaten alone. Let's have dinner together tomorrow afternoon instead.'

Lady Sutton glanced at the two of us to see if we had any objections. Before either of us could open our mouths, she clapped her hands like a child.

'Then it's settled! Lady Eleanor, I'll have a maid fetch you since you don't know the way to my chambers. Lord Holdings, do say hello to your little brother for me.'

'Of course, Godmother. Christopher will be pleased that you thought of him.' Richard bowed and took me by the arm to steer me away from Lady Sutton.

I thought I might have heard Henley hiss, but it could have been the wind.

'Well, Lady Eleanor Shelton, aren't you glad your white knight showed up just in time to come to your rescue?'

'My white knight? And why would I be glad?'

'Because Lady Sutton was already beginning to devour you alive.'

'I wouldn't quite say devour—'

'If you didn't notice, that means you were in even deeper than I thought. She had probably already asked you if you knew any gossip.'

I thought back to what Lady Sutton had asked me and realized that Richard was probably right. I also looked down to find that he still hadn't let go of my arm.

'Thank you,' I whispered, trying to pull back.

He finally released my arm and it dropped to my side. 'Consider me your servant, Lady Eleanor Shelton.'

I rolled my eyes at him as I often did with Henley. 'You're not about to let this go, are you?'

'I'm thankful for two things . . . Or rather, to two people,' he said. 'Whoever made the seating arrangements at the feast and decided to place me next to you, and Lady Sutton for being the shark she is, thereby letting me come swooping in to save you.'

I couldn't help but laugh at that, and Richard looked as if my giggles were a reward.

'I had best be going,' I said, awkwardly trying to turn away from him.

'As you wish,' Richard said. 'So long as I get to lay eyes on you again, Lady Eleanor.' He mock-bowed.

'Eleanor.' I corrected him without thinking.

Richard smiled. 'Till we meet again, Eleanor.'

I shook my head and walked off in search of my room.

Chapter 13

I just wish I could do something, Henley said.

'You are, Henley,' I said, though I knew he hadn't done much since we arrived at court. It wasn't his fault that he found himself in this strange, impotent state. I walked across my room to the chests on the other side. Joan and Helen had placed borrowed garments and dresses of the countess's that I could wear in the chests. 'You can't help it.'

That's exactly it! I can't help it. I can't do anything!

I opened the chest closest to me. 'I wouldn't say that—'

Then what would you say?

I paused, then snapped the chest shut. What *would* I say?

Henley was trying to help. He really was. I couldn't have figured out the identity of Eleanor Shelton without him. But since then he had taken a back seat, and I knew he wasn't accustomed to that. I remembered how back in 1904 – his time – he managed his father's estate and business almost single-handedly, making every decision. Yes, he was definitely not used to taking a back seat.

'I don't know what to say,' I admitted. 'But I do know that I couldn't have come this far without you.'

Henley remained silent, but I could feel his presence. He filled every corner of the space around me.

You don't understand, he finally said.

I wanted to tell him that I did but held my tongue, waiting for him to say more. He never did.

I sighed as I walked over to the bed. Joan had laid out another of the countess's dresses for me to wear to the supper with Lord Empson. This one was black, just like the countess's regular attire. The white dress I had worn to the feast appeared to be the only non-black garment the countess owned.

I slipped off the dress I had been wearing, shivering as cold air hit my shoulders. In 1904, Henley would have objected to me changing clothes in front of him, and I wouldn't have been comfortable doing it, either. But we'd both come to terms with it – besides, it wasn't as if he could see anything more than my outline.

There was a knock at the door and I turned to see Helen letting herself in.

'My lady, would you like me to assist you?'

'Yes, please.'

I couldn't stand bearing Henley's stubborn silence alone.

Helen's fingers brushed over me as she fitted me into the black dress. For some reason, it struck me as appropriate. I didn't feel like wearing anything bright that night.

Joan was waiting outside the door to walk me to the countess's sitting room, where she was always to be found sewing at this time of day. The other ladies played cards, but she didn't approve of such things, especially before supper.

The wooden door creaked open into a room aglow with candlelight, but the countess was not there.

'Her vanity,' Joan said, realising I was looking for her mistress.

Sure enough, she was in the next room, seated in front of the mirror just as she had been when I first met her.

The entire scene was very much as I remembered it. The room's burgundy walls glinted like the facets of rubies in the candlelight reflected by the large mirror. I could see the floral detail of the black lace covering the countess's shoulders and draping onto the rug beneath her chair. The black flowers fell as if cast down from some dark Garden of Eden. Perhaps once vibrant, now they tumbled, lowly and wrinkled, to the ground. They were disgraced in their own eyes, yet unable to forget the splendour they had once embodied.

The countess held a thick strand of diamonds to her throat. They turned red in the light of the room.

'There comes a moment in your life when you realize that you've lost a certain brightness. You see it when you sit in front of the mirror. Others see it in you. All you can do then is try to replace it.' The countess ran a finger over her diamonds.

I sought her eyes in the mirror and they bored into mine, harder than the diamonds.

'I'm sorry about the dress,' she said. 'The young should never have to wear black.'

'Youth is relative,' I said.

'That's what I used to think, too.' She smiled. 'Shall we go?'

She took my arm as if she was family. I couldn't help but note that this was the warmest thing she had done since I got here.

'The Countess Grenville and Lady Shelton to see you . . .'

There was a short pause before the door was opened for us.

'My Lord Empson.' The countess strode into the room ahead of me.

134

'Aunt Marian.' Lord Empson was not to be outdone. He came forward with his arms outstretched. 'I am so glad you could join us.'

'Nonsense. Of course I will join you for supper. It's been too long. You would think we live in entirely different countries given how rarely I get to see you.'

A woman at the back of the room was observing the whole scene, as I was. She looked utterly detached and I wondered if I had the same blank mien. It was as if she hadn't bothered to put on an expression because she knew this wasn't about her. She was merely an outsider looking in.

'Lady Eleanor!'

A smile flickered easily enough onto my face. 'Yes, my lord?'

'Might I introduce to you my dear wife?'

The woman behind Lord Empson stepped forward then, a sweet smile plastered across her face as if it had always been there.

'Pleasure,' she murmured.

'Margarite, this is the daughter of Nicholas Reginald Shelton.'

'Pleasure,' she murmured again.

As Lord Empson went on to describe a little of my upbringing and the circumstances that had brought me here, it became apparent that Lady Empson's minimal replies made up for Lord Empson's endless monologues. When one-word answers were not making their way out of her thin, compressed lips, Lady Empson was tilting her head this way and that. I wondered if she was actually listening, or if she had been taught that this was the way to feign interest and thereby be a suitable mealtime companion.

'Come, come. Why don't we sit down?'

I followed Lord Empson through double-doors on the other side of the room. The countess kept close to me while Lady Empson trailed along behind with the footmen.

The dining room was panelled with wood like all the other rooms I'd seen in the palace so far. The panels sported elaborate carvings, as did the ceiling with its dark, arching designs. I assumed it was the style of the period. I wondered what they would make of stick-on wallpaper. In the middle of the room was a small but ornately set table. Evenly spaced silver candlesticks were angled to greet us in a way that was *just so*.

We sat, the countess across from me, Lord and Lady Empson at either end. The backs of the chairs curved inwards, almost hunching us over the table.

'Though I am far from being the King of England, we only have the best for our most special guest.' With a practised flourish, Lord Empson gestured to the waiting servants to start presenting the food.

And it really was *presented*. Each plate glistened with the myriad sauces covering the peasant, venison and other meats. And they kept coming, every dish on its own plate, each plate placed on the small table with a flourish. Everything was cold – I supposed they hadn't worked out yet how to keep food warm once it left the kitchen. I smiled to myself, wondering what the countess's reaction would be to seeing a microwave work.

I spotted Lord Empson eying me from his side of the table. I hoped I looked appropriately impressed.

'So do tell me,' Lord Empson said, just as I stuck a slab of meat into my mouth. 'How are you finding court?'

I could almost feel the countess's stare as I tried to chew and swallow without spewing my food.

'Very well.'

'Just very well?'

I didn't know what he was probing for, so I simply nodded. 'Yes, very well.'

Giving me a sidelong glance, the countess answered for me. 'Sir Gordon promptly attached himself to her last night, as leech-like as ever. He introduced her to Lady Simnel and her sort. I thought he'd never leave us.'

As I remembered it, the countess was the one who had introduced me to Sir Gordon in the first place, but she appeared not to find it necessary to mention that.

'Ah, of course he would,' Lord Empson said.

The countess went on to list the names of the people I had been introduced to. Some sounded familiar, while others conjured no faces from my jumble of memories when they were mentioned. I found it curious to note that not once did she mention Lord Dormer's name.

'I see that Lady Eleanor is becoming acquainted with court rather quickly,' Lord Empson said. He spoke of me as if I was not in the room.

'Why, yes,' the countess replied. 'She needs to be introduced to the right people. She's having to catch up, given the timing of her arrival.'

I looked across the table at Lady Empson to see if she had something to say about me as well, but her tranquil, tight-lipped smile remained fixed.

'I agree with you, Aunt Marian . . . for once.' It looked as if it pained Lord Empson to admit that. He looked away. 'Eleanor needs to find some leverage, and that leverage will only come by increasing her standing with others.' Finally, he turned to me. 'Now tell me, have you been introduced to anyone else? Did Sir Gordon do anything more useful than leer at you?'

I suppressed a shudder and tried to recall the names the countess had listed.

'I-I don't think so.'

'You don't *think*? What do you mean, you don't *think* so?' Lord Empson massaged his temples.

'Lady Sutton,' I said, remembering the strange woman in the gardens. 'And Lord Holdings, I believe.' I wasn't going to add his name, but something made me include him.

'That old gossip?' the countess said. 'Sir Gordon must have been running out of people to make that introduction. She's absolutely tasteless, not to mention utterly without manners. No one knows if that woman is actually hard of hearing or whether she just likes to hear herself talk over others. She doesn't have one ounce of refinement in that—'

'Lord Holdings?' Lord Empson stopped massaging his temples. 'What a strange introduction. Who introduced you?'

I thought hard. 'Lady Sutton.' That wasn't a complete lie.

'Lady Sutton . . . Why, yes, I do believe she has some connection with the Holdings – their sons' godmother, if I rightly recall. Had they not fallen out of favour with the king, I don't think they would have stooped so low . . .'

Lord Empson trailed off and I craned over the table to hear him.

I knew I shouldn't be so interested and nosy. If I didn't know myself better, I would have thought that I actually *liked* the guy. I mentally chastised myself for feeling glad that Lord Empson was offering additional information. But then again, I reasoned, any sort of information would be valuable right now since I knew so little of the world I was in.

'Though I do believe the relationship with Lady Sutton has come in handy for them. I doubt they would have been able to secure an apprenticeship with the royal alchemist himself for their fourth son had it not been for her. That's the only upside of keeping someone so nosy around.'

I wondered if Richard might be that fourth son. He had mentioned a younger brother – Christopher – but aside from that I knew nothing about his family.

'Alchemy?' I tried to probe.

'Witchcraft,' the countess pronounced. 'Absolutely immoral.'

'No one cares if it's immoral except you, Aunt Marian.' Lord Empson threw up his hands. 'Gold! Gold from something as easy to obtain as this.' He grabbed a candlestick. 'Imagine creating and multiplying gold whenever you saw fit.'

'You have never cared what I regard as seemly,' the countess said softly. 'If you were able to create gold out of practically anything, maybe you could finally quit business. If you quit now, there's a chance you might have some sense of propriety left.'

Lord Empson remained silent as the countess spoke, but he gripped the table with both hands, as if stabilising himself.

After a moment, he said, 'Marian, let's not do this now—'

'So it's Marian now? Not Aunt?' The countess stared directly at him.

Lady Empson looked so pale she was almost translucent. 'Marian, I know you disapprove—'

'Disapprove? That doesn't even begin to describe my feelings on the subject! I *disapprove* of someone like Lady Sutton. This . . . this is dragging our family into the mud. If my husband—'

139

'Go ahead,' Lord Empson said. His voice was shaking slightly, but that was all that betrayed his emotion. 'Say it.'

When the countess looked up, I was surprised to see stark fear on her face. The whites of her eyes appeared to engulf her pupils and her body shied away from him.

'Say it.' It sounded like a warning now. 'By God, if you're going to criticise me, say it to my face!' Lord Empson stood abruptly, jostling the table.

The countess's pallor matched the white linen napkins on our laps. Her lips parted, but floundered soundlessly.

'"If my husband were here" – isn't that what you were about to say?' A vein protruded in Lord Empson's neck as he gritted his teeth. 'Isn't that what you *always* say? Marian, he isn't here. Since he's been gone, I'm all that's left. I know you abhor even the idea of business. I know you think land is the only respectable stock, but even you must see that this is the only way we can preserve the family. As the head of this family, I am doing everything necessary to preserve it.'

The countess remained silent as Lord Empson sat down. Lady Empson picked at the threads in her napkin. I didn't know what to think or where to look, so I simply stared my plate.

Lord Empson cleared his throat. 'Bring out the dessert pastries.'

Finally alone in my room, I inhaled a deep breath. That evening had taken a lot out of me and I found myself too tired to even talk to Henley. He appeared to understand that and kept to himself long after Helen finished preparing me for bed.

Supper had been a long affair made even longer by Lord Empson's outburst. After his flare-up, the dinner ran the rest of its course without incident. The countess kept almost as quiet as Lady Empson. Lord Empson held a one-sided conversation between pauses in which he chewed his food, and rare instances when he looked over at me so I could give him encouraging nods.

Even when we returned to our rooms, the countess didn't say more than two words once we were inside. It was so unlike her and so unsettling that I excused myself for bed as soon as I could.

Now, stretching out on my bed, I watched the room through heavy-lidded eyes.

The edges of the curtains billowed as if the room itself were taking easy breaths. As I sank into the mattress, I felt all the pent-up emotion and fatigue begin to seep out of me. Closing my eyelids, it only took a few breaths to calm my wandering eyes. Soon they stopped moving and I fell into a deep, all-consuming sleep.

And then it happened.

My eyes flew open, but it was so dark that everything looked the same as when I closed them. There was a heavy weight on my chest and something was pressed over my mouth. I tried to yell for Henley but my voice was muffled. Someone was smothering me.

My hands shot out from under the covers and I shoved at the person on top of me. I pushed against the pillow now covering my entire face and obscuring my vision, but whoever it was, they were too strong. They had me completely pinned down. And that was it. I was going to die.

Rebecca!

My head throbbed and my blood thumped in my brain. I felt woozy and wondered if I was about to pass out.

Rebecca! Stay with me.

I thought I felt the weight on my body begin to shift back and forth. I was confused. I had already given up. Why wasn't I dead yet?

The weight on my body now shifted drastically. The pillow covering my face momentarily slipped and I gulped in air. I couldn't see anything yet with part of the pillow still over my eyes, but I knew something was different.

There was a large crash followed by a thud and my lungs suddenly expanded. They burned as if I had been held underwater, but I was still breathing.

'My lady! Is everything all right?' Helen flew into the room with a guttering candle.

I sat up and the pillow slipped easily off my face. There was no one else in the room except for me and Helen.

'Is everything all right?' she repeated.

I surveyed the damage. Apart from the pillow now on my lap and a washbowl of water that had tipped over from the bedside table, everything looked normal.

'What was that commotion?' The countess swept into the room in her nightgown. Joan followed close behind with extra candles.

'Nothing,' I mumbled. 'I fell out of bed. Bad dream. That's all.'

Helen looked worriedly at the countess, who in turn inspected my face.

The countess frowned. 'Just make sure it doesn't happen again,' she called over her shoulder as she left.

'Yes, my lady.'

I insisted I was so tired that I wanted Helen to leave the tipped-over washbowl until morning.

'Are you sure, my lady? It'll be—'

'Yes, yes. I'm terribly tired and out of sorts. I would much prefer it if you cleaned up the mess in the morning.'

After getting her to agree, I waited until both Helen and Joan had left the room before talking to Henley.

Are you all right? Henley asked before I could ask him anything.

'Yes . . .' I walked over to the far wall. There was a small dent and what looked like a smear of blood. Henley must have thrown the attacker.

Are you sure, Rebecca? You still look very pale.

'Who wouldn't after being attacked by a stranger like that? One who vanished before I could see him?'

A stranger? What makes you say that?

I paused. 'I don't know!' I was still catching my breath.

It might be a stranger, Henley began, *but it could also easily be someone you know. It was so dark that even if I went back to see who it was, I wouldn't be able to see their face. And of course in the moment, I was focusing on getting him off of you so I couldn't see his face—*

'What? Lord Empson rushed in here in the middle of the night to suffocate me while I'm technically in his care? Or better yet, the countess tried to smother me with a pillow in her own chambers, but then, failing, went out and came back in to look sympathetic?'

You never know . . .

I threw my hands up. 'What happened in here?'

It was dark . . .

'You mean it was dark *again.*' I thought back to the intruder I'd encountered in the hotel . . . That was the reason I was in this mess in the first place.

So you think it's the same person? It never ceased to amaze me how in tune with my thoughts Henley was.

'It must have been. This wasn't some petty theft. Whoever it was tried to kill me – that was their only motive.'

What I don't understand is that they didn't break in.

I looked towards the windows. Henley was right: none of them was shattered and the latches didn't look broken.

That means the attacker must have come in through the door.

'But anyone could have come in that way,' I said, turning the doorknob. 'See – it doesn't even have a lock.'

I remembered feeling surprised that the door had no lock when Joan first showed me the room I was to be staying in. 'How else do you think we could come in to assist you should something happen to you?' she had said. And she was right.

Anyone who didn't look out of place, Henley corrected.

'It's the middle of the night . . . or maybe even early morning by now. There isn't anyone hanging around to think someone looks suspicious.'

And that, my dear, is where you're wrong.

It was so like Henley to tease, even in a grave situation like this one.

This is court. There's always people about. People who never mind their own business.

Standing by the door, I heard faint sounds of music and laughter.

'I guess you're right there.'

Someone's not used to admitting defeat. I knew that Henley would have a triumphant grin on his face if only I were able to see it.

I ignored his comment. 'Where does that put us?'

Well, someone is still after you. That someone is probably the person who attacked you in the hotel, and they probably have the clock. That person is also probably the same one who killed my m— Miss Hatfield. And since that person's in this time period, I think it's safe to say they're immortal. And they're definitely trying to kill you.

I clasped my hands to keep them from shaking. I didn't want Henley to notice. 'Oh, great. That's uplifting. Thanks.'

Chapter 14

I woke to a sharp knock at the door. The sound echoed
in my head and shook me awake.

'Yes? Come in,' I mumbled into my pillow, but then
resolved to at least sit up to greet whoever it was.

'I'm so sorry to wake you, my lady.'

Seeing that it was only Helen, I slumped back onto
the bed.

'I'm terribly sorry,' she began again, 'but you've been
sleeping quite late . . . and Lady Sutton sent one of her
women for you . . .'

I sat bolt upright.

'What time is it?' I squinted at Helen, who was now
quickly opening the curtains. She moved at a faster rate
than I was accustomed to seeing from her, and that made
me think I had slept in longer than I had intended.

'Ten minutes past noon, my lady.'

'My God, noon?' I sprang out of bed, not caring that
I'd shocked Helen with my profanity. 'Helen, please help
me get ready. I promised Lady Sutton I would take dinner
with her.'

After her standard, 'Yes, my lady,' Helen set to work
pulling a black dress – one of the countess's, I presumed
– onto me and attempted to make my hair look present-
able. Miss Hatfield always told me that to survive in a

145

different time period, looking the part was almost half the battle.

'Ouch.' The hairbrush Helen was wielding snagged in my hair.

'I'm *so* sorry, my lady.'

'No matter,' I said gently. Helen looked terrified, as if she thought she'd inflicted lasting damage upon me, and I wanted to calm her down. 'I asked you to help me get ready quickly. I'm sure Lady Sutton's woman does not want to wait any longer than she already has.'

'Yes, my lady.' She finished fussing with my hair and then tidied the folds of my dress. When she was done, she stood to the side. 'Should I call Lady Sutton's woman in?'

'No, no,' I said. 'I'll just meet her in the sitting room. You may go.'

Helen looked surprised by my instruction, but nevertheless curtsied and left.

In truth, I wanted a second with Henley before I left for Lady Sutton's.

Are you sure this is wise? Henley asked as soon as I heard the door close.

'Going to Lady Sutton's for lunch?'

Someone tried to kill you last night.

'And that's precisely why I need to go. I'm not about to give whoever this is the satisfaction of terrifying me. Besides, it's not as if I'm any safer in my room.'

What about the fact that you're going to Lady Sutton's for lunch when you should be looking for the clock?

'What about it? We've established that it's not among the countess's possessions because it's not in any of her rooms. Now I need to start looking around court, and we agreed that accepting invitations to visit other people's chambers was the best way to go about it – unless you have any better ideas?'

146

Henley didn't reply, but I knew he was deep in thought.

After a moment, he said, *It's easier than breaking in, that's for sure.*

I started for the door.

Just promise me you'll watch out for yourself.

'I'll try.'

Trying isn't good enough.

'Isn't watching your job?'

Henley didn't respond. I had no idea if it was because he had nothing to say to that, or because I was already out of the door.

In the sitting room, I found the woman I assumed to be Lady Sutton's maid. The main reason for that assumption (besides the fact that I had never seen her before) was because she was standing in a room full of chairs. Every chair was empty, yet she chose to stand perfectly still in the corner of the room. Only a servant would do that.

'My lady.' She dropped into a deep curtsy on seeing me enter.

'I hope I haven't kept you waiting for too long.'

She smiled, not meeting my eyes, but didn't respond. She merely opened the door and began leading me silently down the corridors.

It was the middle of the day, and given that court was – as the countess had put it – 'the centre of culture, the learned world and everything else besides Paris', the corridors were packed with people rushing around. I had begun to think that the halls of court were never empty during the day.

Lady Sutton's woman took so many twists and turns through the passages that I knew I would have been hopelessly lost were she not with me. The palace was big and the corridors all looked the same.

147

'Here we are, my lady,' the woman said, stopping at last. 'Lady Eleanor Shelton,' she informed the young man standing by the door.

I couldn't tell whether he served as a footman, a guard or both, but he promptly went in, presumably to announce my arrival, as I followed behind him.

'Lady Eleanor, my dear!' Of course it was Lady Sutton's trilling voice that greeted me before he could get a word out.

She stood from her chair in front of the couch and came flying at me in a whirl of bright blue and chartreuse. Her dress was so bright, especially compared to mine, that I didn't know whether to look away or stare.

'Lady Sutton.' I bobbed a curtsy, acknowledging her, as I tore my eyes away to view the rest of the room.

Though the chartreuse ribbons on her bodice matched the lace on the curtains, beyond that Lady Sutton appeared to have no knowledge whatsoever regarding the concept of a colour palette. Gaudy cloths were draped along one wall like bright tapestries in a range of clashing hues. Vases overflowing with dozens of flowers of every colour filled all the visible surfaces save the chairs.

Chairs lined one side of the room, each placed beneath a window, each upholstered in another absurdly bright colour. I supposed they matched the rugs if you squinted at them a bit . . . but I was supposed to be scanning the room for the clock. It would most likely be hanging on a wall as there were no drawers or chests it could have fit in. Unfortunately, the walls were largely bare, save for the not-so-occasional drape of garish colour.

And in the middle of all that chaos was one longer-than-average bright-pink couch with a particularly handsome-looking man sitting on it. Lord Richard Holdings.

'Richard wasn't certain you'd make it, but I assured him you wouldn't disappoint.' Lady Sutton fluttered around, gesturing for me to sit.

I looked over at the chairs by the windows, but since they were quite a way from Lady Sutton's chair and Richard on the couch, I ended up sitting on the far end of the pink couch, hoping that put enough distance between me and Richard. It wouldn't be seemly to be sitting right next to him, and he also made me feel nervous when I was too close to him.

Richard leaned towards me, close enough that I had a clear view of his five o'clock shadow. 'Couldn't quite escape her after all?'

'I tried,' I muttered.

'I've been trying my entire life.'

I stifled a laugh.

'Now then, since we're all here, I can call for our food.' Lady Sutton nodded at a maid waiting by the door. 'Lady Eleanor, do tell me you've been up to something interesting since we last saw each other. Some interesting titbits might begin to make up for that dreadfully drab dress the countess no doubt picked for you.' She resumed her seat facing us.

'Um . . .' I began, remembering too late the countess's insistence that one should never start a sentence with 'um'. I paused, then tried again. 'Not particularly.'

'Come now,' Lady Sutton pressed. 'What was so urgent that we had to move our meeting from yesterday evening to this afternoon? You said something about taking supper with Lord and Lady Empson?'

'Yes, just d- supper.' I was still finding it difficult to remember that 'dinner' was actually what I would think of as lunch, while 'supper' was dinner.

'And I presume that the Countess Grenville was present as well?'

'Yes,' I said, before adding, 'she was, my lady,' to sound a bit more polite.

'Of *course* that woman was there . . .' lady Sutton looked over her shoulder at the view outside. I didn't know what she saw through the window, but all of a sudden it appeared to interest her greatly. 'And how was supper?'

'Quite ordinary, to be honest.' I smoothed my dress with my palms.

Lady Sutton turned towards me, raising her thin eyebrows.

It felt like betraying family to tell Lady Sutton about Lord Empson's outburst last night, so I decided to keep my mouth shut. It wasn't anything she needed to know anyway.

'And how about you, Lady Sutton?' Richard jumped to my rescue, and I wondered if the expression on my face had made it apparent that I needed saving. 'Surely you had a more interesting night than either of us.'

'Wait a minute, Lord Holdings,' I said. 'I told you what I was doing last night, but you never told us what you were doing.' I smiled to make my words sound lighter. I didn't want to sound accusatory before I had something to accuse him of.

'Ah, nothing particularly interesting.' But as he said this, he looked away from me, flushing.

I wrung my hands in my lap. I had almost forgotten the need to be suspicious of everyone. Had he been nearby when I was attacked? Then I noticed that the cuff on Richard's left shirtsleeve had inched up, revealing a fresh gash running along the inside of his wrist.

'Oh my g-goodness,' I sputtered. I had almost said something completely blasphemous.

Following my line of sight, Richard hastily pulled his cuff down.

'It's nothing. A cat,' he was quick to say. 'It's fine, really.'

But I couldn't erase the image from my mind.

'Now, Lady Sutton,' Richard asked again, 'will you please do us the honour of telling us about your riveting night?'

Richard's question appeared to make Lady Sutton happy, and she proceeded to describe her evening with Sir Gordon and a few other men of the court.

I tried to concentrate on what she was saying, but my mind kept wandering to Richard. I didn't want to believe that he had anything to do with the attack on me . . . but I couldn't rule him out, either. I pushed the thought out of my mind. *Focus*.

'You see,' Lady Sutton was saying, 'I was *positively* embarrassed that they should want, much less ask, me to play cards with them. Imagine that! A lady like me. Gambling with them. Baron Hastings was even in the room!'

'And did you, Lady Sutton?' Richard had an amused smirk on his face, though I couldn't tell if it was caused by the story Lady Sutton was telling or Lady Sutton in general.

'Why, of course not! I am a *real* lady. Though I did stay and help Lord Grey win a hand.' She winked at us and whispered, 'I told him which cards to play.' With a coy giggle, she rose from her seat. 'It appears that our meal is here.'

Two men in red livery entered carrying miniature tables, which they set up in front of the couch and Lady Sutton.

'Come now, hurry up and bring the food in.' Lady Sutton waved them along. 'I don't like to hear my guests' stomachs rumbling. That means I'm not a good hostess.'

Lady Sutton's words suddenly reminded me how hungry I was. Though I had eaten plenty before Lord Empson's quarrel with the countess last night at supper, my appetite was strangely back. Sitting around and doing practically nothing at court appeared to do wonders for it.

The same men returned carrying two plates each, all towering with food. As they set them on the table in front of us, I saw that the plates were filled with various tiny morsels, each no bigger than two of my fingers together.

'The latest from France,' Lady Sutton drawled. 'I recently brought in a French cook I found on my last visit to the Continent, and he is sublime. I was surprised that the Duke of Lorraine could do without him.'

I should have known that lunch would be like this – we were silent and Lady Sutton talked at us. All while the food was sitting tantalizingly in front of us, but since our hostess hadn't reached for her plate, we were required to sit and listen.

'Did I tell you that Lady Sanford wanted a French cook? It is a bit unladylike of me but, between friends, I can say that I was actually glad when she fell ill before leaving for France. It is so important to be unique, isn't it?' Without warning, she took one of my hands. 'We *are* friends now, aren't we?'

She didn't let go till I assured her we were.

'Richard, on the other hand, has no choice about it.' Lady Sutton cackled, glancing at him. 'You aren't tied to me by blood, exactly, but you are family.'

Seeing my confusion, Richard explained. 'Lady Sutton is my aunt's mother by marriage, and also my godmother.'

I remembered Lord Empson and the countess mentioning their relationship.

'Which means that little Richard here can't escape me.'

I swore I saw Richard gulp, and it would have been a funny sight if Lady Sutton hadn't actually looked menacing.

She bared her teeth into a smile before continuing to prattle on about yet more irrelevant subjects.

The rest of lunch went on like that; Lady Sutton talked endlessly while I shrank in my seat, bored beyond belief. I would have been annoyed for allowing myself to be dragged into this lunch – excuse me, 'dinner' – in the first place if it hadn't been for Richard.

Watching Richard and being around him was the most fun I'd had in a while. There was something easy about his manner. I still wasn't sure I took his cat-scratch explanation as truth, but there was a quality about him that made me feel normal. This was someone who made me forget everything – immortality, the clock, the killer. Henley used to be the person who distracted me from these things, but now that he was entangled in the same mess that I was, he was a reminder of my problems, not an escape from them. Things were easy when I was around Richard. So when, after escorting me back towards my room, he asked if I'd like to take a walk with him, I said yes.

'Let me just change for supper before we go,' I said, running ahead of him along the hallway. I knew the countess would want me dressed and prompt, since tonight we were to dine together in her rooms. I threw open my door and ran in.

'Helen!'

'Yes, my lady?' Helen scuttled in, red in the face. I felt bad for giving her such a fright, but I knew I had to hurry since Richard was waiting outside.

'I need a dress for supper.' I struggled to throw off the gown I was currently wearing while Helen just stood there, appalled. 'Quick. Quick!'

That sent Helen scampering about the room, throwing open chests and digging through black skirts. All the

153

countess ever seemed to wear was black clothing, so it was fitting that all the dresses I could borrow from the countess were equally black. I nodded at everything she showed me. They all looked the same. Raising my arms, I tried to help her manoeuvre me into various pieces of clothing. When Helen was done, surprisingly I looked even more pristine than usual – certainly not like someone who had spent the last few minutes running around the room like a headless chicken.

'Tell the countess that I'll be back in time for supper!'

I patted down a loose strand of my hair and shooed Helen out through the door. I was about to follow when Henley's voice stopped me.

God, Rebecca, sometimes you drive me insane!

'Sometimes? Don't you mean all the time?'

Henley ignored my attempt at humour. *There's a murderer after you, and here you are going into the gardens with a stranger. You don't even know who this Richard is, anyway, or what his intentions might be.*

On some level I knew Henley was right, but in that moment I couldn't admit it. I hated to think of Richard like that. He couldn't possibly be in league with – or be – the killer.

'Are you jealous?' I said instead. When there was no answer, I smirked. 'You have no reason to be jealous. Richard's just . . . Richard. And, Henley, you might not understand this, but *this* is my way of dealing with the fact that someone wants me dead. For one thing, I need to remind myself that I'm still alive, and not everyone is like that.'

It's as if you have no sense of urgency whatsoever.

Ignoring him, I went on, 'And for another, if you have a killer after you, changing your behaviour isn't going to help, but keeping things looking normal will. Being around others is good because it's highly unlikely that whoever it is will try to murder me in a room full of people.'

Are you even trying to get back home?

I refrained from correcting Henley and telling him that as an immortal I had no home.

'Have some patience,' I told him. 'If I learned anything while in your time period trying to steal back Miss Hatfield's painting, it was the importance of remaining undercover and waiting for the right moment.'

But I knew that as an immortal, there was a limit to that waiting. Time was slipping away from me. Miss Hatfield hadn't told me much about what would happen if I were to be stuck in a single time period for too long, but she'd disclosed enough to make it crystal clear that it would not end well. The first warning sign was an uneasy feeling in my stomach which would continue to grow the longer I stayed, soon becoming intolerable. Miss Hatfield warned me that the pain would eventually consume me and drive me mad, leaving me nothing but a vessel for that insanity.

'I need to learn to do things my way, and blending in is how I do it. Miss Hatfield's gone, and I'm all I have. Don't you think it's high time I started being a little more independent?'

You also have me.

I looked down, as if to avoid his eyes.

You know I'll always worry about you, Henley said. *That came with the territory of falling in love with you.*

'Oh, woe is you,' I said, finally eliciting a chuckle from Henley.

If this is woe and misery is this sweet, I'm sure hell would be a very happy place indeed.

I shook my head at him, knowing he could see it, and opened the door. Sure enough, Richard was leaning against the wall.

'I've never known a woman to get dressed so quickly.'

I shrugged.

'I've also never known a woman to talk that much with her maid.' Richard smirked and a sheepish laugh escaped my lips. I briefly wondered if he had overheard me speaking with Henley, but if so, he didn't mention it.

'Oh, look! You're not even denying it. You *are* a different kind of woman.'

Richard didn't know how different I was.

'So where to?' I said, changing the subject.

'I have no idea.'

'What do you mean? Weren't you the one who asked me to accompany you on a walk?'

'I didn't think you'd accept,' Richard said. 'It's not every day a lady allows me to walk with her unchaperoned.'

'So you ask women every day?' I teased. 'And here I thought I was special.'

I knew walking with a man unchaperoned was frowned upon and probably something the countess wouldn't approve of, but I figured she didn't have to know. Besides, it was almost unavoidable – how else was I supposed to gain useful information from Richard about the clock or alchemy? Not to mention, I would hate for my time with Richard to be closely watched and scrutinized by someone else. If we avoided the busiest public areas, maybe word wouldn't reach the countess? And if it did, it was better to ask for forgiveness than to ask for permission, right? The people of court could chalk it up to my 'strange Lithuanian ways'.

Richard gazed at me intently, making me feel hot all of a sudden. 'You know exactly what I think of you.'

156

Suddenly things had gone beyond teasing. I thought of Henley watching this scene and grew increasingly uncomfortable. We walked in silence for a bit.

'The gardens are my favourite place,' Richard said after a moment, 'although I prefer them at night. It's so quiet there with no one about. The gardens are even more beautiful then.'

'Isn't it too dark to see them, though?' I asked.

'That's the point – don't you see?'

'Things are prettier in the dark?'

'There's no need to see the flowers,' he said. 'They detract from the beauty of the stars.'

'Now you sound like a tired poet – all fluff and no meaning.'

'So that's how you see me?' he joked. 'Besides, the dark is a nice retreat from the false people at court. They're always putting on one act or another. Everyone.'

I couldn't have guessed that was how he felt about the people at court. 'But you look so at ease.'

'I'm simply putting on an act myself.'

We made a turn that led us towards the back of the gardens, where tall hedges arched over us.

'I didn't know there was a maze here,' I said.

'There's a lot you don't know about court,' Richard replied, but he took my hand and led me into the maze.

'I'm beginning to see that. Court appears to be its own world.'

'It has its own rules and ways of living . . . I'm sure it's different from the Grand Duchy of Lithuania.'

I smiled.

'What's that mysterious smile for?' Richard asked, but he was wearing a similar grin on his face.

'I never told you I was from Lithuania.'

He faltered. 'News travels fast. That's another rule of court.'

I raised my eyebrows. 'Sure . . .'

'My lady, you've caught me. Maybe I have asked about you a little. It's not as though Lady Sutton needs any prompting.'

I was satisfied with his answer. 'No, I like that you're curious about me. It puts us on even ground.'

'So it's safe to say that you've asked about me?'

I shrugged as I tore my hand away from his to walk further into the maze. 'I like to do my research on those I spend time with.' There was a short silence, and I looked back at Richard as he rounded a corner. He looked back at me with a quizzical expression. 'What?'

'Nothing . . . Just that you appear to be planning to spend time with me.'

'Do you have a problem with that?' I planted my hands on my hips and tried to look stern.

'No, oh no! I find you a breath of fresh air here.'

I looked at him. It was such a cliché. I wanted to laugh, but Richard looked so earnest.

'I know that sounded incredibly overused and meaningless, but it's true. I swear I wouldn't say it otherwise.'

'You probably say that to all the women at court.' I meant the comment to be light-hearted, but Richard let it sink in.

He bit his lip, and I couldn't look away. 'How do I make you see yourself—'

'By holding up a mirror?' I tried to steer the conversation to less serious ground but Richard still looked much too serious for my liking.

'You know what I mean. *Really* see yourself. See yourself the way I see you. You're not just a pretty face or

158

a charming woman. There's something in you that I've never encountered before and it has an effect on me.' He coughed. 'If all the people here were stars, you'd be the sun. With you here, I can't even see anyone else . . . And yet you're unapproachable. The same quality that makes you otherworldly makes you distant, alone. You can't be caught and made of this world. Sometimes I think you're fundamentally made of other stuff.'

'Other stuff like what?'

'I don't know . . . sunlight.'

The smile on my face had dimmed during Richard's analysis of me. I never thought that he might be watching me – and further, trying to understand me – as I had been watching him. He perceived a part of me that I found impossible to explain to anyone else. He understood that I was alone.

I quickened my pace and walked further ahead of Richard. When I turned each corner in the maze, I felt momentarily isolated on an island of my own. Isolation brought its own pain, but it appeared manageable compared to facing my insurmountable problems.

'I bet people don't try any more.' I didn't have to turn to know that Richard had caught up and was right behind me again. 'They don't try to reach you when they realize that you're distant and no longer in the same place as everyone else.'

I turned to face him, willing my lower lip to be still. 'I like to be alone. I chose it.'

'You don't have to tell me everything. I'm not asking for reasons,' Richard said. 'I just want you to know that I see through all this. You're not as isolated as you think.'

But there were so many things he didn't know. Sure, Richard didn't seem like the rest of the people at court.

159

He certainly didn't sound like them, but it was wrong to think that he was anything more. Richard *was* them. He was precisely like everyone else. Clueless. Oblivious. And rightfully so.

My life . . . or existence, or whatever this was – didn't concern him. As he said, I belonged in a completely different place, unmoved and untouched by the likes of him. Richard couldn't change anything. No one could. I should have known better than to hope otherwise even for a second. Immortality and the path it put me on were a destiny I could not escape or unwrite.

'I need to go,' I whispered.

I was about to use the excuse that the countess expected me for supper, which was true, but I didn't need it.

'You should go.' He turned away from me and started walking in the opposite direction. He soon turned a corner, leaving me alone between the hedges, leaving me lost again.

Chapter 15

'I'm pleased you're getting along with people here at court.'
The countess took a long sip of wine, as if waiting for an answer.

'I'm very fortunate that you and Lord Empson have introduced me to so many people.'

Though the food hadn't arrived yet, the table already felt too small.

'Not just so *many* people. So many *powerful* people,' the countess corrected me. 'Lord Empson . . .' She swallowed. 'Lord Empson is at least making an effort on your behalf.'

'I guess my father did something right,' I tried to joke, but the countess looked as if she would have none of it.

'Lord Empson sees you as useful. Imagine if your future marriage were tied to someone he had introduced you to at court. He would be very pleased indeed.'

The food came and luckily I didn't have to reply right away.

I picked up something that looked like puff pastry. 'Was that your experience? Of getting married, I mean?'

'The late Lord Empson arranged my marriage, but generally speaking, yes.'

'And it worked out?'

'That depends on what you mean by *worked out*.'

I wasn't expecting the countess to say something like that, especially given the way she had talked about her husband previously.

'But you loved him.'

'Yes, I did.' The countess picked up her wine goblet but, clearly upon second thoughts, she put it down again. 'But love is not all. It doesn't feed or clothe you. Love is just that – one word in an entire world of sentences. I used to think that love was different. That it couldn't be like any other emotion. But I soon found out that it is. It's not enough to sustain anyone.'

The countess said all this in such a matter-of-fact way that I couldn't find it in myself to argue with her. Maybe she was right. Maybe love wasn't the end of all things and the reason for everything.

'You see, my dear Eleanor, having a wonderful, dreamlike ending is meaningless, because it doesn't do anything. You still need to take care of what happens afterwards when you wake up from your dream . . . and that's something love doesn't account for.'

'What do you mean by 'afterwards'?'

'All of this.' She threw up her arms. 'When my husband died, I was nothing. Lord Empson couldn't use me any more, I didn't have anything to my name and I was abandoned. All I'm left with is a title. It's not completely meaningless, but that's it.' The countess closed her eyes and took a slow breath. 'I don't know why I'm telling you this.'

'I asked,' I said.

'I just . . . I want you to be careful.'

Her wording struck me. I knew the countess wanted me – or rather Lady Eleanor Shelton – to avoid being viewed as useless and worthless like she was. But she was smart enough to know that such an ending was almost unavoidable for a person like her or Lady Eleanor. Being careful was all you could do.

162

'And what of Phillip?' I asked. It seemed to me the countess didn't have to be alone.

'Lord Dormer.' She corrected me with a steely gaze. 'I don't know what you're speaking of.'

I lowered my head. I saw my mistake in sounding too familiar, but I was confused. The countess pulled me into her confidence one minute only to push me away the next. I didn't know what to make of it.

Supper finished in silence. It was a much simpler affair than the full court feasts in the great hall, and subsequently ended much more quickly.

I abruptly stood up to leave, forgetting to excuse myself first. The countess looked at me coolly and rose gracefully from her chair.

'I'm sorry,' I said. I took a step back and my hip hit a low table behind me that I hadn't noticed earlier. 'Ouch.' I bit my lip on hearing the sound of something falling to the floor. 'I'm so sorry.'

I looked down to see a small clock, not much bigger than a pocket watch, lying on the floor. The finely engraved metal cover was scratched and dented, and part of the hinge looked broken. I bent down to pick it up but the countess stopped me.

I suddenly realized its significance. 'It was his, wasn't it? Your late husband's?'

The countess took her time answering. She bent down and scooped the small clock into her cupped hands. The hinge looked as if it dug into her palm but she didn't appear to notice.

'I can get it fixed,' I offered. If there were dressmakers and jewellers, there had to be clockmakers at court. And someone who fixes clocks most definitely also makes clocks. *Why on earth did I not think of that before?*

163

The countess did not seem to hear me. She passed the small clock from one hand to the other, not caring if the broken edges scraped her skin.

'I'll have Joan dispose of it later,' she murmured, placing the broken clock back on the table, and left the room.

I couldn't bear to see her like this, and without thinking I scooped the clock up.

What do you think you're doing?

'I'm going to get it fixed. And someone who fixes clocks has to make clocks as well, so I could ask him about the clock I'm after.'

And what makes you think you know where the court clock-maker is? I can see everything in this court, and even then I can't figure out where the clock or this clockmaker is. It's like looking for one grain of sand when you have a bird's-eye view of the entire world. And I'm still learning how to control and work all of this.

I shrugged. 'I'll just ask Richard.'

I could tell Henley didn't like the idea just from his pause before he answered.

So it's 'Richard' now?

'I refuse to call someone "Lord Holdings" when they're my own age and a pain in the butt.'

And yet you're asking this pain in the butt for help . . .

'Who else am I supposed to ask? I don't know which of you is more of a pain sometimes.'

Henley didn't respond and I walked out of the door.

I was careful to leave the countess's chambers without running into her. I wanted the repaired clock to be a surprise. It was the least I could do, having broken it. For the same reason, I didn't want to run into Joan or Helen. Helen's discretion I was more sure of, but I didn't know if they would feel obligated to tell the countess the truth if she asked where the clock was.

I walked along a few corridors that looked familiar, but I wasn't certain. Truthfully, they all looked the same to me, panelled with old stone or wood brightened by the occasional tapestry. I had come to regard the tapestries dotting the halls almost like windows. The colourful scenes of princesses atop white horses and knights holding roses were a welcome relief from the gloom of this place.

I took another right and prayed I was going the correct way. It was dark and everything looked different in the evening from how it had in daylight. I hoped that each turn I took would lead me into the gardens where I had met Lady Sutton and run into Richard. He said that the gardens were his favourite place, especially at night. I just hoped he was there *this* night.

Thankfully the tapestry-lined corridor did end up giving way to the greenery of the garden. I must have entered them from a different doorway before as I didn't remember the fountain in front of me.

'Richard?' I risked calling out. I recalled him mentioning the gardens being empty late at night and figured no one could overhear. Hearing no reply, I began to doubt he was there. I took a seat at the edge of the fountain and stared into the night, watching the marble boy pour water from his vase.

'Enjoying the half-naked boy?'

I rolled my eyes but was glad to see him.

'Or is it the terribly low water pressure that you find so fascinating?'

'I've been looking for you.'

'My lord . . . you sound so disappointed when you say that.'

I laughed. 'Well, I am! I never thought I'd say those words.'

All signs of a smile disappeared from Richard's face and he stared at me so intensely that his honey eyes became searing molten gold. 'I never thought you'd say those words, either.'

'I . . . I came here to ask you about this clock.' I opened my hand to show him the dented cover and broken hinge. 'Do you know where I could get it fixed?'

'The court has a clockmaker in the palace,' Richard said. 'He should be able to repair that in no time.'

'Do you think we could go now? Even though it's night-time?' I looked down anxiously at the broken clock in my hand.

'*We?*' Richard's sly grin was back. 'You'd better be careful – I could get used to this "we".' He took my arm.

'Wouldn't want that, would *we?*'

'This should be it,' Richard said. 'Excuse me,' he called in.

The clockmaker's shop was really more like a den. Being long past working hours, the room was dimly lit with most of the candles already snuffed out. The ceiling sloped down so far that Richard had to stoop to enter. Wooden shelves ran lengthwise along the walls, but most of them were empty. The only items were a few boxes, some wooden, some metal. The entire room was covered with a thin layer of dust, making everything look pale in the scant light. There were probably cobwebs in the corners, too, but there wasn't enough light to see.

'Is anyone in here?' Richard called, then coughed from the dust. I felt it in the air we breathed.

We waited for a response. When none came, Richard shrugged and turned to me. But just as he opened his mouth, we heard a voice.

'Yes?'

An old man hobbled out of the back, bringing a candle with him. Most of his weight rested on the walking stick he carried, and he took the better part of a minute to shuffle across the room. When he finally stood in front of us, he raised his candle and gazed at us with lost eyes. A milky film covered both pupils and I could barely see the original grey of his irises as he tried to focus on us.

'Are you the clockmaker?' Richard asked.

'The king's very own. Now, how may I be of service to you both?

'We're wondering if you could—'

I cut Richard off. 'I damaged an old clock and hoped you might be able to fix it.' I raised the clock to eye level so the old man could see, but he hardly glanced at it, so I decided to describe it. 'It appears to be made of gold with a mother-of-pearl face. I don't know exactly how old it is since it isn't mine, but I'm hoping you can mend the dented case and broken hinge.'

'I see,' the clockmaker said, but he still hadn't looked at the clock.

'Would you like to examine it?' I stretched out my hand.

'No,' he said. 'I remember it.'

Ever so slowly, the clockmaker turned around and started shuffling towards the back of the room. I looked to Richard, but his eyes were trained on the clockmaker. I guessed he wanted us to follow him.

Richard and I trailed slowly behind so as to not to hurry him. The clockmaker took his time opening the door to the back room. He raised his hand and touched the handle several times, only to bring it down and start again as if he didn't have the strength to grasp it. When he finally opened the door, the room beyond it was everything the front room was not.

This space was warm and well lit. There was a kettle warming over a roaring fire in one corner and an abundance of seats and candles. A small girl with strawberry-blonde hair sat in one of the chairs, swinging her legs an inch above the ground.

'Oh, you're finally here. Good,' she said with a smile. But she was looking at us instead of the clockmaker.

It was the strangest thing she could have said. I felt Richard shiver beside me and I instinctively reached out for him.

The girl hopped down from the chair and walked towards us. 'Do you have something that needs to be fixed? Or are you here to place a new order?'

I noticed that the girl's voice sounded much older than she looked. She spoke like a miniature adult.

'Um, we have something that needs to be fixed.' I decided to wait to ask them about the clock I was *actually* looking for.

I showed her the countess's clock, which she examined and then mumbled, 'Oh, yes. You made this one, I think?' She didn't look to the clockmaker for affirmation.

'So can you fix it?' Richard was standing slightly behind me but I could feel his tense posture.

'Of course he can,' the girl answered. She was so proud, she positively beamed.

The clockmaker had taken a seat in front of the fire and didn't appear to be listening to the conversation.

'How long do you think it will take?' I asked. Though the countess had said she would ask Joan to throw the clock away, I didn't want her to be without it for too long. I knew what it felt like to be left with only one thing from the man you loved. Sometimes having a physical object to see and touch is the only remaining assurance that your bond was more than just a memory.

My hand felt for the silver ring I normally wore on my ring finger, but of course it wasn't there any more, not having been created yet. I missed it, but I knew I didn't need it now Henley was with me again. I was lucky to have Henley – or at least some of Henley – come back to me. Others weren't so fortunate.

'The clockmaker is very busy and has a list of orders to complete first. It'll take two weeks.'

Two weeks. I just hoped the killer wouldn't have gotten to me in those two weeks. 'Shall I pick it up then?'

'We can deliver it—'

'No.' I didn't want the countess to wonder how I had arranged for the clock to be fixed. It would be best if I just put it back on the table, good as new. 'I can come here to pick it up.'

The girl looked at me hard but didn't say a word.

'Do you make all the clocks here at court?' My question was directed towards the clockmaker's turned back, but it was answered by the blonde-haired girl.

'Yes, practically all of them.'

'And I suppose he remembers most of what he's made,' I said, recalling his reaction when I described the clock.

'Yes. A true artisan usually does.'

I smiled at how serious the girl was being with me. She wasn't more than a child. Her lips stuck out like two overlapping petals.

'So if he recognised a clock he made, could he tell me who he made it for? Or if it wasn't one of his, tell me which other clockmaker made it?'

'One of his rivals, you mean? Of course. He knows all their techniques, though they don't compare to his.'

Richard looked at me and I could tell he was lost. But this wasn't about him.

'Do you have a quill and some parchment?'

The girl produced writing materials from one of the shelves and I found a space to rest the paper on at one

169

corner of the small table near the centre of the room. I was careful not to disturb any of the miscellaneous clockwork parts scattered about. As I began to draw my picture, I discovered that the table was horribly rickety. I wondered how on Earth the clockmaker could do his delicate work on such a wobbly surface.

'There,' I said, straightening and holding up the parchment for them to see. The point of the quill had leaked some ink onto the page, but other than that, I thought the drawing was a pretty good likeness of the golden clock that used to hang on the wall in Miss Hatfield's kitchen.

'Do you know who asked for this one to be made?'

I looked from the girl to the old man, but neither reacted to my question at first.

'What a strange thing,' the girl said after a few moments and came closer to examine the drawing. 'I can barely call it a clock with those strange markings and extra hands.'

The extra markings she'd noticed should have been for counting seconds but in fact measured years, and the additional hands tallied days and months. The clock didn't work anything like an ordinary clock, but I kept that information to myself.

'I've never seen extra hands like these on a clock,' she muttered.

Of course – the clocks of this time weren't precise enough to measure minutes, let alone seconds. The countess's clock had only an hour hand on its face.

'Does it look familiar?' I tried again.

'I . . . I've never seen anything like it,' she said, her voice breathy. 'Come, Grandpapa. Come and take a look at this. It's remarkable!'

The old man turned in his chair and stood, then shuffled over to us in his unhurried way. He stretched out a single hand, fingers gnarled from age and work, and the girl placed the drawing into his claw.

'This . . . It's not even a clock,' he scoffed.

'Oh, but it is in a way, you see – it should have the same mechanism as a regular clock.' I had no idea if that was true. If it was identical to a regular clock, shouldn't regular clocks be able to time travel, too? But that was definitely a question for another time. 'Just tell me – who has it? Where is it?'

'I'm afraid I do not know. I've never seen it before in my life.'

I felt stricken. 'Maybe another clockmaker made it?'

'My grandpapa is the finest clockmaker in court. There are others, but none with handiwork as fine as his. Certainly no one who can do this.'

'Are you certain you haven't seen it before?' I asked the old man. 'You must have made hundreds of clocks. Surely—'

'No,' he said. 'I remember every single one I make.'

'He remembers *every single one*,' the girl repeated. 'But—' The girl paused and I craned my neck forward.

'But?'

'You see this design around the face? That's a pattern Grandpapa would do—'

'So he did make it?'

'No.' The clockmaker's tone was insistent. 'I've never seen that clock.'

'Grandpapa, I really hope no one's stealing your designs.' Turning towards me and Richard, she asked, 'Where did you see this clock?'

I had to think fast. 'At a friend's house,' I blurted. 'I saw it and thought it was pretty . . . That's all.'

I watched the girl as she studied the drawing, bringing it close to her eyes and away again. Then I had an idea.

171

'Could I commission a clock?' I asked.

'What did you have in mind?' she said.

Nothing ventured nothing gained. I pointed to the drawing. 'A clock exactly like this one here.'

The clockmaker's head came up at this. 'For you?'

'Yes, for me.'

It was a long shot, but it was the only chance I had.

Chapter 16

I sat upright in my chair, pushing the food on my plate around with my fingers. I knew the countess would have minded my manners – or, more accurately, would have *hated* them – but I didn't care. Since I was eating in my room, it was just me at breakfast today . . . Well, me and Henley.

You're making me antsy just looking at you.

'Then look away. Besides, don't you get "nervous" rather than "antsy"?'

Actually, 'antsy' was a word that existed in my time too. But that's not the point – come on, what's bothering you?

'I don't know,' I said. I stared into the food on my plate as if it would give me an answer. 'It's just that . . . you'd think there would be more.'

More what?

'More to go on. More that I could do. More . . . *everything*. I've been here for over a week now and it feels like nothing has progressed, like I'm right where I started. I've been spending the last few days with the countess and at feasts at night. Sure this all helps me fit in more, but it's not helping me get the clock.'

You know that's not true. Lots of things have happened.

'Between dinner parties and a near-death experience, nothing important. Nothing I – *we* could use.'

We've figured out a lot due to that smothering incident.

'That *almost*-smothering incident,' I corrected.

Well, whatever you call it, we confirmed our suspicion that whoever's after you must be an immortal.

'I guess so – but that's it, and that doesn't tell us much. I don't even know how this person came to be immortal. It can't be one of the other Miss Hatfields – they're all dead.'

I only know as much as you do, but I wouldn't rule anything out quite yet.

'What? Like Miss Hatfield back from the dead, even though I saw her die with my own eyes?'

Henley ignored me. *You're just in one of your moods, that's all.*

'I think anyone stuck in 1527, aware that they're destined to literally go raving insane if trapped in a single time period for too long, would be in one of these so-called "moods" you're talking about.'

I think you're the only one in this world who's in that specific predicament.

I caught my breath. 'Me . . . and maybe – just maybe – one other person.'

The killer?

'It would make sense. Let's run through what we know so far. I'm immortal. They're immortal. I can travel through time. They can travel through time. I have – or rather *had* – the clock, so they must have something similar, some mechanism that allows them to time travel – how else would they have been able to travel to the future in the first place to murder Miss Hatfield? I ended up in this period because the tussle in the hotel room turned the clock's hands. The killer might have been transported here by my clock during the struggle or by their own device.'

That all makes logical sense, but when did any of this ever make logical sense? I don't think you should be fixated on that idea. It's a good theory, but it's only a theory.

'You're right. Bottom line, I really do need to find the clock – or have it made.'

You're worried that it hasn't been invented yet?

'It's a definite possibility – 1527 is as far back as the clock goes.'

In that case, I hope it's invented quickly.

'I wonder how he does it.'

How the clockmaker makes a time-travelling device instead of an ordinary clock? Maybe in the same way the waters of Islamorada turned you and my mother immortal – he might use chemicals or some scientific phenomenon. Maybe it's something completely different that can't be explained. But whatever means he uses, it happens and that's our reality.

I wished it weren't, but I didn't say that aloud. I wondered if Henley would have freely chosen this new existence of his.

A knock on the door interrupted my train of thought. Joan peeped her head through.

'My lady, the dressmaker has just sent your wardrobe – Lord Empson insisted they be made quickly. I could instruct Helen to bring them in later, if you like.'

'That would be fine, Joan,' I said, but she didn't leave. 'Was there anything else?'

'Yes, my lady. The countess has asked if you would accompany her to chapel.'

'Not this time, Joan,' I said. 'Could you tell her that I have a bit of a headache?'

'Should I send for a physician?' Joan looked genuinely concerned.

'No need for that, but I think I'll just lie down this morning.' I moved to the bed.

The headache was a lie, but I did want to rest and take the morning slowly. I knew time was running out, but I had to wait another day before I could pick up the countess's clock and check on the progress of the one I'd commissioned. For now I could lie still. It was unlikely that the killer would attempt to murder me while I was wide awake in broad daylight.

Another reason was that I wanted to be alone. Of course, that was impossible with Henley always hanging around in his ghostlike state. It was like being watched every single moment and it set me on edge at times, but compared to the deep pain I felt in my chest when I believed I would never see him again . . . Well, anything would be better than that.

You know . . . Henley started.

I laughed. 'No, I don't know. Unless you tell me, that is.'

But Henley's voice remained serious. *I couldn't help but notice recently* . . .

'Henley, spit it out already.'

You've changed.

His words lingered as we both stopped to think about what he had just said.

'I've changed?' I tried to muster up a laugh but nothing came out. 'You do realize immortals can't change or age, right? At least, that's what Miss Hatfield said.'

You know that's not what I mean.

I did know what he meant but I couldn't admit it. Not to Henley. Not out loud. Perhaps not even to myself. No, because admitting it would make it real.

I'm here for you. I'm always here. And yet . . . you don't confide in me any more. And my God, that hurts, Rebecca.

I didn't want to see it, but I felt it, too.

It used to be you and me together, but now you treat me like some sort of 'other'. As part of the outside world you're trying to keep away.

A tear made its way down my cheek before I could stop it. 'It's different now.'

It doesn't have to be.

'Miss Hatfield's dead. There isn't anyone else—'

And what about me?

'There's no one other than me who's completely immortal, I mean. I don't have someone who's going through what I am any more. You're here, but I'm the one people see. I'm the one who has to blend in, but still do what I need to do. I'm sorry, I'm just trying to find my own way through all this mess.'

There was a pause, and I sat down to steady myself.

What am I to you, Rebecca?

'What do you mean? You know I love you more than anything.'

Henley's voice was faint, but I still heard it. *Sometimes it feels like you've forgotten me.*

There was another knock at the door.

'Come in.' Even my voice sounded tired.

'I'm sorry to bother you again, my lady.' It was Joan, carrying a vase of pink flowers. 'But these flowers just arrived and I thought they might put you in better cheer. They're for you, of course. Peonies. I didn't even know they were in season. Where would you like them, my lady?'

'How about over there on the bedside table?' I pointed to my left.

'Very well, my lady. If there's nothing else, I'll be off to the chapel now.' When I shook my head, Joan put the flowers down and excused herself.

The flowers were beautiful and they did lift my spirits a little. I wondered if they were from Sir Gordon or another of the older men I had met at one of the suppers. After hearing of my father's – or rather Lady Shelton's father's

177

– sizeable fur trade in Lithuania, they all suddenly took an interest in me, my thoughts on mink-trimmed cloaks and, of course, in introducing me to their sons.

I climbed out of bed to see if there was a card.

To my sun.
Because I have to try.
R

So that's what it takes to get you to smile?

I hadn't realized I was smiling until Henley pointed it out.

You're not being fair to him.

I put the card down. 'In what way?'

He's falling in love with you.

I laughed. 'He's just being nice,' I said. 'You should know the difference.'

I do know the difference. And this isn't just him being nice – you're leading him on.

'How? I talk to him the same way I talk to the countess or Lord Empson.'

I don't know if you actually believe that.

I thought I felt Henley's breath in my ear but shook myself out of it. It had to be a breeze.

'Believe what?'

You're blind. And this is dangerous.

'Do you hear yourself? Richard's as harmless as can be. You're jealous and trying to dig up something where there clearly isn't anything to be found.'

If you think 'harmless' is having scratches on his arm the morning after someone tried to smother you with a pillow, than yes, maybe he is harmless. Those were definitely from a struggle. That's hard evidence.

178

I remembered noticing the scratches, but Henley couldn't be right. Richard wouldn't – couldn't – do something like that. That wasn't him.

Oh, really? Henley scoffed. *And you would know what's 'him' and what's 'not him' after only a week's acquaintance?*

I hadn't realized I'd said that out loud. 'Richard's not as bad as you think. He's lost and floundering at times, just like me. I don't know why you think he's evil. He's a perfectly wonderful man. You're just jealous.'

So that's *what you think?*

I sat down at the edge of my bed. We were both breathing heavily, for with the countess and Joan at the chapel, there was nothing stopping us from yelling.

You think I'm just making this up because I'm petty and jealous? You saw his arm, too! I can't believe you're ignoring the proof right in front of you!

'And I can't believe you're letting your jealousy cloud your judgment. He said a cat scratched him!'

A cat? Well, that's *convenient. Have you ever even seen him with a cat? Besides, those scratches were too deep to be from a cat.*

'No, I haven't seen him with a cat . . . But that doesn't mean there isn't one. This is court – there must be loads of cats here!' I felt my cheeks flush red with all the shouting. 'What I don't understand is why you have to paint him as the villain.'

Because he is!

'You're just insecure. You're without a body, without control and completely reeling.'

Oh, are you calling me insane now?

'Sometimes, I just—'

His voice dropped low. *You just what?*

'Sometimes I feel like I don't know you any more.'

Well, for once, that makes two of us.

I was shocked. At the argument. At Henley. At the situation. I couldn't process it. I couldn't think. It was all absurd, and I didn't have the strength to deal with it right now.

I had no desire to sit in silence with Henley perpetually looking over my shoulder, but nor did I want to venture out of my room for fear of running into Richard. Though he always made me feel better, this really wasn't the time.

I tried to look busy, rummaging through the drawers of the bedside table. Most were empty save for a few scraps of paper, but the top drawer had a rosary in it. Maybe it belonged to the countess's late husband or son? I took it out to examine it more closely. The beads were a dark garnet-red, each one smoothed by years of use, and I could see my face reflected upside-down in each bead as I rolled them through my fingers. I must have looked like I was praying.

In reality, my head was still racing. So many thoughts ran across the map of my mind that they blurred together, and I could not distinguish one from another long enough to make sense of any of them. Instead, I forced my eyes down and willed my fingers to continue moving. The rosary beads were a buffer between me, Henley and the world.

Henley could see everything, even beyond the veil of time, into the past and future. But he couldn't see into my mind, and for that I had never been more thankful. It was the last place I could retreat to. The last place that was really mine, and mine alone.

And so I sat there and pretended to pray, gripping the rosary tightly in my hand. Anything rather than hear Henley's words in my head, continuously reverberating in my thoughts. I must have sat there in that same position

180

for hours, maybe even dozed off, because the next thing I knew, Joan was at the door again, asking this time if I felt well enough for supper in the great hall, or if I wanted her to bring up some food to my room. Figuring I had to face the world sometime, I invited her in while I made my decision.

'You're looking a little flushed, my lady. Are you sure you don't want me to call the physician? He's supposed to be very good.'

I assured her that wouldn't be necessary – all I needed was some fresh air and maybe even some dancing.

'Only if you don't overexert yourself.' Joan laughed. 'Those flowers really did put you in good cheer.'

My lips grew taut. 'I'm sure it was lying down that did the trick.'

'Whatever the case, I'm glad you're feeling better and in higher spirits, my lady,' Joan said. 'I'll send Helen in to help dress you for supper.' She dipped into a final curtsy before leaving me.

I was beginning to see the upside of almost never being left alone – I didn't have to deal with Henley.

Just as I pulled myself out of bed, a knock sounded at the door.

'Come in.'

'I'm sorry to hear you weren't feeling well, my lady,' Helen said. Of course news travelled fast within the countess's quarters, especially since she didn't have as many servants as someone like Lady Sutton.

'No matter, I'm feeling better now,' I assured her. 'So what should I wear to supper this evening? Any suggestions?'

Helen opened the chest closest to her, and I flipped through gowns of the lightest blues, the softest greens and the warmest pinks. We settled on a deep-crimson gown for tonight. It was the colour of blood and life. When I stood in front of the mirror, I almost didn't recognize myself.

'The dress looks stunning, Helen. Thank you.'

Helen had a sweet smile upon her face. 'You do look beautiful, my lady. But I think you're thanking the wrong person.'

I fingered the surface of the mirror that reflected my face.

'Are you reminded of someone?' Helen asked. 'Of course, I don't mean to pry, my lady. It's just—'

'No, you're not prying,' I said. 'And you're right – I am reminded of someone I used to be close to . . . Well, as close as anyone could be. She was a private person.'

'I understand. And now, when you look into the mirror, you see her?' Helen raised a necklace to my throat and fastened the clasp.

'Yes. I see her face instead of mine.'

'That's a good thing, my lady.'

'Is it really?' I asked. 'It's as if I can't shake her, wherever I go. It makes me feel as though I'm perpetually in her shadow.'

I watched Helen's face reflected in the mirror as she responded. 'A part of her will always exist in you. You will never be able to shake her because she *is* you. That's what happens when we touch other people's lives – and when theirs touch ours.'

I nodded. Lives didn't exist on their own in a vacuum. They coexisted and overlapped, so there was no grey space between them. And every touch, every graze, shaped both lives, so even when two people parted, they would never be the same.

I thanked Helen one final time, then waited for the countess in the sitting room.

When she appeared, she was dressed all in black as usual. 'Ready to go? I see Helen has adorned you with one of my favourite jewels.'

My hands rushed to my throat.

'It's fine,' she said. 'Who do you think instructed her to give you it? The diamond and garnet look good with that dress.' She stepped closer to me on her way to the door. 'You don't look too ill. Good.' Then she pinched my cheeks hard.

'Ouch!' My hands flew to my face.

'That's for a little more colour,' the countess said with a genuine smile.

I was beginning to learn the route to the great hall. It was simple, actually – all you had to do was follow the throng of people dripping with jewels. To anyone else, I knew I would look like one of them, but I wondered if any of the other people at court felt as lost as I did. Aside from Richard, of course.

As this was my second lavish full-court feast, I felt less preoccupied with trying to fit into all the social rituals taking place around me. I knew the drill now, and because I'd worked out what my role was in all this, I had time to take in the intricacies of court dining I had missed before. I noticed little things, like how the servers placed food from the right of the diners rather than the left; how the younger ladies of the court tried to catch the king's eye, or the attention of one of his men; and how the men started to dance more as their glasses emptied.

'Riveting, isn't it?'

I had heard that voice enough times to know who it was without turning my head.

'Court is truly another world,' he said, trying to engage me again.

I wondered if Richard would go away if I didn't acknowledge him. Henley's words were still fresh in my mind.

'My lady, you blow hot then cold,' he said. 'I don't know what to do with you.'

'What about nothing?'

Just then, the king stood up and the great hall fell silent.

'To God, glory, and this great country!' The king raised his glass. 'This country and this court is blessed by the grace of God, for *we* are the chosen people!

The crowds roared their approval.

Richard coughed as if he had something caught in his throat, but I figured it was another ploy to get me to look his way. I pretended a sudden interest in the balcony that wrapped around the great hall. Tall candelabras the size of two men illuminated musicians perched on one side, while the other side was packed with people socialising and servers milling around them. I thought I saw Lord Empson up there with his wife, but I wasn't sure.

'Ignoring me now?' Richard feigned hurt. 'Cold. Very cold. Especially after I sent you flowers . . . Tell me, my lady, are women not supposed to appreciate such gestures?'

Finally, I turned to face him, but luckily I didn't have to reply.

'There you are!' I had never been more thankful to have the countess swoop in. 'We need to introduce you to more –' she glanced at Richard '– to more *useful* people.'

Taking my arm, the countess led me around the perimeter of the room. It was so large and crowded that one circuit must have taken at least twenty minutes. The countess didn't even look at me once during that time, for she was too busy scoping out the room as if searching for vermin.

'Be patient, Eleanor,' she said at last. 'I can feel your agitation from here.'

I wasn't sure whether she was feeling my angst or my hunger, but whichever it was, I had no doubt that she would neither want nor care to know.

I heard the countess sigh next to me. 'Oh, look who's making her way towards us now . . .'

I glanced up and, sure enough, Lady Sutton was headed our way . . . or rather, headed towards me. In a canary-yellow dress, she was unmissable, shoving people this way and that instead of manoeuvring herself around the crowds.

'Oh, Lady Eleanor! Lady Eleanor!' she called above the music and voices.

Random people turned to see who she was calling and I felt my face turn pink.

'Good to see you here at supper!' Lady Sutton looked me over from head to toe. 'I do wish you'd take to wearing brighter colours. Thankfully this burgundy is a step up from the black you wore last time I saw you. Not that black doesn't suit you, but it makes it look like you've been spending too much time in *certain* people's company.'

Lady Sutton smiled at the countess as if she had only just noticed she was at my side.

'Anyway, I must go and say hello to the French ambassador. I'm told he's brought lots of stories from the French court.' She gave me a nod goodbye, utterly ignoring the countess yet again. 'Let's have dinner again some other time!'

'That woman . . . That's certainly some company you're keeping.'

I opened my mouth to defend myself but the countess cut me off.

'It's good, surprisingly. Lady Sutton is a pain, but she's a pain with useful connections. She's ruined people with her gossip so it's better to keep her close.'

That old saying ran through my head: *Keep your friends close and your enemies closer.*

'She's oddly refreshing,' the countess said. 'Of course, that doesn't mean I enjoy her company.'

'And why do you find her refreshing?'

'Court is a place where you can't trust everybody, for cloaked snakes abound. Lady Sutton, on the other hand . . . There's nothing cloaked about her.' She smirked. 'But remember, even the Devil was an angel once.'

The last thing she said struck me oddly. People do hide who they are, but sometimes they change. I suppose that was scarier in a way. At some point, you look back and no one knows who you've become. You don't even know yourself.

When we sat down to eat, I was pleased to see that Richard was nowhere near me for once. The countess sat across from me, while Lord Dormer and Sir Petley, to whom I had just been introduced, sat on either side of me. Lord Empson walked past us and made no move to sit near the countess. I wondered if there was still tension between them after the last dinner we've had.

'Sir Gordon can't stop talking about his latest conquest. That was all he would discuss when we played tennis today,' Sir Petley said, to which the table roared.

'I'm surprised he has conquests at all, much less a *latest* conquest. I heard he has some sort of large, festering wound on his body from battle.'

'How disgusting!'

'The part *I* can't believe is that he plays tennis! Can that man even move?'

The conversation only grew louder as more wine was poured.

Regarding this sort of gossip as unseemly, the countess mainly kept to herself when others were discussing the people at court. The exception was after Lord Dormer made a comment. Then she was as giddy as the rest of them.

'Oh, Phillip,' she would say, before correcting herself immediately. 'Lord Dormer.'

Apparently even a woman as put-together as the countess got flustered at times.

'Lady Eleanor.'

I turned towards Lord Dormer, who was now pointing at a plate of meat decorated with cherries.

'Have some of the quail. It's supposed to be one of the king's favourites and no visit to court is complete without trying it.'

I thanked him as he took my plate and began loading it.

'What about some more venison?'

'Thank you, Lord Dormer, but I'm afraid I had a large dinner.'

'No matter. We need to make sure you have a taste, at least,' he said. 'More wine for the lady!'

I looked down at my goblet, expecting it to still be full, surprised when it wasn't. I could have sworn I hadn't drunk that much.

'No need to be shy, my lady – everyone loves the wine at court. Only the best for the king and his people.'

Another server filled up our glasses.

'To the fine wine and finer company!' Lord Dormer raised his glass, nodding to the countess. 'Whoever said the French do it best has yet to see us!'

'Hear, hear!' chorused everyone in earshot.

Sipping from my goblet, I felt the wine's warmth slide down my throat. I closed my eyes. The music played on, swelling around us. People's voices rose and slipped under each other's, following the cadence of the violins. I tilted my head up to better hear them and their sound swelled further.

Then a scream pierced through the music and my eyes flashed open. They were met by dark wood and bright candlelight.

One of the huge candelabras from the balcony pitched forward. It was falling towards me – wooden head, stand and all. I couldn't move. I didn't have time. I squeezed my eyes shut as every muscle in my body contracted, waiting for the moment of impact.

And waited.

And waited.

There was silence around me. The musicians had stopped playing and all the voices had died away. Hearing this, I opened my eyes. Slowly. One eye, then the other. Where was the impact? The candelabra was more than twice my size. With it falling towards my head – from the balcony, no less – there was no way I could have survived it.

Was this what death felt like? Painless and silent?

With my eyes fully open, I looked around. I was still in the great hall. The food was still on the table. The musicians still held their instruments. But no one played or talked or ate. Everyone was looking towards me. No, not *at* me – *above* me.

My body was trembling so hard I could barely lift my head.

'By the blood of Christ,' someone said. It was a whisper, but in the silent hall it echoed as if everyone had said it together.

By the blood of Christ, indeed. The wooden crown of the candelabra, still mostly alight with flames – though some candles had fallen out, luckily extinguishing themselves on the stone floor – was less than two inches away from my head. It was hovering above me, as if the whole room had been frozen in time.

188

No person could have caught the candelabra. No human could have stopped it.

Henley.

With a groan, the heavy candelabra tipped back and away from me, apparently entirely of its own volition. It crashed to the floor in a gap between the groups of people, where some ushers immediately doused the flames.

No one else moved, and for an endless minute, not one person dared utter a word. I watched as one by one the ladies and gentlemen of the court made the sign of the cross on themselves. Murmurs grew as people began to say a few words of prayer.

'Miracle.' I heard.

'Witchcraft.' I also heard.

One by one, heads turned as people looked at the king to see what his reaction might be.

I held my breath as he stood.

'God's grace is upon us,' he said. The king made the sign of the cross. 'This is a sign of his blessing.'

I looked at the countess's face, still sitting across from me. Her eyes were brimming with tears. Her lips moved, but wordlessly.

'Miracle.' Someone breathed again. And I supposed it was. Just not the sort of miracle the people in the great hall thought they had witnessed that day.

'What in God's name were you thinking?' I blurted out as soon as Henley and I were alone again in my room.

Funny you should use those words. God was on everyone's mind today.

'This isn't funny, Henley. Y-you crossed the line tonight.' I was conscious that I was erratically pacing the floor of the room, but I felt I would break apart if I stopped moving.

189

'Do you know what could have happened in there? Do you know what you could have caused? They could have accused me – or worse, have me hung – as a witch!'

I know exactly what happened in there. Henley's voice was as smooth and unperturbed as mine was distraught, and it made me pace even faster. *I saved you. For God's sake, without me stopping the candelabra, we wouldn't even be having this conversation! You'd be dead!*

'I know, but—'

No you don't, Rebecca. Do you really think I could just stand there and watch you be killed?

'You could have done it some other way! Just think what could have happened if the king had decreed it as witchcraft instead of a miracle.'

Keep your voice down if you don't want one of the maids to come in, Henley hissed, and I knew he was right. *What other way was there? There wasn't any time. I had to act.*

'You acted in a way that brought so much attention . . . I don't think I could have attracted more attention if I tried.'

So you wanted me to let that candelabra drop on you? Sorry for not abiding by your wishes – I'll know better next time.

'You know I don't mean that. It's just . . . Now everyone knows.'

Knows what? he scoffed. *That you're somehow 'blessed by God'?*

'I don't know what they think. But I do know they won't regard me as normal any more. Any hope of me passing unnoticed, grabbing the clock and leaving is pretty much shattered.'

So what?

'What do you mean, "So what"? You're the one who always insists on making this as simple as it can be – find the clock and go. This is as far from simple as you can get!'

190

The game has changed, Rebecca. That's just it. The game has changed, and the rules have changed, but we're still playing it to win.

'This is more than a game . . . This is my *life*.'

All the more reason we need to win.

'I don't think you fully comprehend the consequences of what you just did. What if Miss Hatfield's murderer was there in the room watching when you pulled that stunt?'

So what? It's not like he could have seen me. Henley chuckled and I had never wanted to smack him more. *And as for you, he'll think you're some sort of blessed angel on Earth. Or maybe even that you have super powers.*

Henley laughed, not caring who heard him. His voice reverberated around the room.

He won't even touch you after that scene in the great hall. You should have seen yourself – you sat there beneath a halo of fire. Everyone was under your spell.

'And what about you?' If the attacker was in fact immortal, I feared he might try to hurt Henley.

You really don't have to worry about me. What could he do to me? Kill me? If only.

I knew he didn't mean it the way it sounded, but Henley's words still hurt. I loved him. I didn't want him to be this way – without a body, with those thoughts in his mind. If only things could have stayed the way they were when we first met. Back then, Henley had no clue about immortality, time travel . . . even who I really was, but things were better that way. At least he was happier.

'It shouldn't have happened this way,' I whispered.

Well, it is what it is.

191

Chapter 17

'Eleanor! Lady Eleanor!'

I jolted up in bed and immediately cursed myself for sitting up too quickly. I held my head.

'Eleanor, wake up!'

I was confused because it wasn't Helen's voice calling me to get up, and it wasn't Joan's, either. As I listened closely, I realized it was the countess herself.

The door blew open and the countess breezed in, closely followed by both Joan and Helen at her heels.

'Good. You're up.'

I was about to make a snarky reply about how it was impossible to sleep through such a ruckus, but as it was the countess, I thought it better to hold my tongue.

'You need to get dressed immediately,' she said.

I slipped out of bed slowly, so as to not make myself dizzy again. 'With the commotion you're making, I'd think the entire palace was on fire,' I muttered.

'Nonsense. Helen, fetch Lady Eleanor's finest dress – the green one. Joan, you brought the jewels?' The countess was standing in the middle of the room like a black pillar, instructing everyone to move around her.

I didn't have a clue what this was about, but I figured the countess would have to tell me sooner or later.

'I've received marvellous news,' the countess said,

turning to me at last. 'I've already notified Lord Empson of this, of course.'

I waited to hear what 'this' was.

'A very great honour has been bestowed upon you, my dear girl. And on us.' The countess moved forward to clasp my hands. 'After the spectacle last night, you are to see the king!'

She paused to wait for my response, but I didn't know what to say or how to react.

'Well?' she said after a second or two. 'What do you say to that?'

'I don't know,' I answered truthfully.

'I know it must be confusing – especially to be chosen by God out of the blue like that, but this is your destiny, child. You can't escape it.' The countess's eyes glittered. I knew she wouldn't be having this sort of reaction if I had been declared a witch. 'And the king . . . The king himself is asking for you! Personally.'

'I guess I'll have to go, then.' I wrung my hands. I didn't even notice how nervous I was until now.

'You guess? This is a great honour.' The countess peered at me as if trying to read my face. 'Now, listen to me very carefully,' she said. 'When you are announced and first walk into the room, you will curtsy and lower your eyes. Do not rise or speak until he speaks to you, and be sure to address the king as "your royal majesty", then subsequently as "sire". Curtsy again when he leaves, or when he dismisses you. I don't suppose they teach you important things such as these in the Grand Duchy of Lithuania.'

'No, they don't,' I muttered. 'And when am I to be summoned to the king?'

'Immediately, of course!'

'Of course . . .'

193

'Now hurry up! The king must not be kept waiting!' The countess began pacing in the middle of the room while I got ready.

I didn't know whether that last comment was more for me or Helen, who was struggling to help me under so much stress. When she lifted the emerald gown over my head, I could feel her fingers trembling against the fabric. I wanted to say something to soothe her but had no idea what, and I didn't want to get her in trouble with the countess.

The countess finally stopped her pacing and exited the room. She looked far more nervous than I felt . . . and I was the one who was supposed to meet the king.

It was all so strange to me. Maybe he changed his mind and thought it was some sort of witchery instead of a sign from God as he originally had thought? Could he do that? Would they threaten to lock me up? In my mind, there was nothing I could say about the incident. But I supposed he felt differently.

'Hurry!' The countess's voice harped above the scuffle from outside the room. 'The king's footman is already here to escort you!'

'There you go . . .' Helen clipped heavy earrings encrusted with pearls onto my ear lobes. 'You should hurry – you don't want to keep them waiting.'

I nodded my thanks and gathered up my skirts to run to the sitting room. The countess and the footman both eyed me disapprovingly till I put my skirts down.

'Very well.' The countess clasped and reclasped her hands in front of her.

The footman nodded towards me, and I took that to mean I should follow him through the door. He made unfamiliar turns and walked down hallways I didn't know existed. Though it was the middle of the day, these hallways were dim, only lit by the occasional torch on the walls.

'It feels as if we're underground,' I said, but the footman didn't even look over his shoulder at me.

When we arrived at a particular door with guards outside, the footman signalled to one of them. The guard to the right knocked, then slipped inside.

'Lady Eleanor Shelton . . .' The words were muffled through the thick wooden doors, but I heard him or someone else announce me.

The guard slipped out of the room and held open the door for me. As I entered, I ran through the countess's instructions in my mind.

Announcement – check. Enter then curtsy, I thought to myself.

I took a few steps into the room before bobbing down to the ground in a deep curtsy, remembering at the last moment to lower my eyes.

So far so good, I thought. *Now, I need to remember to stay in a curtsy and when he speaks to me, it's 'your majesty' before 'sire'.*

I kept my eyes lowered, but under my eyelashes I saw I was in a room filled with maps. They were scattered on the long table in the middle of the room and rolling off the red chair in one corner. All were hand-drawn and looked antiquated to me, like the globe teetering on the edge of the table, but I knew they must be state of the art for this time.

'You may stand.'

I did as I was told, and also remembered to keep my eyes lowered. A few seconds passed, and I couldn't help myself – I decided to sneak a peek.

When I glanced up, I noticed a figure standing with his back to me, facing the window. I would have said he was looking out of it except the curtains were drawn, so he appeared to be staring at the fabric instead. I felt as if I had interrupted something, but I reminded myself that it was he who had summoned me in the first place.

The king turned to face me, and caught my eye. Curiosity got the better of me and I forgot to lower my eyes. I simply continued my staring.

What I saw was a handsome young man with the eyes of someone far older. He stared back at me, unflinching, with the frank and open gaze of a man who didn't see the need to hide anything. There was nothing that he thought I shouldn't see, and that was rare.

I was the one to look away first.

'The feast.'

'Yes, your majesty,' I replied, remembering my manners, thank goodness. 'I know that surprised many people.'

To my great surprise, the king roared with laughter.

'Surprised? It's not every day we encounter a supper guest like that.'

I looked down at the hem of my skirts, not sure how to answer any questions he might have.

He drew nearer. 'It's not every day that an angel comes to the aid of a supper guest, either.'

'I don't know what to say, sire.'

'This must be confusing.' The gentleness of his voice took me by surprise and I looked up to meet his gaze again. 'But how did you do it?'

'I'm sorry, sire, I don't know what—'

'Was it prayer? Did you pray before the meal?'

'No—'

'Leave an offering?'

I was starting to panic in the face of his direct questioning. 'It just . . . happened, sire. I really don't know why. It just happened,' I said. 'I swear.'

196

The king took a step back, eyes still locked with mine. I wasn't prepared for what I saw on his face; it wasn't anger, or even annoyance – it was awe.

I shook my head. 'I'm sorry I can't be of more help, sire.'

He ignored me. 'Was that the first time something like this miracle has ever happened to you?'

'Y-yes, sire.'

'Don't you see what this means? God favours you.'

My palms were sweating and the situation was growing ever more uncomfortable, but I knew that was far better than Henley being discovered. I was fairly sure there was nothing they could do to him, but I didn't want to find out – especially if there was another immortal in court.

'You've been blessed by the Lord God himself, and that was a sign of his favour. Now tell me, have you been seeing any visions lately? At night, maybe?'

'No, none, sire,' I said, truthfully.

The king ran his thumb across his closely shaven jaw. It was a movement I had seen Richard do and I was suddenly reminded of him.

'What do you think about a cure for death?' he asked, taking me by surprise yet again.

'A cure? For death?'

'A potion for immortality,' he said.

I felt cold sweat trickle down my back. 'I'm not quite sure what to think of it, sire.'

'Do you believe such a thing exists?' he asked.

I wondered if he knew something I didn't. What could he possibly know about immortality?

I chose my words with care. 'I have no cause to think immortality possible.'

'And what if there was?'

'I don't—'

197

'I believe it to be possible.' He said it so easily, I didn't know what to make of it.

'H-how?' I stuttered. I realized I had forgotten to use the honorific and call the king 'sire'. Thankfully, I didn't think he noticed.

'My physicians are the best in the country, if not the world, and they have devised cures for many diseases. They are working on others for afflictions like the sweating sickness. Similarly, I have my alchemist working on the means by which a man may attain immortality.'

Hearing the word 'alchemist', I automatically thought of Richard. Wasn't he an alchemist's apprentice? Would he know about this research?

The king gave me a dazzling smile, distracting me from my whirling thoughts. 'But you would tell your king if you found a cure for death, wouldn't you?' His voice, so earnest a few seconds ago, turned cold. 'If you were told the secret by someone . . . or something?' He took one large step to come face to face with me. 'People never have the one thing they want. *That's* my one desire. That's the one thing I need to secure a dynasty.'

'Immortality, sire?'

'It would be even better than having an heir. Think of it – ruling for all eternity.'

My breath drained out of me. 'For all eternity—'

'You may leave.'

I pulled myself together with great difficulty, even remembering to curtsy again before I stumbled out through the door held open by a footman.

Immortality. It was on everyone's lips. I had to track Richard down.

'How was your audience with the king?'

The countess was standing in the middle of the room when I came in, as if she hadn't moved since I left for the king's chambers. Knowing her and how she worried about these things, she probably hadn't.

'Well?' she asked. 'Do speak up. It's rude to keep anyone waiting.'

'It went well,' I said.

'That's it? He asked about last night, did he not?'

'Yes, he did.'

'Did he say anything in particular?' I could tell that the countess was trying hard not to pry like Lady Sutton would. 'How was his mood?'

'He was very pleasant.'

'Very pleasant? Or *very* pleasant?' she asked. 'You do realize there's a difference.'

'The king appeared to be in a fine mood,' I said. 'Do you know anything about the alchemist he employs?'

'The royal alchemist? Did he say something about that?' She frowned. 'For shame . . . Did he ask you if you were involved in some sort of alchemy?'

'No, he did not. What do you know about the royal alchemist?'

'Good. Thank the Lord. Alchemy is not something a well-bred woman should concern herself with . . . Or any woman, really. Alchemy is too troublesome. Too close to the Devil's work, if you ask me.'

I wanted to tell her that I wasn't asking her opinion, but I knew I wouldn't get the information I was after by irritating her because then she would clam up entirely. I just had to let her go on and come back to it in her own time – if at all.

'The royal alchemist, you say?' She returned to the topic more than a few minutes later, after she had extracted as

199

much about the king's mood from me as she could. 'He's Venetian. I tend not to keep his company, but I believe that's what Lady Sutton said when she was gossiping about something or other. They met during her time in the Venetian court. His reputation preceded him, and the king had to have him for his own. Venice has too much gold, anyway.'

'So the alchemist primarily works on making gold out of nothing?' I asked.

'Never start your sentences with "so". It makes you sound absolutely uncouth. I don't know what his primary job is, but yes, I imagine trying to conjure gold is a large part of what he does. I try to keep my involvement with him minimal.' The countess cocked her head. 'Why do you want to know? The king must have mentioned it if you're so curious about alchemy all of a sudden.'

'He did,' I began. I wanted to tell her the truth . . . but not bring up immortality. That was a complication I could live without. 'But only in passing. He called me to his presence simply to ask about the feast last night. The king wanted to know if I had been praying before dinner, or whether something like that had ever happened before.'

'And has it?' The countess looked at me, her eyes wide.

'No, it hasn't. You would be the first to know about it if it did.'

Apparently pleased with my answer, the countess bade me continue.

'That was it,' I said. 'That's pretty much all he said.'

'Hmm . . . So he wasn't upset at all.' she said slowly.

'I don't think so.'

The countess visibly relaxed.

I took the lull in conversation as an opportunity to go back to my room. Internally, I was a mess and needed some quiet to sort out my thoughts. I knew the countess wouldn't be able to provide me with that unless I closed my door.

I sat on the edge of my bed. Apparently this was the spot I'd picked to do most of my thinking – not to mention panicking – nowadays. I just didn't know what to think. Things were starting to look ever more interwoven. If there were a court alchemist searching for the secret to immortality, did whoever was after me know about him, too? What if the immortal murderer who killed Miss Hatfield was also connected to this? Would Richard's apprenticeship mean he knew more than he appeared to? Was he tangled up in this, too?

The more I thought about it, the more afraid I became. Immortality and time itself used to be my only enemies. Until now it had been a race against the discomfort I always began to feel after staying in one time too long. Now it was more than that. Now there was someone after me. And if time didn't get to me first, I knew *he* would.

Immortality was complicated, but once you figured out the rules, it left you in peace . . . more or less. But you had to know your limits: don't stay in one time for too long; don't make connections with people; certainly don't fall in love with someone. I had broken so many of these rules and had to live with the consequences every day.

But this was different. This situation had no rules that I could follow. I didn't know who this killer was. But more importantly, I didn't know why they were after me. That made the situation almost impossible. And I knew I couldn't do anything at all until I got my hands on the clock.

Chapter 18

Sitting in my room, I wished Henley would say something to me. Anything. We hadn't talked since we'd argued the day before, and so far, it didn't look as if that would change any time soon. I couldn't stand knowing he was so close yet out of reach.

'Henley?' I called out into the empty room. But empty it indeed was, for there was no reply.

So that's how he was playing it now? Outright ignoring me?

I didn't call again. I had no desire to give him the satisfaction of knowing that I needed him.

The clock, I told myself. That was what I had to concentrate on.

It had been a couple of weeks since I dropped off the countess's clock to be fixed, so I figured I could pick it up today. It wasn't as if anyone needed me, anyway.

Retracing the steps I had taken with Richard was more difficult than I had imagined, as we had visited the clock-maker's at night. I must have gotten lost a few times, but the corridors looked so similar it was hard to tell. As I continued through the corridors, for the first time in a long while I felt truly alone. Miss Hatfield was still dead, the countess was in her chambers and Henley was gone. My chest hitched as I tried to take a deep breath. It was a much longer walk than I remembered. When I found the right door, I shook my head and tried to clear my mind. Just as I raised my hand to knock, the door swung open.

'My dear, come in.' It was the old man. 'You look distressed.'

I supposed I probably did look a bit upset given the depressing turn my thoughts had taken, but I brushed it off. 'Oh, it's nothing. I'm just having a rough day.'

'A rough day can be an apocalypse to some, while an apocalypse can be a rough day to others.' The old man waved me in.

I followed him through the grey storefront to the back room, where the clockmaker's granddaughter was sitting on a workbench.

'I suppose you're here for your clock?' she asked.

'Yes, if it's ready,' I said.

'It is. The damage was minor – just the broken hinge and some dents that needed to be hammered out of the metal.'

As I watched the clockmaker rummage around behind her, I wondered how to broach the topic of the clock I'd asked him to make. Luckily, I didn't have to – the girl did it for me.

'The clock you commissioned,' she started.

'Yes – is there any issue with its manufacture?'

'Not at all – it will be ready in a week.'

I knew a week was fast for something so intricate and complex, not to mention larger than a normal clock, but this was urgent. As the days passed, I was starting to experience the effects of staying in one time too long. The nagging feeling in the pit of my stomach had already turned into something more.

'Is there any way to speed the process up? Money wouldn't be an issue.' I figured Lord Empson would pay for it without so much as a single question. He seemed to want to go out of his way to please his business partner's daughter. And if he asked, I could always tell him it was a gift for my father. 'A week just might be a bit—'

The girl cut me off with a solid and resounding 'No.'

I hoped I had that long left.

The clockmaker handed me the countess's clock. Sure enough, the damaged hinge had been replaced and the metal backing was once again without a scratch or dent.

I thanked both of them and assured them that Lord Empson would take care of the expense. The old clock-maker was the only one to give me a small smile as I left.

I was eager to see the countess's reaction to the repaired clock. I felt like I needed to make up for breaking her husband's clock in the first place. I walked back to the palace with a smile.

I practically ran down the corridor with the clock in hand. Passers-by looked at me strangely and turned to watch me go. Swinging open the doors to the countess's chambers, I waltzed in and walked with purpose to the table in the dining room on which the clock had been placed before I bumped into it and sent it off the edge. I stopped dead when I saw the countess sitting in the room.

'My lady.' I dropped into a curtsey.

The countess didn't take her eyes off the sampler she was working on in her lap.

I placed the clock carefully on the table. When the metal hit the wood, I looked for a reaction from her. Nothing. Even when I excused myself, the countess didn't look up at me or the clock on the table.

Later, I caught the countess fingering the clock's engraved case. I don't know exactly what went through her mind in that moment, but her expression was familiar to me. Her lips were tightly pressed together. Her eyes were shut tight.

It was the face of someone wishing for a different world and a different life. I knew that expression so well because I often wore it.

I spent the rest of the afternoon with the countess, watching her work on her sampler.

Though not as exciting as the rest of court, there was something I enjoyed about being in her presence. She wasn't any real relation of mine and we had no formal connection, but a part of me still strove for her approval.

'Are you sure you wouldn't like to start a sampler while you're here?' the countess asked.

'I'm fine just sitting – I'm enjoying having some peace.' Truthfully, I didn't know how to sew, but I had no desire to let the countess figure that out.

'I hope you're contemplating something worthwhile,' she said. 'An idle mind is a greater sin than an idle body.'

Ever since Miss Hatfield had come into my life with a vial of the Fountain of Youth's waters, I was never at a loss for things to contemplate. There was always the fact that my . . . I was about to say 'life,' but perhaps 'existence' would be a more accurate word – that my *existence* would never be the same again.

'I have a confession to make,' she started.

Those were the last words I expected to hear from the countess's mouth, since she gave the impression that she never did anything wrong.

'Lady Empson invited us for dinner at noon and I declined on behalf of us both.'

I shrugged. 'I don't mind.'

'Thank goodness,' she said. 'I'm sure Lady Empson means well . . . or perhaps Lord Empson put her up to it . . . but in either case, I can't endure an hour or so of her not talking, or worse – talking but blandly not having an opinion.'

I tried not to laugh at how much the countess hated Lady Empson's shrinking-violet act.

'If she were a wallflower, you could use her for wallpaper,' I said.

The countess's brow furrowed and I immediately saw my mistake. Did they even have wallpaper yet?

'Tapestries,' I sputtered.

'What is a . . . wallflower?' she asked hesitantly.

I guess that word hadn't been invented yet either.

'Oh, nothing. Slip of the tongue,' I said. 'Just a word we use back home.'

She nodded and thankfully returned her attention to the sampler on her lap.

A week went by quickly in this way, the pain in my stomach growing more and more intense with each passing day. The ache caused me to retire to bed earlier and wake up later, as only during sleep did it subside sufficiently to become tolerable. My days became shorter and appeared to fly by ever more quickly.

Henley still wasn't talking to me. I admit that was in part because I was avoiding being alone with him. Although I didn't attend any feasts or dinners with Lady Sutton or Lord Empson, I spent my waking hours looking busy with the countess, or Helen, or Joan. I threw myself into social situations during which I knew Henley could not talk to me.

I avoided Richard, too. I stayed in the countess's chambers, where I knew he would not try to visit me. He sent me a pastry each night from the court feasts, as if to remind me he existed. Each night, when Helen helped me undress, she mentioned that Richard had brought a sweetmeat for me and enquired after my health. She even thoughtfully set the pastry on a platter in my room, but seeing it untouched the next morning, she whisked it away. Richard sent me pastries until the fourth night. After the fourth was returned untouched, they suddenly stopped coming. I didn't want to ask Joan, but I knew Richard had also stopped coming.

I sat with the countess for hours, making light conversation. Occasionally, when I slipped up and mentioned an object or a phrase she was unfamiliar with, the countess nodded and blamed it on my Eastern upbringing. She didn't question me about Lithuania any further, firmly of the belief that Henry's court was the only place worth talking about.

I was spending so much time with the countess that she appeared to have grown used to having me by her side at certain times during the day – before and after breakfast, dinner, and supper. When I mentioned I would be taking a walk after supper one evening instead of sitting with her as I usually did, she looked surprised.

'Do you want me to sit with you a little longer?' I asked. 'I could always go later.'

'Oh, no – you go on ahead. Fresh air would be good for you. It's always good for the young. But it *is* late, so do be careful.'

She may have said she didn't mind, but I didn't believe her. Though the countess would never admit it, I was pretty sure she would miss me. I appeared to be the only person who spent time with her – besides Joan and Helen, of course, but she didn't really communicate with them beyond giving them lists of things to do.

In any other circumstance I would have made time to sit with her, but I couldn't put off any longer my trip to the clockmaker's to pick up the clock. I excused myself, saying that I was tired and was going to retire to my room, but snuck out into the still-bustling hallways instead.

I squeezed between extravagant skirts and velvet leggings to get where I was going. I pulled the hood of the cloak I was wearing to make sure it concealed my face, but no one seemed to pay me any heed. I didn't know how the countess would react if word got back to her that I was wandering court at night without a chaperone.

Eventually I stood before the clockmaker's door. This was it. There might be a way out. I knocked and waited. On the other side of the door, I heard the girl's soft footsteps.

When I opened the door, she did not greet me politely.

'Here for your order?' she said, as sullen as ever.

'I am,' I said. 'Where is your grandfather?' I recalled the young girl had called him 'grandpapa' during our first meeting.

The girl's tone became even harsher. 'The clockmaker is not here.'

'Should I come back another time?' I was disappointed to say the least. With every day wasted, the risk – both of the murderer finding me and of me slowly going insane – only grew.

'That will not be necessary. Your order is ready.'

I followed her to the back room. Today it appeared to be lit with more candles than on my previous visits. As the girl looked through boxes and miscellaneous items on the shelf, the flames behind her created a halo effect and the hair flowing down over her shoulders glowed warmly in the light.

'Here you go,' she said.

I held out my hands, expecting a great weight to be put into them. But that didn't happen.

I looked down when I felt a small disc, cold to the touch, placed in the palm of one hand.

'This isn't what I ordered. I don't understand.'

'You *are* Lady Eleanor Shelton, àre you not?' The girl looked up at me and cocked her head.

'Yes, I am—' I had no recollection of giving either her or the clockmaker my name, but they must have known that Lord Empson had a girl named Eleanor Shelton staying with his aunt at court.

'Then this is yours,' she said.

I began to grow frantic and my voice rose. 'This clock looks nothing like the one I drew.'

Turning it over in my hand, the silver case glinted in the candlelight. I could feel it ticking in my palm. The cover, which snapped open, had flowers growing on vines engraved onto it, like climbing roses.

'I've never seen anything like it.' The girl peered into my hand. 'He calls it a "pocket watch". The clock-maker must have thought it would be more becoming for you to have this instead of the one you drew. He does this from time to time – free of charge – when he feels strongly about it. I've never seen anything so small, so intricate.'

'But it's not what I wanted.'

'I know,' she said. 'But it's what's better for you.'

'If I'm the one commissioning a clock, I think I should get what I ask for,' I said.

'Don't worry, it'll grow on you.'

Don't worry? How could I not. My last resort had just disappeared down the drain.

'I'll pay extra—'

209

'It isn't about the money,' she said. 'Though we could certainly use it, money has never been important to the clockmaker. It doesn't drive him.' The girl shrugged, and I felt as if I was having this conversation with a thirty-year-old woman rather than a child.

'I only want what I came here for.'

'I know,' she said. 'That's what they all say, but soon you'll realize you're better off this way.'

She started towards the door and I had no choice but to follow her.

'Will you at least tell me when the clockmaker will be in again?' I asked. 'This is really important to me.'

'He'll be back later tonight,' she said. 'He only went to the neighbouring village for some parts. But if you're planning on trying to change his mind, you might as well give up now. He never changes his mind on things like this. When he feels strongly about something, that's the way it goes.' She laughed. 'You look like you ate something sour.'

I couldn't reply.

'On the bright side, it often works out for the better when people take his suggestions.'

I wanted to reply that this wasn't a suggestion. He had made me a clock I hadn't ordered. This was a far more important matter than someone at court ordering a clock to please their sweetheart. But then she smiled sweetly and shut the door, so I had no choice but to take the pocket watch and put it into the small velvet pouch that hung from a belt like fixture on my dress. I couldn't leave it lying around for Joan or Helen to find. With its minute and second hands, it barely looked like something from this time. I couldn't have anyone – least of all the countess – asking questions. No, it was safer to simply keep the watch with me.

210

My nails dug into my palms. This couldn't be happening. Henley's words came back to me: *Well, it is what it is.*

I wanted to scream.

I spent the next day with the countess as she worked on her sampler, just waiting for night to fall. I was scolded when I began to pace.

The countess looked up from her sampler just long enough to say, 'Whatever can you be so impatient for?'

If only she knew.

I spent hours making small talk with the countess. The weight of the pocket watch in its pouch against my side was unfamiliar and caught me off guard whenever I moved.

After another supper with the countess, I excused myself, pretending I was going to my room.

'I'm just feeling a bit tired today,' I said.

'My, my,' was all the countess said, but she didn't try to stop me.

I slipped into my room, quickly pulled on a cloak I had set aside earlier and tiptoed right out again once I made sure that Helen and Joan were nowhere to be seen. The cloak was one of the garments the dressmaker had made for me. The countess had told me it was the latest fashion and that the deep-blue colour would show my station, but I hadn't found a use for it until now.

I walked quickly down the corridors. Everything was dark, save for the occasional torch that lit the way. I tried to stay out of the light. I didn't want to run into anyone who could give me more trouble.

Just as I found the clockmaker's door in the dark, I heard something in the corridor behind me. I pulled up the hood of the cloak to hide my face and flattened myself against the wall. I held my breath. The dark-blue melded with the shadows, and I hoped that would be enough to keep me concealed.

The sound sounded like someone rummaging near the door, but the closest torch was set too far to see who it was.

The rummaging sound stopped.

'Show yourself.'

I froze.

'Lady Eleanor, I know it's you,' the figure said.

My heart hammering, I stepped forward into the light of the torch.

I squinted into the light. I took a risk and stepped closer to the voice to see who it was. It was the clockmaker.

'What are you doing here?' he asked.

'Looking for you.'

I waited for him to unlock the door and let me in, but he made no move to do so.

'There's no need to thank me for your gift,' he said. 'I do that often for clients I take a special . . . interest in.'

'I am here to talk to you about your . . . gift.' I hadn't been intending to call it that, but wanted to stay on his good side. 'I love it,' I began. 'I think it's very beautiful. But it's not what I asked for, and I really had my heart set on the gold clock exactly as I drew it.'

'I know you did, my dear. But this one better suits you and your needs.'

He was being stubborn, but I had expected that. I just had to be more forceful. 'I know you believe that. But as the patron, I'd like what I ordered. It's something I need.'

He didn't say anything.

'I'll pay more money.'

He studied my face. 'You insult me, my lady.' He unlocked and opened the door. 'Goodnight.' As he shut the door behind him, I felt my hopes crashing to the floor.

I took the pocket watch out of the pouch at my side and ran my fingers over the engraved cover. Glinting in the dark, it almost looked like it was taunting me. This stupid, damned watch.

I was almost certain he was the creator of Miss Hatfield's clock. Hadn't the girl said that my drawing looked like one of his designs? And yet the clockmaker wouldn't make it for me. I had felt so close to getting out of here and returning to whatever 'normal' was for me but, in reality, I was no closer to leaving than the day I was dragged here.

I returned the watch to its pouch and climbed back onto the horse. I rode towards the palace walls, knowing there was nothing more I could do tonight except sleep. I resolved to go back again the next morning. The clockmaker would soon see I was just as stubborn as he was. This wasn't something I could give up on.

Chapter 19

The next morning, as soon as Helen had finished dressing me, I marched straight to the clockmaker's. I must have looked quite a sight, for neither Helen nor Joan said a word. They both looked scared.

Arriving at the clockmaker's, I rapped on the door and thought I heard voices on the other side.

'Lady Shelton, I won't be changing my mind.' I heard the clockmaker's voice quite clearly through the wood.

I rapped again, this time even more insistently. 'I just want to talk to you,' I said. 'This matter is very important to me.'

'I'm sorry, my lady, but I don't want to talk with you.'

The door remained closed and I stood there dumbfounded. I didn't know why he was doing this to me.

I stood with my back supported by the opposite wall of the hallway until my legs would no longer hold me, then sank down to my knees. There went what I thought was my last and only chance.

'You look quite mad.'

I glanced up to see Richard standing in front of me. 'Not now, Richard.'

'No "Hello, Richard! Why, isn't the weather marvellous today?"'

'No,' I said.

214

'I was about to say that you look beautiful, but in truth you look more mad than beautiful. Angry, even.' Richard took my hand and drew me to my feet. 'Now, if you don't have anywhere to be, come take a walk with me and tell me what's wrong. Fresh air will do you and your anger some good.'

He was right, and I didn't have any place to be. I took his arm and walked beside him. As we ambled along, I told him about the clock.

'Ah, yes – the clockmaker is famous for doing that from time to time,' Richard said, after listening to my tale. 'Of course, he would never do such a thing to the king himself. I'm afraid the king would not find that very amusing.'

'Well, I certainly don't find it very amusing.'

Richard smirked but agreed with me.

'I was so specific with the design! And he refuses to do it!'

'Eleanor . . .'

That startled me out of my rant. It was the first time he had called me by my first name . . . or rather, by Eleanor Shelton's first name.

'If I may call you by your first name,' Richard said quickly, seeing what must have been a rather stunned expression on my face.

'Of course,' I muttered.

'I feel we know each other well enough by now,' he said with a smile.

'Certainly.'

'Now, Eleanor . . . As I was about to say before I digressed, could you loosen your grip on my arm a little?'

I looked down to see that my knuckles were turning white where I was holding on to Richard. Embarrassed, I pulled my hand away.

'You don't have to take away your hand completely,' Richard said. 'In fact, I much prefer having your hand there.'

My cheeks must have flushed an even deeper shade of red as he brought my hand back up to his arm.

I tried to act as if I hadn't noticed. 'What were you going to say? You just interrupted yourself.'

'No, that was it. I only wanted to ensure I still have a functioning arm after my stroll with you is done.'

I didn't think it was possible, but my cheeks grew redder.

'You're even more beautiful when you're embarrassed.'

Of course he didn't know that part of the reason why my cheeks were burning was because Henley might be watching all of this. Richard's words, my reactions – everything. It would be just like him to focus in on this moment to see how things played out. And that made my cheeks burn all the more.

'Tell you what,' Richard said. 'If this means so much to you, let me try talking to the clockmaker myself.'

'Be my guest,' I said. 'But I'm warning you, he's very stubborn.'

'I've been told I can be very persuasive.'

'By who?'

He looked away. 'Lady Sutton.'

We erupted in giggles and Henley flew out of my mind. He wasn't here – not in person, at least. Even if he was watching, he couldn't stop me from enjoying myself.

Things were so natural between Richard and myself that it just felt right, whether we were talking, or walking in silence. It was all intuitive, no difficult explanations required. I couldn't help thinking that this was the way all human relationships were meant to be. And Henley . . . I wished my relationship with Henley was like this. I knew even forming that thought in my mind was a kind of betrayal, but I couldn't help it. Our relationship used to be like this

216

– Henley always joking around and me laughing along with him. I missed that. And, realizing what I was thinking, I tucked that dark thought at the back of my mind, hoping it wouldn't spring up again.

'Tell me something I don't know,' I said suddenly.

'What I had for breakfast, perhaps?'

'Anything you think I need to know.'

He thought for a bit before responding. 'I believe in people.'

I smiled to myself. No one else would think to say that.

'I believe in their abilities. And I believe that purity exists in this world, whether it be religion or some other thing,' he said. 'Does that fulfil your request?'

'Yes.'

I saw his brow furrow.

'What is it?' I asked.

'No one's ever asked me a question like that before. I've always had to do the asking myself, and even then, I've never had to articulate what I believe in.'

Richard and I were poles apart in so many ways – from different times, with disparate backgrounds and experiences – and yet I knew exactly what he meant. Like him, I was always alone with my thoughts, and that became exhausting after a while.

We all need someone. That's how we are built. We spend our entire lives trying to find someone we can connect with – someone who will ask us those questions – and fearing our loneliness if we don't find that person. That's all anyone ever wants. That's all I ever wanted.

When Richard walked me to the door of the countess's chambers, he gave my hand a squeeze.

'I wish that walk were longer. Oh, why do you have to live so close?'

217

I chuckled and wished him a pleasant rest of the day.

'Pleasant? I think it'll be anything but pleasant without your company,' he said as I walked into the sitting room.

'I don't know if I like that boy.' The countess was sitting by the window.

'R–Lord Holdings?'

'He is from an old family, I'll give you that. And they are wealthy, but not incredibly so. He's not the oldest son, either . . . He's a very nice boy, or so they say, but I think you could do better,' the countess said. 'I'm sure your father would also want you to do better.'

'Lord Holdings is just a friend.'

'A lady does not have friends like that. And friends don't walk unchaperoned.'

'I was asking him for a favour,' I said.

To my surprise, the countess did not scold me. 'Do be careful,' was all she said, disapprovingly, before waving me off.

After that strange conversation with the countess, I no longer told her when I was out with Richard. The fact that she hadn't criticised me openly affected me more than if she had. I almost wished she had scolded me! Anything would have been better than the cold disapproval in her tone.

I knew it was juvenile, but I couldn't help wanting to please everyone at once. In order to please the countess, it was easier not to tell her I was seeing Richard so much. I didn't outright lie to her; I just didn't inform her where I was going. Occasionally, when she asked, I told her I was wandering, which was true in some sense.

On one of our meandering adventures, Richard and I walked arm in arm through some of the court's more deserted halls. Instead of people, the hall was dotted on either side with short pillars, atop which decorative Greek vases were artfully placed. I didn't know such a deserted place existed in a place where so many lived in such close quarters, but he knew all the ins and outs of the palace and its inhabitants.

'You appear to be fingering that pouch at your side quite often,' Richard said.

'I hadn't realized.' It was the truth. I had become accustomed to the weight of the pocket watch at my side and no longer noticed it was there.

'It's almost as if you're guarding something of great value.'

'Really?'

Richard shrugged. 'Just trying to figure you out, my lady. You have so many facets.'

I didn't want him to figure me out. I didn't know how he would look at me if he did.

'So what is it like living at court?' I asked, changing the subject.

'Shouldn't you know the answer to that question as well as I do?'

'No, it's not the same for me,' I said. 'I haven't been here as long as you.'

'True, but you do realize I had a life before court, too, don't you?' Richard said.

'With your family?'

'With my family. I used to live in a quieter place than this.'

'I can imagine that almost any place would be quieter than court.'

'We didn't have so many festivities at home, no.'

'What was it like there?' I asked.

I was curious what 'home' was to Richard. I wanted to get to know him better, and that meant knowing all of him. I couldn't shake Henley's words about the scratches on Richard's arm even though I was sure he was wrong, so I wanted the whole picture, to prove to myself that he was exactly what he appeared to be.

'As you would expect, I imagine,' he said. 'Mother. Father. Brothers. I have a good enough relationship with all of them. I've been fortunate.'

'No sisters?'

'One stillborn, but that was before my time. After that, all boys,' Richard said. 'I'm sure we drove my poor mother crazy, but my father loved it. He always said we kept him young.'

'Do you still see them?' I wished I could have a family like that, but tried not to let it show in my voice.

'Of course. I see my father and my oldest brother when they visit court to pay their respects to the king. My mother sometimes accompanies them. They don't come too often, though – Father prefers his home in the country – but that's fine by me. I'm learning to be on my own now. I think that's something everyone needs to master at some point or other in their lives. Besides . . . I have Lady Sutton to keep me company.' He smirked.

I nodded. It reminded me of Henley's father, but I was glad Richard had a better relationship with his father than Henley had endured with his own.

'And how about you?' Richard asked. 'I've never heard you speak of your family.'

I thought about Eleanor Shelton and her father back in Lithuania. I thought about my own foggy memory of my – Cynthia's – mother. In a way, Miss Hatfield was the only real mother-like person I had . . . or used to have.

'I don't want to talk about it,' I said.

I thought Richard would question me further but he let it go. That was one of the things I was growing to love about him – he knew when to let things go.

'And what of the future?' he asked, catching me off guard. 'Talk about the past is all well and good since that makes us who we are, but what about the future?'

'I'm not sure where I'll go from here,' I answered truthfully.

'That's a good answer,' he said.

'I imagine you were looking for something a bit more concrete.'

'No. Just something honest,' Richard said. 'It's normal not to know. That's all for the better – it makes you create your life instead of just choosing a path laid out by someone else.'

I paused and let his last words linger. 'I'm not sure I agree with that. Sometimes we're given choices we can't run from.'

'True – but that doesn't mean you have to take them.'

I let it go, as Richard had let go the topic of family for me. There were some things even he didn't – or couldn't – understand.

'I almost forgot. Eleanor, I have a surprise for you. Maybe this is something you can accept because it's not pastries.'

His tone was cheerful once more, but I couldn't meet his eyes when he said that.

'I was worried about you.' His voice was still playful, though there was a softness to it now. 'But enough of that. As I was saying, I have a surprise for you—'

I automatically looked towards his hands.

'No, no. I don't have it with me.' He laughed, showing me his empty palms. 'Perhaps I should not have called it a surprise since I did tell you about it earlier. It concerns the clock you commissioned.'

My legs almost froze, but I willed them to keep walking in pace with Richard. I couldn't show him how big a deal this was.

'What about the clock?'

'I convinced the clockmaker to try to construct one to your design.' He said it so simply, but his words changed my world.

'Oh, Richard!' I stopped in my tracks and looked up at him.

'That makes you so happy?' Richard said. 'I mean . . . I had a feeling you would be pleased, but not like—'

I hugged him. He stiffened up. He never did finish his sentence.

We walked on in silence for a while, my body barely a foot away from his, before Richard spoke up again.

'Eleanor, I'd like to show you something . . . With your permission, of course.'

'As long as it won't spring out and bite me, sure.'

Richard only smiled, and I wondered if this was something serious.

'I want you to get to know me,' Richard said. 'That may sound silly, given that you discern parts of me very well already, but I want you to understand all of me.'

I didn't know where he was going with this, but I let him take my hand.

'So this is it?' I turned around to get a good look at the room. So many twisting tubes and pipes full of God knows what surrounded me that occasionally I lost sight of Richard.

'If by that you mean is the place I disappear to, then yes.' Richard's voice scattered, hitting the copper tubes and echoing back to me. 'The Royal Alchemist's domain.

And you're here as an official guest of the apprentice to the king's Royal Alchemist Sir del Angelo, brought to this place from Venice by the king himself . . . but if anyone asks, I don't know a single thing about you ever being in here because it's forbidden.'

'It's remarkable.' My whisper carried to him.

A tabby cat sauntered over to us and stretched against Richard's leg. He bent down to stroke him behind his ears. I thought back to the scratches I had seen on Richard's arm. So there *was* a cat after all. I felt more and more silly for ever having doubted him.

The room was unusually large for court, but the myriad tubes and vials of simmering liquids and arcane equipment I had no names for made it feel a lot smaller. Some of the items were arranged in rows on countertops, as if someone had started out with good intentions of keeping everything neat. However, more recent additions crowded the table tops and bulged out into the walkways.

'I wanted to show you where I work,' Richard said. 'It's another part of my life I want to share with you.'

I moved slowly, carefully, trying not to knock anything over. Everything looked terribly important.

'Would you like me to explain what some of these things do?'

I nodded and walked over to Richard's side.

'According to Sir del Angelo, the king is most concerned with two things. The first is gold, of course – what monarch in their right mind isn't concerned with gold?' Richard cracked a grin in my direction. 'There are two types of alchemy,' he explained. 'The first makes gold out of a completely different substance, such as copper. The second multiplies gold – you take a small amount of gold to start the reaction to make it into larger amounts of gold.' He pointed to what looked like a blackened kettle of some sort. 'We use that for melting gold. As you might imagine, the second method is somewhat easier, and the one we're most concerned with.'

Richard paused to make sure I was following.

'Go on,' I said. He looked pleased that I was interested.

He described different processes of melting and preparing gold, using metals that were inert but also had high melting points. Most of it went over my head, and I knew they would never really create gold, of course. But the scientific advances they were pioneering were amazing, and I told him as much.

Richard's cheeks flushed. 'Well, we haven't quite managed to make gold yet. But we're close.'

'That's still incredible.'

He looked adorably embarrassed.

'And what's the second thing?' I asked.

'The second thing?'

'You said the king is primarily concerned with two things: gold and . . .?'

'Immortality.'

Richard smiled but I felt my skin go cold. I had tried to put my audience with the king to the back of my mind, but of course, this was what he had been talking about.

'By God's grace, the king still has many years ahead of him. But not even kings are immortal, and that frustrates him.'

'Have you found anything?'

Richard laughed. 'If I figured out the secret to immortality, I'd be one of the first to take advantage of it.'

'Wouldn't that be something.' I was horrified that we were even talking about this. All of a sudden, Richard wasn't my escape from my reality any more.

'It would! And the king would be very pleased.'

'So it's safe to say you haven't discovered it yet?'

'Unfortunately not,' Richard said, but I didn't find myself sharing the same sentiment. 'About a year ago, Sir del Angelo thought he had made a significant discovery. He had been working on a solution for months, studying Greek texts and collecting the necessary herbs and metals to trigger the reactions. He was so excited – so sure that it would work this time.'

'And?'

'It didn't work.' I saw a flash of disappointment in his eyes.

'Is there any of the potion left? May I see it?' I had no idea what made me ask that, especially after Richard had admitted that it didn't work.

Richard took my hand and I didn't pull away. The gesture was so warm, I wanted to sink into him. It reminded me of what I had felt with Henley before . . . before all of this.

He led me down a row of violet-coloured liquids and silver vials.

'This is it,' Richard said. 'Failed distilled life.'

He gestured towards a single bottle standing alone on a countertop. Amid all the clutter, it drew the eye even though the bottle itself was only as big as my thumb. The liquid inside was as clear as the glass. The only way I could tell there was anything inside it was by the distorted image I saw through it. It looked a lot like the vial of liquid Miss Hatfield had used to turn me immortal.

'And you're sure it doesn't work?'

'We both tried it,' Richard said. 'We also experimented on animals with shorter life spans, and on elderly people whose time was almost done, but none survived. We started out with at least a gallon of it – the vial you see here contains all that's left after our many trials.'

I stooped to take a closer look at the liquid in the vial, and when I straightened again, I found Richard's expression amused.

'I've never seen a girl so engrossed with something like this,' he said. 'If I had known it would help my cause with women, I would have brought all the ladies of court up here years ago! All the ladies save for Lady Sutton, of course . . .'

I smirked at his attempt at being cute.

'Here, since you appear to be so enamoured with that little thing, why don't you keep it? I have instructions to dispose of it anyway.'

My eyes went wide. 'The bottle?'

'Yes. Why not? It serves no purpose any more. Besides, I like the idea of you keeping something of mine.'

I laughed off the comment but still took the vial. I slipped it into the pouch that hung from my belt.

'I know you secretly find me dashing,' he said, leading me by the hand through the maze of tubes and out of the room.

I looked up at him. 'Do you expect me to confirm or deny that claim?'

'No.' He patted the back of my hand. 'I just wanted you to know that I know.'

When we were back out in the more spacious hallways, I turned to him, narrowly missing one of the pillars that balanced a vase precariously on top. 'So why alchemy?'

He shrugged. 'My oldest brother, the first son, took over the family estate, of course. The second son went into the church and the third became a soldier, as is customary. I suppose my father didn't know what to do with me. Alchemy was the next most useful thing he could think of.'

'And do you actually like it?' I had to ask.

'It's more than just liking it. It makes me a . . . somebody.'

I recognized something in him then: that feeling of not mattering in the world, as if you could die and not be missed. Everyone else would keep going, keep living, because you weren't a crucial part in the machine. Perhaps not even a part of it at all.

'Just like you make me feel as though I'm a somebody.'

I was surprised. When I looked up at him, I couldn't see the warm honey colour of his eyes through my tears.

The hand that was still holding mine pulled me closer, till we were touching nose to nose. And then he kissed me.

And I didn't pull away. I knew Henley was almost certainly watching, but in that moment I couldn't bring myself to care.

Richard kissed me. Hard.

There was a crash as one of the vases on the pillars fell and I took a step backwards. I knew that was Henley.

Chapter 20

What in God's name was that?

I had run back to my room without so much as saying a word to Richard after I kissed him. I was in such a panic, I didn't know what to say.

Henley was speaking almost before I managed to close the door to my room.

Every word Henley uttered was low and punctuated with a tension I didn't need to see his face to feel. I knew he was talking about the kiss with Richard, but neither of us wanted to say it out loud.

'I have no idea.'

I wish I could say the room was spinning and that I felt guilty for kissing him back, but both the room and I were fine. Instead, I saw everything with a perfect clarity I hadn't known in ages. Sure, I was still confused about a lot of things, but I kept waiting to feel that guilty knot in my stomach and it just wasn't there.

'I don't know where that came from.'

But that must have felt right – at least on some level – because you didn't fight him at all. I know. I saw.

I hated that Henley had seen what had happened, but I had no control over that.

I-I'm at a loss—

I sat down at the edge of my bed. It wasn't just Henley;

I had no words to say in this situation, either. I knew it must have felt worse for him, and there wasn't anything I could say to make it better. If there was, I would have said it in a heartbeat.

You try to leave me behind, but I'm always here. God, Rebecca . . . You . . . you've really hurt me this time.

'You don't understand—'

You always say that. 'You don't understand.' 'You don't understand.' When will I understand? When I lose you for ever?

'You know that's not possible.'

Is that it? Are you running from me because you feel trapped with me always here?

'I always feel trapped, but that's regardless of whether you're here or not.'

You know I can't change this. If I could, I would.

'It's not you. You're not at fault. Richard . . . Richard is just . . . different.'

Is that supposed to make me feel better?

I ignored him. 'Don't ask me to explain it because I barely understand it myself. He has this irresistible draw, this . . . passion. I don't expect you to understand. You're removed from it – disembodied – and he's here. Actually here.'

Silence followed my statement, and had this been any other conversation, I would have thought Henley had lost interest and stopped listening.

I do understand that feeling – that draw. That's how I feel about you.

Invisible though he might be, I could plainly see how much he was hurting and I hated myself for being the cause of it. I had known this would happen. And yet I couldn't stop it.

Richard. Richard was different. I know everyone says that, but it was true. There was something in Richard so animated – almost fervid – that it made even someone like me feel alive for once. For the first time in a long while, I was *seen*. It was an energy that scared me – something I had never experienced with anyone else.

I knew it was natural to compare Richard with Henley in my mind, but it was sickening at the same time. I didn't want to do this to Henley. I kept falling and Henley was always there to see me fall.

'Henley, you know I love you,' I said.

I pray every day that's still true. But you love Richard, too.

I opened my mouth but Henley cut me off before I had a chance to speak.

Don't even try to deny it. I know it's true.

I shut my eyes.

And I'm not angry.

'No.' I opened my eyes to feel warm tears rushing down my face. 'Be angry. Be furious with me.'

Rebecca—

'I want you to shove me. Hard. I want you to be so angry you feel like tearing me apart.'

You know that won't solve anything.

'It would make me feel better.'

I heard a disembodied sigh.

It's not worth it. You love him. You can't control that. No one can control love.

'It's different with him,' I repeated. 'It's almost a different sort of love. This love is maddening, all-consuming, terrifying.'

And ours isn't.

'No. It isn't,' I said. 'You and I are something entirely different. We're safe, constant, reliable, even with you as you are.'

I guess neither of us can fully have you.

'You know I'm yours,' I said, but I was met with silence.

It didn't make sense, even to me, but something about that conversation with Henley made me throw myself further into my growing relationship with Richard over the next week. I had always looked forward to spending time with him, but now there was a part of me who spent time with him out of desperation, since he was the only person I could talk to. I knew it was the wrong reason to want to be with him, but I didn't care.

The feeling in my stomach was incessant. I would have to leave as soon as the clock was finished but that only made me throw myself towards Richard even more. I didn't know why I thought my relationship with Richard would be any different from my relationship with Henley. Maybe I was making a huge mistake. I didn't know any more – and I didn't care.

Richard had this *normalcy* around him. When I was near him, I became 'normal', too. I knew that when I left this time, I would never see him again. He would grow old and die. It was the same as when I thought I was leaving Henley for good in 1904.

So why did I do it? Why was I hurting myself even more? With the murderer still out there, it wasn't as if I could stay even without this immortality business. I wished I could be like Miss Hatfield – *don't get any closer to people than you need to, don't make friends you know you'll have to leave, and certainly don't love anyone.* That would be so much easier. I knew Miss Hatfield didn't have this ability from the beginning – having fallen in love and having had a child. But she learned to distance herself. And I knew I couldn't. I didn't know if I was constitutionally weaker than Miss Hatfield, but I just couldn't not love. I wasn't built that way.

So I became more proactive in planning outings with Richard rather than leaving it up to chance and hoping to bump into him. Richard didn't appear to mind. In fact, he was always rather pleased when I asked him when I would see him again. Maybe he saw me as eager. If so, he was correct.

Since showing me the alchemy lab, Richard hadn't tried to kiss me again. I didn't know how I felt about that. Combined with my desire to spend more time with him, it only confused me all the more. I had become a stranger to myself.

My eagerness did loosen Richard up a bit, who took it as a sign that it was okay to occasionally put his arm around me. He sometimes brushed a hair from my face and sat closer to me – close enough that I could smell him on my skin when I retired to my room for the night.

Even now, Richard did it again, sitting down with his back to the fountain in the garden, drawing me close. It was a week since we kissed.

'What are you thinking right now? You look so pensive,' he said.

I shook my head. 'Nothing. I'm just enjoying the company.'

'You mean to tell me that for once, that pretty little head of yours is completely blank?' He played with my fingers. 'You're not cooking up some plan or other to take over a foreign country, are you?'

He narrowed his eyes in mock-suspicion and I giggled at the face he made.

'You expect too much of me!'

'Never.' Richard wove his fingers through mine and it felt like the most natural thing in the world. 'I'd give anything for a glimpse into that mind of yours.'

'I don't think you'd want to if you knew what actually went on in there.' I meant it, too.

'You underestimate me.'

Just then, Richard had a coughing fit. He withdrew his hand from mine and turned aside, covering his mouth.

'Richard, are you all right?' I raised a hand to rub his back but he shuffled away from me.

As the coughing fit dragged on, I grew increasingly worried. He began to wheeze and it sounded as if he couldn't get breath into his lungs. I had half a mind to yell for help, but slowly the coughing eased and he began to catch his breath.

'Are you all right?' I asked again.

'Yes, yes. It's nothing, just a little cough. My throat felt a bit irritated.'

I raised my brows. 'A little cough? That wasn't a little cough at all. Come here—'

As I pulled him towards me, I froze. There was blood on his hand.

'My God . . .'

'It's nothing,' Richard said, following my gaze.

He tried to pull his hand away and wipe it on his hose, but I firmly held his wrist.

'That's not nothing, Richard. You just coughed up blood.'

'That, I'm aware of,' Richard said slowly.

'You must see a physician. This really can't be—'

'I already have.' In the mid-afternoon sun, Richard looked more tired than I'd ever seen him.

'And?'

'And it didn't help.'

'Did he prescribe anything?' I asked. I thought through what little I knew about the medicine of the time period. 'Did he leech you?'

'Nothing helps. The physician himself told me that.'

My body grew cold at how callous he sounded. 'What do you mean, nothing helps?'

'Do I have to spell it out for you? I'm dying.'

His words dangled in the air between us.

'Dying?'

'Dying.'

'My God.' I sat back and put my hands to either side of me to steady myself.

'Consumption,' he said.

I almost couldn't hear him through the ringing in my ears.

Chapter 21

'Lady Sutton would like to invite you to dine with her this evening.'

Those were the dreaded words spoken by Helen the next morning. The invitation came out of nowhere and I wondered what had prompted it. I almost declined before rethinking. It would have only done more harm than good if I had tried to avoid Lady Sutton. Maybe *avoid* was too strong of a word. I simply didn't want to see her. It seemed like a hassle. But even if I had declined the invitation, she seemed like a woman who would make it her mission to hunt me down.

I spent a particularly difficult day trying to ignore the pressing feeling of discomfort in my body. It was growing increasingly urgent as time went on and I didn't know how much more of it I could take.

'Do you have a specific dress you would like to wear for tonight, my lady?' Helen asked that evening.

Maybe Lady Sutton would serve as a welcome distraction.

'Something bright,' I said. I was sure Lady Sutton would approve.

Helen pulled out a lapis lazuli dress I didn't even know I had. I nodded and she began dressing me.

'Did Lady Sutton say why she wanted to see me?'

'Not that I know of, my lady.'

This made me more nervous for some reason and I hurried to get ready.

'Would you like me to come with you?' Helen asked when I started for the door.

'It's all right,' I said. The last thing I wanted was a bigger audience. It was a full-time job figuring things out and keeping myself in check without worrying about Helen watching me, too. At least Lady Sutton would keep my mind off my aching stomach.

When I knocked on Lady Sutton's door, one of her servants opened it. Before he could make a sound, Lady Sutton yelled, 'Bring her in!' from within. I felt like I was about to be fed to the dogs.

When I entered, Lady Sutton was lounging on the bright-pink couch, fanning herself. Wearing an equally pink gown, she almost blended in with the lumpy cushions.

'Lady Sutton.' I curtsied.

'Now, now. Sit by me, Lady Eleanor. Come and talk to me.'

I looked around for a seat near the couch since Lady Sutton was taking up all of it. The servant who had let me in moved a chair close to Lady Sutton for me.

'Thank you,' I said, sitting down.

If it was gossip she was after, I wanted no part in it.

'I've been noticing you spending more time with my Richard,' she began.

I didn't know if she meant 'noticing' or 'hearing', but something told me it was more likely the latter.

'Yes, I've been enjoying Richard's company.'

As I said that, Lady Sutton's eyebrows shot up. I really did need to remember to call him 'Lord Holdings' when I wasn't talking to him directly.

'So I've heard—'

'Would you prefer me not to spend time with him?' I asked.

I hadn't the slightest intention of following through with not seeing Richard if she asked me to. I just wanted to gain some sense of where this conversation was going.

'Not at all! I think you're quite good for him,' she said, and I relaxed into my seat. 'I haven't seen him this excited in months, since . . . You see, he's in a . . . fragile state.'

'I know,' I said.

Lady Sutton sighed. 'So he told you?'

'He did.'

'I suppose it's better that he told you himself, rather than me accidentally letting it slip. You know I have a big mouth.'

I wasn't going to deny that.

'I'm glad he told you,' she went on. 'It wouldn't be right if you didn't know what you were getting yourself into.'

It did still hurt me when I realized how long Richard had kept such a big secret from me. He wanted me to know him and understand him to the point that he risked smuggling me into the alchemy lab, and yet he had tried to hide the fact that he was sick. I couldn't help wondering when – or maybe even if – Richard would have told me he had consumption if I'd not caught him coughing up blood.

'How long has he known?' I had to ask.

'That he was ill? A while.'

My chest tightened and something must have shown on my face because she reached out and patted my hand.

'There, there. I know it's horrible to think of someone so bright and vibrant being ill, but he's learning to live with it.'

He's learning to live with it till it kills him. That was the part Lady Sutton was avoiding saying.

'He's strong,' Lady Sutton said. 'Stronger than you or I give him credit for sometimes. When the physician first told me he was ill, I cried for hours. And you know who consoled me? Richard. He came into my room with a glass of sack and brandy, telling me everything was going to be all right. Imagine that! He comforted me!' Lady Sutton clapped her hands together and laughed.

I wasn't sure how that was supposed to make me feel better.

'I know he's strong, but—'

'No buts. He doesn't want anyone to worry about him.'

'I can't help but worry about him,' I admitted.

'That's because you're a good person.' She patted my arm. 'Which is why he likes you. I can hear it in his voice when he talks about you. We all worry about him. It's what people who care do.'

'He talks about me?'

'Oh, don't be silly. How can a boy in love not talk about his girl?'

I didn't realize it till then, but my eyes were brimming with tears.

'There, there. Aren't you glad that two you found each other before . . .'

She trailed off but the unspoken words hung in the air. *Before he died*. Richard was going to die. And I had to sit here unable to do a thing about it.

'I'm so sorry. That was insensitive of me.' Lady Sutton fanned her face more furiously than before.

It was insensitive, but that was just Lady Sutton.

'Were you ever married?' I asked.

'Of course I was. I still am!'

I was about to apologize for not knowing, but Lady Sutton cut me off.

'It's a wonder the old idiot's still alive!'

'Excuse me?'

'With the kind of life he lives, I expected him to die years ago, but he keeps on surviving.'

'He . . . doesn't live with you?'

'Of course not,' she said. She sounded so pragmatic. 'I wouldn't be able to do a thing with that man breathing over my shoulder. It's better when we leave each other to our own devices. He has his life and I have mine – that's how happy marriages are kept happy.'

This sounded as far from a happy marriage as it was possible to be.

'And you don't ever wish to see him?'

'My dear young Lady Eleanor . . . The last I saw of him was about three years ago at a wedding of some sort. That was enough for a lifetime.'

I knew Lady Sutton was one to gossip, but it surprised me to hear her speak so ill of her own husband . . . Her words sounded particularly harsh after praising Richard only a moment ago.

'I'll be frank with you, Lady Eleanor, because I value frankness above all else – even loyalty. My husband is a good-for-nothing scoundrel. Simple as that.'

Her tone was so matter of fact that I didn't know how to respond. I was about to try to change the topic of conversation but Lady Sutton ploughed on. She didn't appear to want to abandon the subject yet.

'Even at that wedding – or was it an engagement? No matter – even at that gathering, do you know what he did?'

Lady Sutton looked at me expectantly. It was a few beats before I realized she was waiting for an answer.

'Umm . . . No?'

'Of course you don't, sweet girl. You haven't been exposed to the horrors of this world, and I hope you never will be. Anyway, at this feast celebrating whatever it was – wedding? – of the son of some dear friend or other of mine, he had the nerve to gamble.'

239

I tried to think quickly of a response that would make it at least sound as if I was interested in her story. 'I can't believe he gambled!'

'It wasn't the fact that he gambled – that's fine, I occasionally gamble, too. But the difference is that I win.' Lady Sutton sat up abruptly. 'Do you understand me?'

After reassuring her that I did know the difference, Lady Sutton rolled over onto her back again.

'Thank goodness somebody does!'

As she cackled, I wondered how much she'd drunk before I arrived. I had noticed that the wine flowed freely practically from breakfast onwards here at court.

'He lost enough money during the course of that one evening that I could have bought a hundred dresses . . . not to mention a house to store them. And best of all . . . Do you know what was best of all?'

I shook my head. No, I didn't know what was best of all, especially since I hadn't been there.

'He didn't even show up to the actual ceremony itself.' Lady Sutton roared with laughter, slapping the sofa arm. 'He drank so much the night before that he was too sick to get out of bed! Can you believe it?'

I told her I couldn't.

'What a man . . .' she said.

She continued her monologue about her husband's faults while I ate her food, but eventually the dessert pastries came and went, so I felt I could excuse myself. I told her that the countess was probably expecting me.

As I was backing out of her room, Lady Sutton was still muttering to herself.

'What a man . . . What a stupid man.'

Chapter 22

Richard and I walked through the palace gardens together the next morning as we often did. He told me it was 'as natural as court would ever get with its false people'. Of course, I had to remind him that every plant here was meticulously chosen, not to mention trimmed to an exact shape and strictly confined to its appointed place.

'It's as if you enjoy ruining my small pleasures,' he joked, to which I wrinkled my nose.

I noticed another couple across the green expanse of manicured grass.

Richard looked in the direction of my gaze. 'Another pair enjoying this beautiful day?'

The woman's black dress contrasted starkly with the white flowers surrounding that section of the garden. The man wore a dark crimson cloak with some sort of gold trimming that caught the light as he solicitously escorted his lady.

'I suppose days like this bring people together,' I said.

'But certain people are destined to find each other, no matter what the situation. Sometimes it's just meant to be. You can't argue with *meant to be*.'

He chuckled and I tried not to cringe as his chuckling turned to wheezing. There was nothing I could say or do but pat his back. Luckily, it didn't take him long to recover on this occasion.

'Are you sure you want to spend time with this invalid?'
he asked.

'I do! Especially when this invalid needs me to even
breathe.'

That brought a smile to his face and I felt warm, as if
staring into the face of the sun.

'Don't flatter yourself,' he said.

That was the Richard I had come to love.

We walked once around a statue Richard claimed was
of the Roman goddess Diana.

'But couldn't it be just any Roman woman?' I pointed
out. 'There's nothing about it that says it has to be Diana.'

'She's the goddess of the hunt and there are arrows at
her feet.'

'That still doesn't prove anything.'

'You wouldn't be satisfied unless there was a plaque with
her name on it,' Richard teased, but his teasing sounded
half-hearted.

I glanced away from the statue to see that he looked
a bit pale.

'Are you feeling all right?' I asked.

'Just because you know I'm ill now, you don't have to
ask how I'm feeling every two seconds.'

I didn't want to push him but his face looked a bit grey.
'Are you sure?'

'Oh, so now you treat me like an old man. What's next?
Making sure I remembered to pull my hose on this morning?'

I was about to apologize for being overbearing when
Richard interrupted me.

'Perhaps I should sit down,' he said. 'Just for a moment.'

I wasn't going to argue with that and led him to the
closest bench I could find. As soon as the backs of his knees
touched the marble, I felt his weight slump against me.

I panicked. And screamed.

In the back of my mind I knew he had only lost consciousness, but in that terrifying moment, I couldn't access the logical part of my brain. I was so scared. I thought he had died.

And with the logical part of my brain nowhere to be found, I didn't know what to do. So I sat there, and screamed, and screamed. I clutched at Richard's body, pulling him close to me as if that would help somehow.

CPR. First aid. None of my modern knowledge came to me. It was as if a plug had been pulled, and when Richard lost consciousness, I couldn't function any more either.

I knew I had to snap out of it, but it took me far longer than it should have.

When I came back to reality, the first thing I saw was the man in the distance start sprinting towards me. The woman clutched at her skirts and ran after him, but he reached me first. It was Lord Dormer.

'He . . . He just dropped.'

'We must get him to bed and call the physician.'

I felt helpless and grabbed Richard's clammy hand. It was quickly turning cold.

Just then the woman rushed up to us. I had to blink twice. It was the countess. It didn't make sense that she would be alone with Lord Dormer, especially since she believed so staunchly that no woman should go out with a man unchaperoned, but I couldn't think about that now.

'Good, you're here,' Lord Dormer said to the countess. 'Keep his head propped up so he doesn't choke on the blood while I summon the physician.'

He ran off as the countess was settling Richard's head in her lap.

Richard's body was slumped lengthwise across the bench. He was almost as pale as the stone on which he was lying, and I now saw what Lord Dormer had been talking about – his lips were parted in the middle of his mouth but the edges were stuck together with a rusty substance that could only be dried blood.

Had I not screamed before, I would have at that moment. But there was nothing left in me.

Two men dressed in palace livery took Richard away. I wanted to go with them but the countess pried my hand from his and told me I would only be in the way. I stood there, staring at the shapes her lips made as she talked at me. She held my hands and sound was coming out of her mouth, but I could barely comprehend a word of it.

'Let's get you back.'

I had no idea how the countess conveyed me from the gardens to my room. Everything went blank, and then I was suddenly aware I was sitting in my own bed.

As soon as the countess stepped outside for a moment, Henley took over trying to talk to me. It didn't matter what he said, it was more the sound of his voice and the knowledge of his presence that comforted me.

He's going to get better, Henley said.

'You can't know that. He's . . . He's dying.'

I hated to repeat Richard's own words – finally saying them out loud made it feel more true. I couldn't take them back or change the outcome.

He'll find a way to pull through. You'll find a way to pull through.

'You can't promise that. This is consumption. No one survives consumption. Not in this time, anyway.'

Henley was quiet, and I had even shocked myself with that bald statement.

I wish I could make him better.

But I knew better than most that wishing wasn't enough.

I stood up. 'I need to go and see him.'

Are you sure that's a good idea?

'As opposed to not seeing him? Miss Hatfield told me I have nothing to worry about in terms of getting sick or being infected by diseases. Immortals can't catch any of those.' I knew that wasn't what he was objecting to, but Henley didn't respond.

I passed the countess on my way out. She didn't try to stop me, either. I figured she knew where I was heading.

When I stepped into the corridor, it struck me that I didn't know where Richard would be. I had never been to his rooms and had no idea where they were. I thought back to his comment about Lady Sutton being the only family-like person he had at court. If anyone knew where he was, she would.

I walked with deliberate, sure steps, moving quickly but not wanting to run. All the faces I passed in the corridor were turned towards me. *That's the girl who almost died with the candelabra . . . That's the girl who's different.* I shrank away from their eyes.

It took all my strength to knock. I was surprised when Lady Sutton opened her door herself, instead of having a footman do it for her.

'I had a feeling it would be you,' she said. 'Hurry, come in.'

This time when I walked into her parlour, the garish colours didn't faze me.

'Where's Richard?'

'I had the men bring him here, to my chambers – they're far more comfortable than his quarters.'

I made for the first door I saw, but Lady Sutton laid a hand on my arm.

'The physician is attending to him,' she said. 'We must wait till he's done. That would be best.'

I had to see Richard for myself but I knew she was right. Waiting would be best for him. I perched on one of the brightly upholstered chairs near the window.

'You were in the garden when . . . *it* happened?' Lady Sutton asked, taking a seat across from me on the couch Richard and I had sat on during our last visit.

I hated the way she said 'it'. It made my blood curdle. 'Yes.'

'I suppose you didn't know how ill he is,' she said. 'Poor girl. Perhaps no one did. Not entirely, at least. But have no fear – the physician is the best in the country. When Lady Boyle had complications with—'

'I-I'm sorry.' I didn't mean to cut her off, but Lady Sutton looked as if I had slapped her.

'What did you say?' She pronounced her words slowly, deliberately.

'I can't listen to that right now. The gossip. Not when Richard's suffering and we're sitting here unable to do anything.'

'The gossip.' Her voice was low and somehow dangerous. 'That's what people think of me, don't they?'

I opened my mouth. To say what? I didn't know. Maybe to apologize, or try to take back what I had just said.

'Do you think I don't know what people whisper about me?' Her voice was low, and she was looking straight at me. 'I'm not as much of an idiot as everyone believes me to be. I need this – the gossip, the news – to have staying power in this world. To not be forgotten. This is what people use me for – and yes, I'm conscious of the fact that they're using me – but it's better to be used and know it than to be forgotten. In a harsh world like court, I wouldn't wish that on anybody.'

I took a shaky breath.

The door behind me opened.

'If anyone would like to see the boy, I suggest they do it now. He's fatigued and should rest.'

Lady Sutton nodded to me.

When I rose to enter the room, the physician tapped my arm. 'Only a short while,' he warned. He didn't appear to mind that I was going in unchaperoned, but perhaps visiting the sick was governed by different social protocols.

The room Richard was in was unlike most of Lady Sutton's other rooms. It wasn't flamboyant in any way. The only colour came from the walls, which were a robin's-egg blue. Everything else was white. In the middle of it all was Richard, propped up on a mess of pillows and swaddled in white blankets.

'You came.' There was a sigh to his voice that was new to me. He was normally so lively and passionate. It hurt to see him bedridden like this.

'Of course I did.' I tried to muster up a smile.

Richard patted the side of the bed and I walked over to sit by him.

'They have me so swaddled, I feel as though I've regressed to infancy.'

Seeing the sweat on his brow, I was about to ask if he was hot when a violent shiver ran through him. I settled for covering his hand with mine. It was the only thing besides his face that peeked out from beneath the blankets.

'How do you feel?'

It was a pointless thing to ask but I had to say something.

247

'I think you know the answer to your own question,' he said. 'Remember, I see through you all the time.' He tried to laugh but coughs hacked out of him instead.

Richard turned away from me and covered his mouth, but I could see the fresh blood that smeared his hand.

The physician rushed in and helped Richard sit up straighter while he coughed. He looked at me and gestured for me to leave.

'I think he needs his rest now,' the physician said.

Richard didn't even look at me as I left.

Chapter 23

Days went by as I visited Richard. I ignored the increasing tension in my stomach as I sat at his bedside every day, hoping that by some miracle he would be better than when I last saw him. And every day Lady Sutton gave me a sympathetic look as I emerged from his room.

'My Lord . . . He's only a boy. Such a good boy,' I heard her saying one day. I didn't know whether she was talking to herself or praying.

Sometimes Richard was awake, but often he was asleep or wracked by fitful dreams. Though he shivered, his fever climbed higher. He had night sweats and complained of a pain in his chest as he grabbed at it and struggled to breathe. I much preferred it when he was asleep, for though he had lost weight and his skull showed beneath his skin, at rest he was still Richard, and when I closed my eyes, he was the same as before in my mind's eye.

'The physician said there's nothing more he can do. He's accompanying the king on a hunting expedition tomorrow – one of the king's men isn't feeling well and requested his presence,' Lady Sutton said.

'Then he shouldn't go hunting,' I replied. 'Richard needs a physician more than he does.'

'Like I said, child, there's nothing more he can do.'

I didn't want to hear that. Those were the last words

people said before someone died. They couldn't be said now. It wasn't Richard's time. He would live. He had to.

Lady Sutton shook her head, as if she had heard my thoughts. 'The best we can do for him now is make him comfortable.'

'No.'

I turned from Lady Sutton and ran out into the hallway. *Rebecca!*

I was vaguely aware of Henley trying to say something, but soon I was surrounded by people. I pushed and shoved them aside to get air. I ran into the countess's chambers just as tears began to flood my vision. I swallowed them and tried to compose myself.

'My own dear.' The countess came towards me with outstretched arms and embraced me. 'There, there. I know this must be hard.'

I wondered if this was how the countess had felt when she lost her husband. It felt as if the earth was being ripped out from beneath me and I was falling without end.

'I know this is a difficult time but there's something we need to discuss,' the countess went on. 'I know Richard is . . . a dear friend, but I'm afraid it's not seemly for you to go on visiting him like this.' She raised a hand, perhaps to comfort me, but I flinched away.

'I *love* Richard.' I was surprised by how easily those words came out of my mouth. 'I love Richard.' It sounded right. 'I have to see him.'

'Visiting the bedside of someone ill is admirable – once, but visiting repeatedly raises eyebrows. I don't want you any more involved in this than you already are,' she said.

Thinking quickly, I remembered the night the falling candelabra had almost killed me. 'My lady, I believe this is

250

my duty – a calling bestowed upon me by a power greater than either of us.'

She stood in awe. 'A calling bestowed upon you by the Lord?'

'I heard a voice one night, instructing me that I must do this,' I said.

She stood dumbfounded and I figured she wouldn't try to stop me again.

As Richard's health deteriorated, so did mine.

It was close to the middle of the night, yet I was lying wide awake in a cold sweat. I felt a pressing pain all over my body and I tried not to moan out loud. I wondered if Richard were awake in a similar manner. I hoped not.

The nervous feeling in my core had progressed beyond a queasy uncertainty to a permanent dull ache encompassing my whole body. At times, tremors shook my hands, and I tried to hide them in the folds of my skirts.

I had never let it progress this far before. Miss Hatfield had always moved us from one time period to the next before we started feeling much discomfort. The only other time it had come close to this bad was when I was with Henley in his time period. I remembered the nausea I endured day in and day out, and trying to fight it for one more day with Henley. But even that couldn't compare with what I was experiencing now. This was the first time I had felt actual *pain* associated with staying too long, and it frightened me all the more.

I missed Henley. I wanted to talk to him about this . . . about everything, but I knew he would only worry and insist we find a way to leave this time period immediately after the clock was made. He always thought about what was best for me. And of course I couldn't talk to him about my confused

251

feelings for Richard. I didn't want to hurt him more than I already had.

I knew I had two choices: leaving before the murderer found me or choosing to stay with Richard. As soon as I realized I needed to make a decision, I knew I had already made it long ago. I would stay with Richard.

Henley wouldn't like it . . . Actually, Henley would hate it. He would try to talk me out of it. That was why I wasn't going to tell him yet; he didn't have to know until I had the clock. Damn Henley for looking out for me.

I thought back to the last night I had spent with Miss Hatfield, in front of the old television coated with dust. I didn't know why that memory came to mind, but it made me smile. I remembered how we bickered over the characters and what we made of them. Miss Hatfield always thought that any way other than her way was foolish. And for once, I missed hearing that certainty.

I remembered the extended family on the show – the older father, his two grown-up kids and their respective new families. I loved that although they had their own complexities and issues, they always managed to come together as a family in the end. It might take them a while to work out their problems, but they realized that all they ever really needed was family and the support they offered.

I remembered wanting – craving – that so badly. I wanted a family. I just hadn't realized at the time that I already had one. Once in Miss Hatfield, and now in Henley. We would always bicker, but we'd also always find our way back to each other.

Henley was my family.

I turned over and threw up.

Chapter 24

The next morning, as I readied myself to go to Richard's room again, Henley spoke.

Are you really in love with him?

There was no one else he could be talking about, but apparently he couldn't bring himself to say Richard's name.

'I do love him,' I said, quietly. 'I realized it even before I knew he was sick, but that only confirmed my feelings.'

But are you in love with him?

Love, in love, did it make a difference? I hated that Henley knew and could see the effect Richard had on me. I hated that I couldn't turn it off like a switch.

So you're not in love with him . . .

I still couldn't say anything.

If you're not, I still have a chance.

'I can't think about this right now with Richard dying. It's not the time or the place.'

So you'll talk about this after he's dead?

I grabbed the first thing I saw – the washbasin on the bedside table – and hurled it towards Henley's voice.

Helen threw open the door and came running in. 'My lady, are you all right?'

'I'm fine. I'm fine.'

Her eyes darted from me to the washbasin now in fragments by the wall.

Helen had already suspected there might be something amiss with me today when she saw that I had thrown up in the chamber pot. I had convinced her that I was fine and there was no need to inform the countess of a minor upset stomach from something I ate at dinner last night. But I supposed there was no convincing her to keep quiet about this.

'Is the countess up?' I asked, walking past her into the sitting room.

'In her room, my lady.'

'Very well,' I said and headed in that direction.

When I entered, the countess was sitting at her vanity with her back towards the door, as usual.

'I gather you have had an eventful morning already?'

I figured she had heard the crash of the washbasin, so I didn't bother lying about it.

'I'm sorry about that,' I said.

'Nonsense. Let he who is without sin cast the first stone,' she said, running a brush through her hair. 'When my husband died, I went through about twenty plates. There wasn't a piece of china that was safe from me.'

It was hard to imagine someone as perpetually refined as the countess throwing a tantrum.

'You really loved him,' I said.

'I did. And the loss of him hurt all the more for it.'

'How did you get over it?' I asked.

'I never have.'

The countess went on brushing her hair as if we were having an entirely different conversation. To a passer-by who couldn't hear our words, it would have looked like we were discussing the weather.

'All I can say is this: don't try to prepare yourself for the pain,' the countess said. 'You can't prepare yourself for something like that. It's unimaginable.'

254

The countess's words resonated with me and remained stuck in my mind for the rest of the day.

I was beginning to learn that there are a handful of people in your life who affect you like no others can. It doesn't matter how long you have with them, you'll carry their mark for ever. It was exactly as Helen had said when she found me staring at the mirror and thinking of Miss Hatfield.

Richard was one of those people. I could never forget his intensity and passion – and I didn't want to. I wanted to be a living testament that he had existed. I suppose that's what love is. I loved Richard. But I wasn't *in* love with him.

I wondered why it had taken me so long to realize that, why I hadn't grasped what Henley had been getting at. It sounded so simple now that I knew, but I guess that's always the case with the hardest things we have to learn. I had fallen in love once, and I knew that because it felt like I couldn't breathe and the sky had opened up. It was a different kind of love from what I felt for Richard. Not more significant, or less so – just different.

You could love more than one person in a lifetime. It didn't mean you were replacing or comparing them. I wondered if the countess knew that. She had looked so happy with Lord Dormer, both in the gardens and the first time I met him, in the great hall. It was clear to everyone save herself how good he appeared to be for her.

I laughed as I recalled the countess telling me that it was unseemly for any woman to go out alone with a man when she herself did the same thing with Lord Dormer. Lord Dormer was the kind of man who could persuade the countess to do anything. It was obvious how he swept her off her feet with the smallest things he did and said. I knew the countess still loved her late husband and that would never change, but she had room to love Lord Dormer, too. There wasn't anything unseemly about that.

I walked to the countess's door and knocked.

'Come in.'

Ever the picture of propriety, the countess sat still, poised, working on her needlepoint again.

'I don't think you're going to like what I have to say,' I began.

'I don't think anyone will if you start your conversations that way, Lady Eleanor.'

Ignoring her, I plunged ahead with my observations. 'I think you need to give Lord Dormer a shot. And by shot, I mean a *real* chance.'

The countess betrayed no emotion at me barging into her room to say something so personal to her.

'I think it would be a shame for you to let what you have with him disintegrate because you are too cautious to act on it.'

I paused, waiting for her to say something.

When she finally spoke, her response was short. 'Is that it?'

I was taken aback. What I had said wasn't something small.

'I am guessing that is all you have to say since you have stopped speaking,' she said.

I wondered how someone could be so disengaged from their own life. She reminded me of Miss Hatfield in this way.

'There are things we'd all like to do in an ideal world. But we don't live in an ideal world. I'm sorry if you haven't realized that yet.'

'You can't live by society's rules for ever,' I said.

'Spoken like someone who doesn't know the true consequences of not living by the rules.'

'I've given up more than you know,' I said. 'An entire life.'

'And you expect me to do the same? Not every story has a happy ending, my dear. At some point, we have to learn to be satisfied with something less.'

'What use is a life you have to be *satisfied* with? Don't you want more?' I asked.

I knew what she was like around him. She couldn't make me believe that she would prefer a life without him.

'Wishful thinking doesn't do anything—'

'You're wrong. Not taking risks is what doesn't do anything.' I knelt at her feet and chose my next words carefully. I knew she was finally listening. 'You've seen Lady Empson—'

'What about her?'

'She frightens me. Not because of who she is – I obviously don't know who she is since she hardly ever talks without echoing someone else – but because she doesn't have an identity.'

A smile played over the countess's lips and I chuckled.

'So you've seen it, too?' she said.

'It's really not difficult! She's her husband's shadow. My point is that she is an example of someone who doesn't take risks. I don't think she's ever taken a *single* one.'

'Not even deciding what to eat?' said the countess, laughing softly.

'Not even that,' I said. 'You don't want to become that, do you?'

She smirked. 'I'd rather die.'

'Then don't always live according to what society says. There's a time for that, but there are also times when you have to *do* something else.'

'Like run after Lord Dormer?' The countess looked at me.

257

I laughed at the idea of the countess running after anyone. 'Like giving this . . . whatever may be between you and him a chance.'

'You sound like an old married woman giving advice,' she said, after a while.

'I feel like one.'

About an hour of peace went by before I heard a knock at the door. Knowing it was Helen, I called for her to come in. I had been here long enough to grow used to Helen's soft knock and differentiate it from Joan's more peremptory rap.

She curtsied, as always, and I wondered if she ever got sick of doing it.

'I'm sorry if I'm interrupting, my lady,' she said.

'No, no. Go on.'

'I was told to tell you that the clock you commissioned is ready.'

The clock!

'Oh, yes. I'll pick it up as soon as I can.' I waved her out of the room, trying to look bored and not reveal how much this sudden pronouncement meant to me.

The clock. Richard told me he had somehow convinced the clockmaker to create the golden clock. I could hardly believe he had succeeded after my many failed attempts . . . but I was incredibly thankful for his efforts. And yet . . . the ecstatic feeling I experienced when Richard first told me he had persuaded the clockmaker was all but gone. It meant almost nothing to me emotionally now that I knew Richard was sick.

Still, the clock was my only means of escape and survival, and I went promptly to the clockmaker's court workshop to pick it up. I didn't want to jinx anything.

The clockmaker was there when I arrived.

'Lady Eleanor,' he said. 'I'm pleased you could come so quickly.'

'I've been looking forward to this for a long time,' I said, but left it at that for fear of provoking him.

'I'd ask if you were still sure you wanted this clock, but you look very certain.'

'I am.'

'Shame about your friend,' he said. 'I liked him. Almost better than you.'

I shook that off as he handed me the clock.

'I could have it delivered to your rooms, if you would like. It is rather heavy.'

I assured him that delivery wouldn't be necessary. Now I finally had it, I had no intention of letting the golden clock out of my hands. It looked practically identical to the one hanging in the hallway across from Miss Hatfield's kitchen, albeit a bit shinier. So many memories came flooding back to me – memories of things that didn't exist in this time period.

The weight of the clock felt comforting in my arms and, for once, seeing the strange hands indicating days, months and years brought me relief me rather than the usual uneasy sensation that the clock was slightly askew to the world. Funny what a few hundred years could do to a person's perceptions.

I traced the design surrounding the clock's face with a fingertip. The familiar lines had new meaning for me now that the man who painstakingly created it was in front of me.

There was a small inscription towards the bottom of the clock's face. I vaguely remembered noticing it when Miss Hatfield first showed me the clock, but I had never actually read it. I raised it up to my face now to better see the small words.

'Time is the devourer of all things,' the clockmaker said. 'I wrote it for you to remember and think about, but although you look young, I suppose you already know the truth of it.'

'Thank you,' I said. 'You have no idea how much this means to me.' And yet, somehow, I felt as though he *did* know.

I said my goodbyes and left for my room, running. I passed the countess on the way there.

'Lady Eleanor, you weren't searching for me, were you?' She looked concerned.

'No, I wasn't,' I said, continuing to my room.

At the end of the corridor I remembered something I needed to ask the countess. When I turned back to call out to her, I saw her meeting up with a man – Lord Dormer, of course. I hoped the conversation we shared earlier had meant something to her, but there was no real way to tell at this distance.

When I shut the door to my room behind me, it slammed with a sudden bang. I cursed under my breath, hoping Helen or Joan wouldn't come running to see what the commotion was about.

I'm not going to pretend I'm pleased that Richard became involved with the clock, but thank God you have it back. Now you can finally escape.

Henley's words stuck with me in an odd way. *Escape.* But I didn't *want* to escape. I *couldn't.* Not with what I had tying me here.

Henley sensed my hesitation immediately. *What's wrong?*

'I-I can't.' I gently placed the clock down onto the bed.

You came to court to find the clock, and now that you have it you can escape, he said. I knew he was right, but

260

I couldn't shake the feeling that I wasn't done. *I know you've become attached to the people here but your life is in danger. That has to come first.*

'I know, but—'

No, you don't. You're immortal, but not invincible. You have a killer after you. And even without the killer, you can't stay in one time for too long. I heard you throwing up last night – I know what that was about.

Henley sounded exactly like Miss Hatfield, and in any other moment that would have made me laugh. I knew he was worried for my safety. I was, too, but I also had other concerns.

'Richard—'

What about Richard?

'He's dying.'

I know he is. I also know how much you've been suffering because of it. I've seen it in your face. But we can't do anything about it. No one can.

Henley was right again, no matter how much I wished he wasn't.

'I can't leave him,' I said. 'I can't just disappear from his life.'

This wasn't only about Richard any more. This wasn't the first time I'd had to abandon someone I loved.

When I left Henley in 1904, I had never felt agony like it. I thought it would ease as time went on and we both continued with our lives. Instead, it was a wound that wouldn't heal. It festered, a daily reminder of the pain. I had sworn I would never do that again, not for any reason.

'I've experienced that pain once,' I said. 'I can't go through it again.'

I knew Henley was thinking of the same moment – when I'd had to walk away from him. He hadn't been aware of the reason then, but even now that he understood everything, I knew it didn't lessen the suffering for him.

'I can't go yet.' My voice started to get stronger. 'I just can't.'

Rebecca, that's not a decision you can make. You're putting your life at risk. And I . . . I can't let you do that.

'You think I don't understand but, Henley, I really do comprehend the gravity of the situation. It's also my life, and my choice. I have to stay with Richard until he . . . dies . . . and I *will* do it. I'd just rather do this without fighting you every step of the way.'

Silence answered me and I knew I had won.

At the slightest indication – whether it's the murderer reaching for you or you feeling even worse because you've stayed here too long – you're getting out of here.

Henley and I both knew he couldn't enforce that, but I agreed purely to pacify him. Staying with Richard till the end was something I knew I had to do.

Chapter 25

Visiting Richard every day, time went by both slowly and quickly. I brought the clock with me whenever I went to see him. No one had questioned me about it. It had taken me so long to get my hands on it again that I didn't want it out of my sight for as much as a minute. Even when I slept, I hid the clock under a pile of clothing. When I brought it to Richard's bedside in the evening, I placed it on the table next to the bed, where it caught the light of the disappearing sun and almost seemed to glow. Its warm glimmer almost made me forget the unabated ticking.

The hours I spent by Richard's bedside were long, but they still felt too short every time Lady Sutton came to escort me out so Richard could get his rest. Day by day, he grew progressively worse. It got to a point where the deterioration was so fast that he looked sicker and closer to death every time I saw him.

'Lady Eleanor,' Lady Sutton said to me one day as she was walking me out, 'maybe it would be best if you didn't come any longer. I know you want to be supportive till the very end, but Richard . . . He's not responding to anyone any more. You've seen him – he appears to be forever caught between feverish dreams and delirious reality.'

It was true – on the few occasions when he woke to see me at the foot of his bed there was no spark of recognition in his eyes.

'Perhaps it would be best, for you and him both, if you stopped visiting. You could remember him as he was, and not as what he's become.'

I swallowed and shook my head. 'I need to see him till the end.'

'Very well,' she said. And that was the last she ever said on the matter.

I was there through it all, and to Lady Sutton's credit, so was she. I was there when Richard started hallucinating; he yelled at something only he could see in the corner of the room, and cried during a one-sided conversation with his mother. I was there when Lady Sutton couldn't take it any more and broke down crying while wiping his damp forehead. I was even there when Lady Sutton called the priest to administer the Last Rites.

I waited in Lady Sutton's sitting room with her, the clock in my lap, as the priest went straight into the bedroom to hear Richard's last confession. I held Lady Sutton's shaking hands in my own while we waited for him to call us in.

'The family may enter now,' we finally heard.

Without a moment's hesitation, Lady Sutton pulled me in with her.

'I'm the only family he has here,' I heard Lady Sutton telling the priest. 'His parents, his brothers – they started towards court as soon as a letter was dispatched with news of Richard's fast-declining health . . . but they didn't arrive in time.'

The priest, who Lady Sutton had said was visiting from Spain, had anointed Richard with what I guessed to be blessed oil. Lady Sutton remained solemn, and judging from her expression I assumed the anointing was a standard practice. The priest laid his hands on Richard and continued to pray.

'Through this holy anointing, may the Lord in his love and mercy help you with the grace of the Holy Spirit.' The priest had a familiar voice that rose and fell, comforting me. 'May the Lord who frees you from sin save you and raise you up.'

He placed a wafer between Richard's half-parted lips, but he was too far gone to accept it. The priest had to push it further in before Richard instinctively swallowed.

Soon after, the priest left. I wished I could have thanked him for administering the Last Rites, but I couldn't take my eyes off Richard, much less turn them to the priest for conversation.

Lady Sutton also had to leave the room. She was sobbing too hard, and simply squeezed my hand as she passed.

Finally, I was alone with Richard. I placed the clock on the bedside table. When I moved to sit down next to him, I felt a weight roll in the pouch at my side. Reaching in, I withdrew the silver pocket watch the clockmaker had made for me and placed it on the table next to the clock. My hands shook, and I wondered if it was a sign of my body finally being rejected by this time period, or if it was because of the goodbye I knew I had to say.

I sat at the edge of the bed and wondered what I would say to Richard. I only had this one chance left.

'Oh, Richard . . .'

I had known him for such a short time, but I felt I knew him. *Really* knew him. I understood the passion that lived within him, and he in turn had recognized what lived inside me. I wished I could have known him longer, but I was certain I had already said everything I wanted to say to him. We understood each other, and we didn't need words for that.

And so I took his hand, which felt dwarfed and lonely in mine, and brought it to my lips.

'Thank you.'

Richard's eyes flickered to me and looked confused. My whole body ached with that one look. Richard was someone who had always been so sure of his place in the world, and now he was so lost that he couldn't even find himself. He coughed violently, barely managing to turn to his left. Blood dripped down his chin. It was the only colour on his face now. His eyes skittered under their lids, as if he was reading something I could not see. His lips mouthed words over and over but no sound came out. So this was it.

I wished I could have said goodbye to the real Richard. The person in front of me wasn't even a shell of the man I loved. He was a completely different person.

I shut my eyes, but not soon enough. Fat tears rolled down my cheeks.

It'll be all right, Henley said.

I looked at Richard but he didn't react to Henley's disembodied voice. He simply stared past my head.

He's just returning to the place he came from before he was alive.

I turned to see what Richard was staring at and followed his gaze towards the window in the corner of the room. It was dark now and the glass reflected the image of the scene playing out before me.

Richard stared and stared, and as a last effort to connect with him, I squinted at the window pane. I blinked quickly to rid my eyes of the tears that shrouded them. And then I saw it.

266

The window wasn't reflecting what was happening at all. It was reflecting me, kneeling beside the bed. The figure in the reflection knelt, clasping her hands as if in prayer. Her face was open, her expression strangely serene, as if she was waiting for a miracle.

The window reflected a lie. There was no miracle. The tears streaked down the young woman's face didn't show in the reflection and her lips were parted not in accepting prayer but because she was sobbing out loud. None of it was captured as it was, but when I turned to face Richard, his greying lips were fixed in a smile.

'Henley, you have to do something.'

I clasped my hands together to keep them from shaking. My fingers turned white from the amount of pressure I put on them but I didn't care.

Richard started coughing again, but this time his body hardly moved. He looked too tired to force another cough out.

'Please, Henley,' I whispered, because I knew my voice would shake if I spoke any louder. 'You have to try.'

I had no idea what I thought he could do, but I was at a point where even him making the attempt would make me feel less helpless.

I am trying, but there's nothing I can do. Henley's voice sounded pained, and I knew he was doing everything in his power. I knew it hurt him to see me like this, but I couldn't stop crying.

I tried to take a breath but cried out instead, seeing Richard's body shudder.

Rebecca, I'm trying.

Through my tears I was only vaguely aware of Richard's body rising an inch off the bed from the force of Henley attempting to influence the physical world. A palpable energy ran through the room.

My shoulders shook, and I didn't know whether I was crying out loud or in silence any more. Henley *had* to do something. He just had to.

Richard's chest appeared to struggle to rise. And then it stilled.

'Oh, God. Please.'

My head bowed with the pain in my own chest, and in that instant I felt Henley in every part of the room and every molecule of my body. It was as if he expanded in a crack of energy.

I felt the bed shift as if a weight moved upon it.

I looked up but could only see a blur of disorientating images. I wiped my eyes and tried to focus them on the shape on the bed.

There, right in front of me, Richard sat up. His curly brown hair was plastered to his forehead with sweat, but other than that he looked fine. His skin was already losing the grey sheen that had marred it only seconds ago, replaced by a natural flush.

I couldn't believe it. I blinked, and he was still there.

My eyes ran across his face, watching him come alive. His hands twitched and his lips regained their colour. I swept my gaze over him, then froze when his eyes met mine.

His eyes were still warm and the colour of honey, but there was something different about them. Something . . . *off*. Perhaps the light was hitting them in a different way. I stared into his eyes, and although what I found there was familiar, it wasn't Richard at all.

'Henley, what have you done?'

The voice that replied was Richard's in sound and tone, but everything else was different.

'I don't know,' he began hesitantly, stopping and starting. 'I was trying to help, Rebecca. I was trying to do something.

Anything. It was the way you looked. Devastated. Small. I was trying so hard to keep him alive. When Richard died, it felt like a vacuum was created. I was trying so hard to sustain him, even for only a minute longer, that I somehow . . . fell in. What I mean to say is that it felt like falling . . . or being sucked in—'

'My God . . .'

It really was Henley.

I reached out a hand, almost still testing if he was real. He placed his hand against mine, palm to palm.

I had lost a man I loved but regained the man I was in love with.

We both straightened, hearing footsteps outside the door. The priest? Lady Sutton?

I looked Henley in the eye and nodded. The ache in my entire body had become almost too much to bear.

Reaching towards the bedside table, he felt past the silver pocket watch and grabbed the clock. He held my hand in one of his as he moved the clock's hands with the other.

'No, that's too far into the future,' I said. 'You're in a mortal body – you can't survive that.'

'I'm not supposed to be able to, but I wasn't supposed to be alive either. We'll see.'

Now that he had come back to me, I didn't dare let go of him.

I lunged at the clock, but it was already happening. The colours around us started melting, morphing. It was too late. It was all I could do to keep hold of his hand.

Henley had come back to me. I wasn't about to lose him again.

Epilogue

They say a dead man walked that day. That he rose from his deathbed, hand in hand with the one who was blessed by God.

Others say he simply vanished, along with the woman who went into his room but never came out.

It was on everyone's lips. Some say it was witchcraft, but others say it was a miracle. It was the very image of a resurrection – God's work.

They say she was an angel. She came out of nowhere, sent by God himself to deliver the dying man. The first sign of God's favour was when she was saved from certain death beneath a falling candelabrum.

Those who knew him say he was a good man. He never did anything wrong. The most deserving. He was chosen by Our Lord.

They say the two walked, one foot in front of the other, through Death's door and into the light. Others say they floated towards the ceiling, disappearing into the air. But all agree they were gone. Gone to God. Leaving no trace behind.

'My lord . . .'

Everyone was fervently making the sign of the cross and reaching to kiss the door.

'It's a miracle!'

'We are witnessing God's work!'

Hearing these cries, a priest came running down the hall; the very priest who had given the dying man his Last Rites. The people made way for the man of the cloth and bowed their heads reverently as he walked past them and into the room.

'Father, this is a testament to God's power!'

'It's a miracle!'

He closed the door behind him.

'No,' he said. 'It is the Devil's work. Death should be final.'

He picked up a silver pocket watch from the bedside table.

'This cannot stand.'

Acknowledgements

A huge thank you to my agent, Maggie Hanbury, and my editor, Marcus Gipps. Thank you for making this book a reality.

Thank you to Lisa Rogers, Sophie Calder, Jennifer McMenemy, and the whole team at Gollancz for all the work they've put into this book; without them there would be no book.

Laura Ackermann and Anna Kreynes, you guys are the best! Thank you for everlasting enthusiasm.

To Rhean, thank you for all your support and guidance over the years.

Corinne, thank you for feeding me (even if baked goods aren't all that nutritious) and thus ensuring my survival. Katie, thank you for practically being my unpaid therapist. That's what friends are for, right?

To my parents, I don't know how you've managed to put up with me for 18 years. That's a lot of kindness and resilience, but most of all, that's a lot of patience. Thank you for always being there.

BRINGING NEWS FROM OUR WORLDS TO YOURS . . .

Want your news daily?

The Gollancz blog has instant updates on the hottest SF and Fantasy books.

Prefer your updates monthly?

Sign up for our in-depth newsletter.

www.gollancz.co.uk

Follow us 🐦 @gollancz

Find us ⓕ facebook.com/GollanczPublishing

Classic SF as you've never read it before.

Visit the SF Gateway to find out more!

www.sfgateway.com